The Rosetta Stone

A harvest waiting to happen.

Partially based on a true story.

The Rosetta Stone

Part one and two

What a reader has said about the Rosetta Stone novel.

This book has really encouraged me over the time I was reading it. From the faith of Bryce in his Saviour to the perseverance of his mom Aubrey, in prayer, it never ceases to show Gods kindness and love to all his children. His healing power is real and you can see it in this book. Plant your seeds carefully! God has shown me through this novel that faith isn't a word, it's perseverance, prayer, belief and a relationship with Christ. A gripping novel!

Josie, Surrey, 13

For my mama who has been strong through it all and for Siena, who loves these characters almost as much as I do. (I said almost;)

Any scripture references in this book comes from the NLT, NIV and the NKJV.

Disclaimer: This is a fictional book, any likeness to people you may know or circumstances is entirely coincidental.

Front cover design: copyright Mannaministries(2021)
Back cover design: copyright Mannaministries(2021)

Copyright: Arialle-Lily Crick (2020)
All rights reserved. No portion of this book may be copied, reprinted or reproduced without prior written consent from the author.

Editor's Note:
Siena Weingartz

Life is an adventure. We never quite know what's going to happen next. Twists and turns arise, mountains and valleys come before us, yet we all trudge on, because that's the way we're trained.

We're expected to rise up to the challenge, to get on with it and carry on.

This is all good and well, but what happens when the challenge is just too big? What happens when we can't attack it like we normally would; with our logical thoughts and pre-planned strategies?

This book is a story of a family whose biggest challenge arrived unexpectedly, whose mountain seemed to grow daily, whose pain cut more deeply day after day.

The only way to succeed was to stay on their knees and fight from the ground.

It has been a privilege to edit this book, Arialle-Lily, and beautiful to read some of your own story hidden in the chapters below.

Readers, may you learn more about who your Creator is and how He works as you read the story of the Rosetta Stone.

Foreword

This is real life … Jesus is all we need Him to be. 'The Rosetta Stone' was needed to decode Egyptian hieroglyphics, Jesus shows us how to unravel this life.

Arialle-Lily so clearly explains how in turmoil, doubt and fear, the members of a family that span three generations each discover plans revealed in God's word for the present and their future. Fear challenged their faith. Trust and encouragement became a reality as they persuaded their own hearts to stand and believe against all odds. United, they overcame, growing in wisdom and understanding.

Arialle-Lily grippingly communicates how we can experience intimate friendship with God. At 8, home schooled, a beautiful dancer and choreographer, she believed God for the same miracle referenced in this book. I love her passion and courage to share her heart in this first book about The Walker family.

A fiction story based on the author's life. She has a powerful gift to relate how nothing is impossible for God, He is only a heartbeat away.

Written by Ann Gruber

Isaiah 53:5

He was wounded for our transgressions, he was bruised for our iniquities. The chastisement for our peace was upon him, and by his stripes we are healed.

1 Peter 2:24
Who himself bore our sins in his own body on the tree, that we, having died to sins, might live for righteousness - by whose stripes you were healed.

~*Chapter One*~

To have a harvest you have to plant the seeds and cultivate them. It's just the natural way things work.

Bryce laughed as the school bell went, "Summer vacation here we come!" He rubbed his hands together and then fist-pumped the air.

The boy next to him tossed his red hair out of the way and laughed. "And while you slave away on the farm I'm going to be relaxing on the beaches of LA."

Bryce rolled his eyes and shoved Randy playfully, "Yeah, as if your parents will really let you out of their sight while you over there. It's a business trip for your dad, 'member?"

Randy snorted and adjusted his backpack, "I'll show you who has the good summer."

Bryce laughed "This is gonna be a summer to remember, I just know it, I've got this feeling it's gonna be pretty neat."

"Uh-huh," Randy tipped his head back and drained the last of his Dr. Pepper can, crushed it and tossed it into the trash on his way down the steps. "Have fun with that."

"I just can't wait to feel that sun on my face." Bryce grinned, throwing his head back, strands of blond hair trailing down his neck.

"The smell of cows, the heat while working hours on end, the stench of horse manure-" Randy ended on a laugh as Bryce shoved him across the hall. He crashed into one of the lockers, "Hey, watch it dude." He smirked rubbing the back of his head.

"*You* watch it dude." Bryce walked ahead of him, pulling his denim jacket on as he did so. Warm air hit him in the face as he stepped out of the school doors.

Randy followed, nodded and lifted his hand in a farewell greeting as he jogged the other way down the sidewalk towards his bike.

"See ya in the fall." He hollered.

Bryce returned the movement, "Yeah, see ya!"

A car horn blared and he turned to see Ivar hanging out the truck window.

"You comin' little brother? Or you going to make me late for picking up Savannah?" Ivar called banging on the outside of the car with his fist playfully.

Bryce shook his head as he hurried over. "I'm coming I'm coming, don't get your knickers in a twist."

Ivar gave him a look as he climbed into the passenger seat. Bryce stared at him. "What?"

"Don't get my *knickers* in a twist?" Ivar repeated slowly. Bryce nodded, a smile playing across his mouth,

"Yeah, Mrs Thompson said it today when Kelly tried to do the science project and it failed. She got really upset and I mean really upset." Bryce laughed, "There was foam going everywhere and Kelly was standing on the chair in the middle of the lab screaming like anything. Oh man, Randy and I thought I was the best thing ever."

He grinned and shrugged, "Mrs T told Kelly not to get her knickers in a twist, it was just a failed science experiment. Not the end of the world."

Ivar's eyebrows rose, "You know that saying only works when talking to a girl, right?"

Bryce cocked his head, "Really? Ah, maybe I should try it on Sav."

Ivar put the brakes on suddenly and threw the car to the roadside just as he pulled out.

He spun in his seat and stared at his brother. "Don't you even."

Bryce hooted with laughter and held his hands up, "I won't, I won't, don't worry. I was just messin' with ya."

Ivar glared at Bryce for a moment before his face split with a grin. He shoved Bryce's ball cap further down his face.

Bryce laughed. "You should have seen your face."

"Shut up." Ivar grinned as he started the truck's engine up again and indicated the pull out once more.

"Nah, I don't think I will." Bryce tipped his cap back and wound down the window.

"You oddball."

"Takes one to know one."

Ivar's lips twitched.

Bryce smirked as they rode in silence for the next quarter of a mile.

Ivar pulled the truck to a stop at a red light, "Oh hey, Mom is taking you to Grandpa's. I'm going to help Dad out at the garage after I've picked Savannah up and dropped her home."

"Okay," Bryce pushed the car door open as they pulled up outside the café.

"Mom will meet you here." Ivar instructed, grinning as Savannah left the café and got in Bryce's seat.

Bryce laughed and shook his head, waving them off as he went inside.

Savannah's dad was behind the counter. "Ah, young Bryce, what's it gonna be?"

Bryce hoisted himself up on one of the bar stools, "Ah one double chocolate banana shake, please Sir."

"Righto,"

Savannah's dad went out to the back, returning a few minutes later with a tall milkshake glass, filled to the brim with the sweet foamy chocolate drink.

Bryce grinned and placed a few dollars on the countertop. "Thanks," he said before sticking the straw in his mouth and drinking it. He had drained half the glass when his mom pulled up and sounded the car horn.

Bryce looked regretfully at his drink, discarded the straw, tilted his head back and drained the glass until it was empty in a matter of seconds. He jumped up and ran outside, leaving Savannah's dad laughing and shaking his head.

~Chapter Two~

"-I know, life is busy...And time's short, honey!"

Aubrey smiled at Bryce as he got in, she backed the car out of the parking lot. "Was that nice?"

"What, the milkshake?" Bryce wiped his upper lip with the back of his hand.

His mom nodded, "Yeah, I was watching through the window. You drank it fast."

Bryce laughed, "Yeah it was real good. Did ya know Mr Van-Dyke has started putting a spoonful of honey roasted peanut butter in his chocolate banana milkshakes?"

"Huh, does it work?"

"Yes, definitely." Bryce leaned out the open window, the wind blowing back his hair. He rolled up his shirt sleeves and pulled his upper body out the car window as they hit the country roads. He let out a wild yell.

Aubrey grabbed him by his belt, "Bryce Andrew Walker, get your head back in the car."

Bryce grinned at her as he ducked his head back through the window, "Aw man," he sat back in his seat watching the seas of green and golden crops roll past.

Sometimes, Aubrey wondered to herself as she watched her youngest son. *Sometimes I wonder wether he got his spark from me or Caleb.*

She paused her train of thought to switch to thinking about her childhood. Visions of radical escapades filled her mind and she grinned to herself. *Definitely me.*

Bryce fiddled with the radio dial until he found the country station.

Music blared through the speakers at high volume.

Aubrey rushed to turn it down. "Why does your dad need it so loud on the way to school?" She groaned.

Bryce shook his head, "So he can drown out my talk about how boring school is." An impish smile on his sun tanned face.

Aubrey ruffled his hair. "Well, next time keep it below thirty five. I don't want a husband who can't hear me when I speak."

Her voice was firm but Bryce saw the twinkle in her eyes. He leaned back in the seat, "Yes Ma'am."

~

The ear of wheat crumbled away into a fine, powdery dust as Jason rubbed it back and forth between his thumb and forefinger. He blew out his breath and scanned the golden fields with aged blue eyes that were accustomed to keeping watch over his life's labour.

Something bobbed up and down among the tall wheat stalks. The curly blond head was only waist-high and crashed through the field, the faded denim dungarees standing out brightly against the sea of gold.

Jason crouched down and spread his arms open wide, the child's small chubby hands clasped together around the back of his grandpa's neck.

A deep laugh rumbled inside Jason's chest as he lifted his grandson onto his broad shoulders. "You ready to go home buddy?" Jason bounced slightly as he walked, making the child laugh.

"Daddy will be reawlly happy that wheat grows bwig and strowng! Won't he, Grandpa?" The boys voice chimed.

Jason nodded his white head, "He sure will be, Hunter."

"Good," Hunter nodded, a smile spreading across his cute face causing little dimples to appear in his cheeks.

Jason laughed quietly to himself whilst marching across the fields back towards the farm house.

~

"And you're back, finally."

"Yes Ma'am." Jason grinned as he strolled in through the back door and set Hunter down, patting him slightly on the backside, "Go find one of your siblings to plague." He joked.

Madison leaned back on the wooden countertop wiping her hands on a towel, watching their grandson scurry off. Jason walked over and stood next to her taking the offered cup of steaming coffee, "Mmm," he inhaled the smell of freshly ground coffee beans.

Taking a long drink he put an arm around his wife.

"You're late," Madison's attempt to remain firm failed as she glanced at Jason.

His eyes twinkled over the edge of the mug at her.

"I know," he said, "but you don't mind, do you love."

He kissed her cheek.

Madison hid her flushed face in the hand towel. Her voice muffled, "Oh stop! You always manage to work yourself around me," she said, her words ending in a choked laugh.

Jason beamed broadly and drained his mug, striding across the kitchen to place it in the sink.

He pulled a sunflower out of the vase that stood on the kitchen table.

Moving back towards his wife with large, over-exaggerated dance steps somewhat resembling the tango, he presented it to her. "Missy, you wanna go for a hayride?" He drawled, his eyes sparkling.

Madison whacked him with the towel, "Oh shush! You got around me when I was eighteen and you still do now. I can never be firm around you." Madison trailed a hand through her husband's greying hair.

"Yup, now you're an old lady, it's even easier than when you were a young gal!" Jason grinned and ducked another towel swish.

"Get out my kitchen, old man!" She said half-laughing whilst failing once more to be firm with him.

Jason winked and grabbed the biscuit jar from the cabinet shelf before heading towards the door.

"Nuh uh." A younger voice cut in and hands removed the jar from his hands.

"What, Aubrey?" Jason whined, following his redheaded daughter back into the kitchen, dragging his feet. "Those were my ginger snaps."

Aubrey smirked and placed the glass jar on the highest shelf she could reach. "I'm with Mom on this one, you let that sweet tooth run away with you too often."

Madison laughed and Jason grumbled, "Open your mouth and I shall fill it. That's in the Bible, those biscuits are just the Lord's way of filling my mouth." He pointed out.

"Ha!" Madison snorted, "you find that verse in the Bible for me and you can have the jar! Besides, you have that verse outta context." She added.

Jason grinned.

"Watch it Mom, Dad's gonna try and find it now." Aubrey laughed.

"You bet." Jason said, his grin growing bigger. Maddison blushed as his crystal blue eyes twinkled at her again.

The two wrapped their daughter in a hug, "The whole family with you?" Jason asked looking over towards the door.

"No, sadly not, Sean needed to stay in town as we have a possible buyer coming for the truck today. Ivar stayed with his dad in case he needed help with anything around the garage."

Madison nodded, "He's a good lad," she said, grinning like the proud grandma she was.

"I brought Bryce with me though." Aubrey commented.

Jason cried out triumphantly, "Haha! Bryce, Hunter, Jade and Reese, all in the same house. What a scream!"

Aubrey grabbed a pitcher of lemonade from the fridge freezer, "Are Caleb and Emma here then?"

"Ya, your brother and his troops are here." Madison said whilst getting several glasses out of the cupboard.

"Good! Bryce needed his uncle's help with fixing something." Aubrey placed the pitcher on the table and walked into the hallway.

Jason walked with her, "So, how's Sean holding up with everything?"

Aubrey bit her lip, thinking of her husband's overloaded workload now that their eldest son was in New Orleans.

"He's stressed. With Cameron still working over in New Orleans he has to rely a lot on Ivar and Bryce and both boys are finding the workload tough, and Sean's worn out most days."

"You wish Cameron was back home with his family?" Jason asked.

Aubrey nodded and then shook her head, "Yes, I mean no. I mean I'm proud of everything our son is doing. I just miss him." She rubbed a hand over her face, "It's just hard sometimes. Not to fear for him and stuff with his work."

Jason winked and took hold of the stairwell banister, "Don't worry, honey. Everything will work out."

He paused and studied his daughter, he knew the struggles his oldest grandson had gone through

He knew of the fears that both his daughter and son in law had for him. "I'm sure Cameron will be home soon for a visit."

Jason reached over the banister and gave her shoulder a affection squeeze, "But until then," He nodded towards the lounge door, "I think your brother wants to catch up. It's been a long time since you and Caleb have had a laugh together."
Aubrey's lips twitched, "I know Dad, but life's-"

"-I know, life is busy," Jason said whilst mounting the stairs. His steps slowed a little and he called back "And time's short, honey!"

Aubrey laughed, she combed her strawberry-blonde hair with her fingers and walked into the lounge.

She smiled as she looked up at the dark, wooden beams holding up the whitewashed walls and roof.

The familiar sofas and armchairs circled the open fireplace. Her mom's piano stood off to the side next to the porch door.

Through the window, Aubrey saw a tousled blond head. A weary smile crept up on her mouth as Aubrey headed towards the door.

As her hand rested on the doorframe, her phone buzzed in her back pocket.

Pulling it out she said, "Hello?"

"Hey Mom, it's Ivar,"

Aubrey let out the breath that had been pent up inside her lungs, "Hey kiddo, how's dad?"

Ivar's voice came across the phone in a laugh, "He's stressing out a little since we're still waiting for the buyer of the truck."

Aubrey smiled as she heard him flop down onto the ground, the sound of wind rustling through the grass filled the phone's speaker.

"Well, you tell your dad that I left you both dinner in the fridge freezer. Tuna pasta on the top shelf for your dad and the spicy chicken in the tupperware is yours."

"Cool, thanks Mom," Ivar yawned over the phone. "Oh hey, Dad's calling. See ya later, Mom, say hi to Grandma and Grandpa for me."

"Will do,"

"Thanks, bye,"

"Bye." Aubrey sighed and pocketed her phone as she walked onto the porch.

~Chapter Three~

"...he. Certainly has spirit,"

As soon as Grandpa told Hunter to go plague one of his siblings he made a beeline for his dad who was sitting on the porch talking with his mom.

Hunter watched from the shelter of the porch doors' shadow as his dad swung his mom's hand back and forth, their fingers interlaced and genuine affection showed on their faces.

"So what're you gonna do while I wait for my sister?" Caleb asked his wife gently.

Emma laughed and pushed back her brown curls. "I'm gonna go help Reese and Jade in the barn. They're trying to groom down the horses."

Caleb rubbed his jaw, "Ain't Bryce gonna help?"

Emma shrugged and smiled, "You know that boy, he's either playing truant, playing that fiddle or up to no good."

Caleb grinned, "Our nephew certainly has spirit."

Emma twirled a lock of hair around her finger and nodded,

"Mmhmm. When he and Aubrey arrived, you know what the first thing he did was?"

"What?"

Emma leaned forward and pointed at a large tree that grew up from the ground a few feet from the porch.

"He climbed up that and hopped into Reese's window giving her the fright of her life."

Caleb's lips twitched.

He swallowed and ran a hand over his face.

He let out a long breath trying to regain his composure. Emma sniggered and Caleb swatted her playfully on the shoulder. "Go groom a horse."

Emma laughed, kissed him and ran towards the barn.

Caleb watched her, feeling like a teenager again who was crushing big time on the girl from his senior homeroom.

Hunter grinned as he watched his dad, the little boy toddled quietly forward and stuck his hand into his dad's back pocket pulling out his dad's phone.

Caleb froze and raised both eyebrows as he felt the small hand reach into his pocket, then he heard it.

Like a bird song.

Wind chimes or joy overflowing.

Hunter's laughter bubbled up and spilled over.

"Aha!" Caleb spun around catching his son in the act of taking his phone.

His small, pink chubby fingers grasped the phone's glass screen and brown leather case tightly.

His blue eyes were as large as saucers sparkling with mischief and joy.

Caleb grinned, picked him up and threw him in the air. Hunter squealed, grasping the phone tighter. His little legs kicked against the air as his blond curls scattered across his forehead.

Caleb caught him and held him in the crook of his arm, tickling him with his other hand.

Hunters laughter turned into screeches of delight.

"Daddy!" Hunter screeched.

Caleb grinned with fatherly pride and hoisted the little guy up onto his shoulders, running down the porch steps quickly and into dizzying circles, relishing the sounds of Hunter's delighted squeals.

"Daddy! Daddy! I wanted to tell wou something!" He laughed and slapped his dad's forehead with his small hand and the phone.

Then with a sudden lift Hunter was flying through the air again.

He spread his arms out as if he where a plane, or a bird. "Wheeeee!" The small voice called out.

Caleb caught him around the waist again, and putting his son back on his shoulders, he mounted the porch steps, sat on the swing seat and bounced Hunter on his knee, trying to pry his phone out of the small, loveable hands.

"Well, what's this you wanted to tell me little man?"

Hunter eyed his dad's hands as they inched their way slowly towards the prize he was clutching.

Holding the phone tighter than ever he lifted his cute, loveable round face towards his dad like a flower who lifts it head towards the sun.

The clusters of blond hair around his small face made Caleb think of the sunflowers growing along the front garden's border.

"The wheat is big, and strong! Grandpa says it's weady to be harvwested."

Caleb leaned forward taking Hunter's face between his hands, and leaned in more till his nose touched Hunter's small one.

"That's the best news yet buddy!" He turned as he heard a voice just inside the porch door.

Aubrey walked out and Caleb grinned lazily at her, he crossed his legs and rocked the swing seat back and forth.

Hunter still sat in his lap playing with his phone.

"Hey little sis."

Aubrey laughed and sat down next to them. "Hey, Emma not here?"

Caleb yawned and rubbed the back of his neck, "Yeah she's around here somewhere with Jade and Reese." He grinned and gave her one of his cheek-filled winks.

Aubrey nodded, "I didn't know you were up here,"

Caleb inclined his head to the side.

"Staying with Dad, I mean."

"Ah," Caleb said. "Yeah, Emma and I brought the kids up here yesterday. Dad needs a hand with bringing the harvest in." He nodded towards the sea of golden fields.

"I wish Sean and the boys could help." Aubrey frowned "But, with Cameron away," she shrugged "as I was telling Dad, Ivar and Bryce have their work cut out for them."

"I help Uncle Sean!" Hunter chimed, having lost interest in Caleb's phone after too many incorrect passcodes had locked him out.

"Sure you can, buddy."

Caleb stood, placing Hunter onto his shoulders, "As soon as you're bigger."

"I am bigger now!" protested the little boy.

Aubrey watched the father and son disappear into one of the large storage barns.

A few moments later, Emma ran out, Caleb and Hunter following her with a hose. Their two teenage daughters followed, each with a bucket of water.

Aubrey rocked the swing seat and laughed at the sight.

The porch door swung open and Jason, followed by Bryce ran out, "Come on Mom!" Bryce hollered as he ran towards the garden tap.

Madison leaned on the door frame, "Only *your* brother and dad would advocate a water fight when work needed to be done."

The sound of tires on gravel filled the air and dust filled the driveway as a large red pickup truck rolled to a stop.

"Looks like we got here just in time," Sean drawled, getting out the front. He grinned, removing his hat and rumpling up his hair.

Ivar bounded out the back of the flatbed and ran to join in the war of the hoses with his brother and cousins.

He waved to his mom quickly and smiled as he passed where she sat.

Aubrey laughed and leaned back on the swing seat.

Sean's boots clomped on the wooden boards as he mounted the steps, "Mornin' Madison," he grinned and sat down next to Aubrey, draping an arm over her shoulder,

"How's it going?" Aubrey asked, "Did you sell the truck?"

Sean shook his head, "The buyer called, he can't come until later this week now." His mouth curved into a frown, "Well," his eyes scanned the land surrounding him. "I've got plenty of work at the garage in town, but I'll try to lend a hand around here as much as possible, Madison."

He smiled at his mother-in-law and hooked an arm around Aubrey's waist.

Jason ran past and waved, several grandkids tailing him with water. "C'mon Maddie!"

He dashed up the porch steps, grabbed his wife's hand and pulled her into the fray.

"Whoop! Get Grandma!" Bryce called, letting out a wild yell.

Aubrey and Sean chuckled as Madison lifted her skirt, chasing after her husband.

~Chapter Four~
"Yeah, it was fun. I'll give you that."

Monday was warm, and as the day headed into mid-morning, the temperature rose.

"So what's this that dad said that your mom said you needed help fixing?" Caleb said laughing as he rubbed dirt off his hands and perched on the fence that ran around the edge of the wheat field.

Bryce hoisted himself up next to his uncle.

He stared at the familiar Stars and Stripes that fluttered in the wind outside of his grandparents farm just on the outskirts of woodland park Colorado.

"The neck on my fiddle snapped and I was wonderin' if you could fix it, bein' good with your hands and wood and all." Bryce crossed his ankles and leaned forward.

Caleb nodded, "You bring it with you?"

"Yessir, it's in Grandpa's workshop."

"Cool," Caleb jumped down, he arched his back. "Come on then, let's check out this fiddle so you can get back to fiddling." He winked and started out towards the workshop built onto the side of the house.

The door creaked open and the smell of must and wood shavings smacked Bryce full on.

He breathed deeply, rolling his eyes heavenwards at the amazing scent.

"Okay," Caleb picked up the instrument that lay on the table. He let a low whistle.

Bryce came over to stand next to him. The sixteen year old shoved his hands into his pockets as he looked at his uncle.

"That bad?" He asked as his uncle glanced down at him and smirked, "Nah, I just wanted to get your attention."

He winked again and fitted the two neck pieces together. "Here, pass me the wood glue."

Bryce handed the thick tube to his uncle.

"Thank you kindly,"

Caleb moved the wood apart and filled the gap with the thick glue and then pushed them back together.

"And ta-da!" Caleb placed the now-fixed fiddle gently on the table, Bryce beamed, "Thanks, Uncle Caleb."

He reached to pick up his musical instrument but Caleb swatted his hand.

"No not yet, young man. The glue needs to dry first."

Bryce grinned and nodded.

He tapped his foot and glanced around the barn.

His eyes fell on an old metal wagon. "Hey, Uncle Caleb,"

"Uh yeah?"

Caleb looked up from the pile of wood he had been inspecting.

Bryce's eyes were sparkling and a mirthful grin tweaked the corners of his mouth.

Caleb tilted his head to the side, "Why are you smiling like that?"

Bryce cleared his throat, "Does that wagon still work, or are the wheels rusted up?"

"It still works, why?" Caleb asked slowly.

"Can I take it?"

Caleb rubbed his forehead.

"Please!" Bryce begged,

"Why?" Caleb squinted up at the bright red painted wagon. He looked back at his ambitious nephew, "What do you plan on doing with it?"

"I promise not to get into trouble." Bryce said. "Well, not too much trouble anyway." He shrugged.

"Mmm," Caleb looked from Bryce to the wagon. "Er, well, who else is gonna be involved?"

Bryce grinned impishly, "I promise Hunter won't be injured or anyone else involved in the making of my enjoyment, er," he coughed, "our enjoyment, I mean." He gave his uncle a toothy smile.

"Nuh uh, Hunter isn't having anything to do with any of your crazy ideas. You are *so* your mother's son." Caleb placed the wagon on the ground.

"Hey, what's that supposed to mean?" Bryce asked, taking hold of the handle.

"Well," Caleb said, "when we were kids, your mom would have all the crazy ideas, I swear she gets them from Dad, Grandpa, I mean." He smiled, "One time during a heatwave she had this idea to get an old fence panel and lay it on the top of that hill over there."

He pointed towards a large grassy slope that backed onto Jason's land.

At the base of the slope, a crystal clear lake shimmered in the midday heat as if inviting people to go and jump in.

Caleb chuckled. "And as always I followed along, we sat on the fence panel and Aubrey pushed off, we flew down the hill and splash! Landed in the lake. I hadn't had so much fun in years." He winked "Then she grew up and lost every ounce of mischief in her body." He crossed his arms as he said this.

Bryce laughed, "She didn't, but that sounds awesome. Let's try it!"

Caleb shot up out of the seat he had perched on, "Whoa, hold it Bryce! Bryce-" Caleb gave up, his nephew was already halfway back to the house, the old wagon bouncing along behind him.

He sighed and called after him, "Just don't go breaking any bones and keep Hunter outta it," Caleb bit his lower lip, "What's the bet Hunter's gonna be on that wagon ride." He said to himself. "Maybe I should warn Emma?"

~

"Okay," Bryce rubbed his hands together, eyes shining. "Who wants the first ride down the hill?"

Reese, his cousin, poked the wagon with her foot, "Is this safe Bryce?"

"Suuure!" Bryce drew the word out, "I mean, what's the worst that could happen?"

"Famous last words," Jade held a struggling Hunter away from the wagon.

"Ivar, you're the oldest. Here, you go first." Bryce turned to his dark-haired older brother.

"Whoa," Ivar held his hands up and backed away a step. "I think I'll stay outta this one and let you have the fun. Besides, isn't it ladies first?" He winked at Jade and Reese. Jade glared at him, "Yeah. You're just saying that because you're scared to go first."

"Me, scared? Never!" Ivar said. "I'm just being polite, I mean, I'd hate to steal all of your fun." He grinned.

"Well, someone's got to go first," Reese stared uncertainly at the wagon.

Bryce worked the handle up and down, "If Ivar won't, then I guess I will." He clambered in and sat down gripping the sides while everyone else stepped back. "Oh come on, you pack of sissies, not one of you gonna ride down with me?" His eyes swept over his cousins and brother.

"I go with wou, cousin Bryce!" Hunter gripped the wagon and lifted his leg as if to climb in.

"No way! It's on my life that I don't let you on that thing. Mom will fry me if you get hurt," Jade picked him up,

"Aww Jade! No fair, me wanna ride downhill." Hunter kicked his sister.

Bryce laughed, "Hey buddy, ya know, I don't think Auntie Emma would be happy with you bombing down the hill and into the lake alone."

Jade breathed a sigh of relief, Bryce's eyes twinkled, "But."

Jade narrowed her eyes ever so slightly.

Reese raised both of her blonde eyebrows and Ivar glanced nervously about.

"Maybe," Bryce went on, "she wouldn't mind if you rode down if everyone went down with you."

Ivar breathed in sharply, "you're a crafty one." He hissed as he climbed on behind his younger brother.

Hunter and the girls got in front.

"Ready?" Bryce asked.

"No," Reese replied shakily.

"Well, here we go anyway!"

Bryce used his hands to push off the ground, the wagon started to roll slowly, gaining momentum as it went downhill. Reese and Jade screamed the whole way down.

Hunter would have stood up just for the fun of it if Jade hadn't locked him against her chest with her arms.

Bryce yelled wildly, Ivar's hands turned white with his intense grip on the wagon. His jaw clenched tightly.

The wagon tore down the hill so fast that even Bryce felt his heart doing somersaults in his throat.

Bryce caught sight of both his dad and uncle running towards them. Sean was waving and shouting for them to stop. Just behind them Jason was running, he turned suddenly and bolted down to the lakes edge and waded in up to his waist. Aubrey, Emma and Madison came out at Sean's cry.

Bryce winced as he heard Emma scream Hunters name.

"Jade!" Bryce hollered as the lake got closer, "Get Hunter out!"

Jade stood to her feet, her knees shaking.

"Jade! Jump."

Sean came up alongside, keeping up for a brief moment before falling back.

Momentarily Bryce saw Jade and Hunter rolling on the grass as they jumped off.

Then the lake's water flooded the wagon, Reese turned and clung onto him, dragging him under the water, the water closed over Bryce's head, Bryce's lungs burned as he held his breath, he surfaced, pulling Reese with him as the wagon sunk and Ivar kicked it away, Reese gasped for breath, Bryce spluttered for a moment before grinning, "That was awesome!" He splashed the water with his fist.

His blond hair hung down over his eyes several shades darker.

Jason came towards them and helped Reese out as Ivar and Bryce splashed towards their dad.

Bryce laughed, "Tell me that wasn't fun!"

Ivar stared at him a grin slowly spread across his face.

"Yeah, it was fun. I'll give you that."

~Chapter Five~

Our walk with the Lord is a lot like a field...

"I think we are in for a good harvest, don't you hon'?" Madison watched the spiral of steam rise from her mug and glanced at her husband.

Jason nodded absently, rocked the porch swing seat and put an arm around her.

"Mmm," he drained his own cup and ran his thumb around the edge. "Maddie,"

"Yes?" She looked up at him.

Jason grinned down at her, feeling like bashful young man again. Madison nestled into the crook of his arm, "What's that face for?"

Jason played with her hair, gently twirling it around his finger. "I found the verse."

Madison arched her eyebrows and snuggled against him even closer. "What?"

Jason leaned in and planted a soft kiss on her forehead. "The verse."

He wiggled his eyebrows at her. Madison's eyes flew open and she sat up right. "As in the *biscuit* verse?"

Jason threw back his head and roared with laughter. He brushed her cheek. "Yep." Mischief lingered in his eyes. "Would you like to hear it?" His mouth tilted in a teasing smile.

Madison nodded, her forehead drawn together, a knowing, almost expectant look in her eyes.

"I've been wondering how long it would take you to find it, Jason."

Jason grinned and pulled her into a hug, he loved the way his name sounded when she said it.

Clearing his throat, Jason started to repeat the verse he had found, "I am the Lord your God who brought you out of the land of Egypt; open your mouth wide, and I will fill it."

He grinned as he finished, dipping his head in a small dramatic bow. Madison blinked, sat up and stared at him as if he had lost his mind.

"That doesn't count." She said soberly.

"What? Why not?" Jason gaped.

Madison winked, a slow smile spreading across her face.

"Because you haven't been anywhere near Egypt."

Jason snorted and ran a hand through his greying hair. "Ha," he retorted. "Well, it counts to me."

Madison leaned against him again, "Well then, if it counts to you, it counts to me." She said loyally. "You can have your reward later as promised."

Jason smiled. For a while he sat still, stroking her hair with one hand.

"I think Aubrey's struggling a little with her busy life and her relationship with the Lord." Madison breathed deeply. The music coming from Bryce's fiddle floated through the top window. "Sean told me that she hasn't had as much time as she normally would have with the Lord each day." She said after a moment.

Jason started to rock the swing seat.

He nodded, "That would be it, to remain in the Lord's peace always is to be walking with him always. To know someone you have to invest in them and spend time with them." He paused the rocking motion by placing both feet on the wooden porch. "Come on," he stood up and took Madison's hand.

"Where are we going?" Madison asked as Jason pushed the gate to fields open.

"Just come on."

"Okay, okay, but we're getting too old for this." She said laughing slightly as Jason helped her over a fallen tree.

"Maybe you are." Jason replied over his shoulder, a smirk tugged at the corners of his mouth. Madison rolled her eyes and pushed a strand of strawberry-blonde hair, laced with silver threads, behind her ear.

"If I'm old, then you're ancient!"

Jason grinned.

"So what's this thing you had to show me? It had better be worth it, I think I just walked through some animal mess." Madison made a face and wiped her shoe on a patch of grass.

"Ah don't worry about that," Jason said. He took her hand and pulled her forward. He kept going until he was standing waist-deep in a field of wheat.

Firebugs crept out of hiding as dusk settled across the county. The fading light shone through the few trees that scattered the piece of land. Jason exhaled, allowing all the breath in his lungs to escape.

"You wanna know something?" He asked, tucking his wife under his arm to keep her warm as the twilight brought a slight chill.

"Depends on what it is," she said with a smile.

The pale blue eyes of her husband became sober and once more he did what he always did when he had a lot on his mind. He allowed his eyes to sweep the fields, before rubbing an ear of grain between his hands.

"Our walk with the Lord is a lot like a field,"

"Oh? And how did you come up with this profound piece of knowledge." Madison asked teasingly.

"I'll tell you." Jason tilted his head and started to explain in soft tones.

~Chapter Six~

*'Satisfy us in the morning with your steadfast love,
that we may rejoice and be glad all our days'
Psalm 90:14*

Aubrey watched the bow glide across the strings and listened as the music filled the air. "You love that, don't you?" she asked.

Bryce looked up from his concentrated daze, "What?"

"You love that fiddle."

"Yeah, I do." He drew the bow back and forth quickly over the strings. His gaze focused on a point far off out the window.

Aubrey listened to the country folk music he played. Bryce smiled fondly as he made the music leap from the strings and fill the room. The sound was sweet, melodic, soothing.

He slowed his playing a little as Caleb, Emma and Sean walked in. Sean dropped down on the sofa next to his wife, "Keep playing Bryce, I like hearing my son play that fiddle."

Caleb and his wife perched on the other sofa across the room.

"That plays mighty fine," Emma commented.

"Yeah, I'm just glad it's fixed," Bryce smiled at his uncle, his hands still moving. His right hand drew the bow back and forth whilst his left hand pressed down on different strings. Caleb winked.

"Ya know," Sean said, he stretched out his long legs and pushed his hat down over his eyes. "Bryce is the only one of his brothers with blond hair."

"Oh?" Aubrey laughed.

"No really!" Sean protested, "I mean, Ivar is a dark brunette and Cameron is a dark reddish brunette."

His mouth puckered, "Actually, we don't have any Brunette's in the family aside from Emma. But they couldn't have got it from her."

"My dad, he was a brunette." Aubrey grinned, "Bryce though, he gets the blond from you Sean." She knocked Sean's cap off to reveal tousled blond hair. Sean's green eyes twinkled up at her.

"He looks a lot like you, thinking about it." She added affectionately.

Sean smiled warmly.

"Is that a good thing?" Bryce grinned wickedly. Sean's cap flew through the air, smacking him around the face.

Bryce chuckled and threw it back.

"Hunter looks like his dad," Emma noted, holding onto Caleb's arm as the small boy ran into the room and started spinning around making airplane noises.

"Wheeee," the little boy called as he span in dizzying circles. Bryce sidestepped to avoid a collision, stopped playing the fiddle and watched his young cousin.

Caleb laughed. "Come into land there, please buddy. Bryce is making music."

"I want to make music!" Hunter decided, stopping. He went over to where Madison's piano stood and started hitting his grandma's white ivory keys.

Bryce made a face and lifted his hands, balancing the fiddle and covering his ears. The adults laughed.

"Okay squirt." Jason said walking in and picking Hunter up, "You dance with Jade and Reese whilst Bryce plays the fiddle and Grandma plays the piano." His voice brought Madison and the two girls into the room.

Reese grabbed one of Hunter's hands, Jade took his other hand and joined hands with her sister. Creating a circle, they danced around the sitting room.

Halfway through a side gallop Reese bumped into Bryce, he grinned at her, shook his head and winked.

Walking in circles around her, he continued to play the fiddle. Reese laughed and clapped her hands in time to the music. Aubrey grinned and leaned into Sean's shoulder as music filled the old house.

"You okay?" He asked, glancing down at her and pulling playfully on her strawberry-blonde ponytail.

"Yeah," She sighed contently and nestled closer, *I am blessed.* Aubrey thought to herself. *Very, very blessed.* She almost laughed. *I never want this to end.*

Aubrey stored the picture of Bryce playing music with his grandma and his cousins playing around them all in her mind along with the feeling of Sean's arm around her. After a moment more of watching and feeling blessed beyond measure, Aubrey sat up, "Hey, where's Ivar?"

Sean shifted slightly, suppressing a yawn, "I think he went outside to call Cameron."

Aubrey nodded and relaxed again, "Okay. Have you heard how he's holding up recently?"

"Cam?"

"Yeah," Aubrey took his hand and started drawing patterns on the back of his hand with her index finger. Sean grinned and leaned down, kissing her forehead.

"I spoke with him earlier, he's getting better and is thinking of making a trip out this way soon."

Aubrey smiled gently, "Bryce and him have a lot to sort out. Did he ever tell you what happened that day?"

A cloud passed over Sean's face, "You mean the day he was on call for the fire station in town? Before he moved to New Orleans?"

Aubrey nodded slowly, twirling a strand of loose hair around her finger.

"Yeah, he told me and Ivar a day or two afterwards. He said if he didn't tell someone he would go crazy." Sean rested his cheek on the top of her head as they watched their nieces and nephew play with Bryce. "Oh, and that guy after the truck is coming Friday."

"Okay, you gonna need Bryce and Ivar around the garage?"

"Yeah, you think Jason will mind?" Sean asked, worry hidden in the depths of his eyes.

"No, I think Dad and Caleb can handle the first few days of the harvest, and besides it will take all week to bring it in. You boys can help out Saturday."

"Yeah, good point." Sean yawned, slid down the sofa, crossed his ankles and jammed his cap back on his head. "So I'm gonna take a nap before I hit a week of work." He gave her a toothy smile from under the cap's rim.

~Chapter Seven~

"Why does everyone name their cow Daisy?"

Tuesday morning dawned with the promise of warm weather. Jason led the cow into the barn, the only other animal kept on the farm aside from the horses and chickens. The cow tossed its head and protested slightly from going into its stall. "Come on you! Don't be difficult," he frowned as he pulled on the rope, "Oi, Reese, Ivar get in here and help me."

He called out to the two passing teens. Ivar trotted up, Reese right behind him.

"Ivar push this old thing from the back would you?"

"Sure, Grandpa, but then I really gotta go help Dad and Bryce down at the garage in town."

"Sure, sure, just give her a little push." Jason said, his cheeks going red as he puffed, pulling on the rope.

Reese stood to the side watching, a slight smile tilted her lips. Ivar braced his shoulder against the cow's backside and pushed, his trainers digging into the barn floor. "Move it cow!" He muttered.

Jason tugged on the rope until his fingers burned, "Come on old girl. Move already." He grunted. He held the stall gate open with one foot. Reese glanced up at the board hanging above the stall.

She smirked, "Maybe try using her name. She has one for a reason."

Ivar stared at his cousin incredulously, "It's a cow." He said bluntly, "She's not going to understand whether we use her name or the name of the grocery store clerk."

"Okay, let's try it then." Reese grabbed a handful of hay and ran inside the stall, she waved the hay in front of the cows eyes.

"Come on, Sarah."

Ivar and Jason raised their eyebrows and stared at her.

"What?" Reese asked.

Jason motioned towards the sign, "Her name's not Sarah."

"I know, Sarah is the clerk at the grocery store." She said, a look of mischief gleamed in her eyes.

Ivar shot her a look.

Reese laughed and waved the hay in front of the cow again.

"Here girl, look what I have for you." The cow's tail swished and her front hoof lifted off the floor. "Come on Daisy, come on." Reese backed up slowly, the animal watching the hay as it came towards her. "Good girl, Daisy." Reese said, patting her leathered back.

She dropped the hay on the ground, skirted around the cow and stepped out of the stall, closing the gate with a satisfactory clang.

Ivar glared at the cow. "Why does everyone name their cow, Daisy?" He threw his hands up and tried to sound miffed, but his mouth curved into a smile that couldn't hold back his laughter.

"Well, do you have a better name for a cow?" Jason asked reaching over the gate and tethering Daisy's rope to the metal feeding rack.

"Yeah, what about Bryce?" Ivar grinned.

Jason clipped him around the head.

"What about Ivar," Reese retorted.

Ivar stuck his tongue out in protest and Reese returned the favour,

"Go help Bryce and your dad in town, Ivar, before Reese names the horses and your aunt's chickens after you as well." Jason grabbed the pitchfork that leaned against the barn wall and started gathering up the hay that littered the floor. Ivar shoved his hands into the pockets of his jeans and tossed his dark hair back.

"Ha, yeah right."

~Chapter Eight~

"Because we all need a reminder now and then that He will never leave us."

Bryce jumped from foot to foot as Ivar pulled up in his car outside their dad's garage.

"What's wrong with you?" Ivar asked, getting out and closing the car door. He had just been out with Savannah and his mind was on other things.

"C'mon." Bryce grabbed his arm and pulled him into the garage. "Dad wants this shelf restocked, then we can go."

"Go where?" Ivar picked up a pile of car tires and moved them to the other side of the garage.

"Do you remember that stream down at the base of Pike's Peak?" Bryce started stacking oil cans in a haphazard way.

"Careful, Bryce. And yeah, I remember it why?"

"That new field Grandpa bought last week has that stream on it, let's take the girls and Hunter down to see it." Ivar tossed a cloth he used for wiping down the cars from hand to hand.

"I guess we can," He glanced at his watch, "It's almost midday. If we can get this done in the next half hour, we can go back to the farm. Mom's there anyway and I think Dad planned on joining her later today."

"Awesome," Bryce pushed his hair back and piled his dad's spanner collection on the top shelf.

~

"Okay," Bryce said, "it's this way." He pointed northward.

"No, it's that way," Ivar shook his head and pointed behind him, southwards.

Jade frowned she looked around the large field they were standing in. "I'm sure it's more eastward." She put her hands on her hips.

"No!" Hunter giggled, he pointed backwards, back towards the farm, "it's that way." He threw his head back laughing. Bryce grinned, scooped him up and put him on his shoulders.

As he did, Bryce felt something shift beneath his shirt. Once Hunter was safely on his shoulders Bryce undid the top button on his shirt and pulled out the small wooden cross hanging on the end of a leather cord.

He smiled fondly and gripped it. He still remembered the day his dad had given it to him.

"Bryce,"
Sean sat down in front of his fifteen year old. "I wanna give you something."

Putting down the brush he had been using to groom down his horse Bryce faced his dad. "Yeah?"

Sean held out a thin leather cord, hanging off the end was a simple wooden cross.

Bryce had seen his dad wearing it before, he'd always liked it.

Sean smiled softly at Bryce's wide eyed expression. "First it was your great grandpas, then my father in law and then dad me."

He flipped it over and pointed to the back, his great grandpas initials where engraved at the top.

Then his grandpas, then Jason's.

At the very bottom where the letters, B.A.W.

"Bryce Andrew Walker." Bryce said, his voice filled with awe and wonder.

Sean nodded and dropped the leather cord around Bryce's neck, the wooden cross bounced against his chest. "Thanks dad," Bryce fingered it carefully.

Sean nodded, and leaned forward, his elbows in his knees. "It's been passed down through years,"

"But why not give it to Ivar or Cam? Cam's the oldest."

Sean pulled his cap off and fanned it in front of his face, "when we pass it down we give it to the person who we feel needs it. Your grandpa Jason isn't my dad but my father in law. He could have given it to Caleb his son. But both Caleb and him felt I needed it. I was given it the day of your mom's and mine wedding."

"What they think you need help with mom?" Bryce sniggered.

Sean swatted him. "No, but as a reminder to keep Christ as the centre. I was a new Christian back then and was still learning."

Bryce looked down at the cross hanging around his neck, he slid it under his shirt.

"So why me?"

"Because we all need a reminder now and then that he will never leave us. You'll know when it's time to pass it on."

Bryce grinned at the memory, he pulled the leather cord out and let the cross hang again this shirt.

Jiggling Hunter, who was leaning heavily on his head, he called to the others, "I'm the leader of this expedition. We're going this way."

He started northwards, heading for the back fields. Ivar glanced upwards as a few dark clouds speckled the horizon. He bit his lip and hoped the storm would stay away until they were back safely at the farm.

~Chapter Nine~

"And let them find us soon, God."

The smell of freshly-cut grass filled the room as Caleb and Jason wiped their boots on the mat and stepped into the kitchen. The smell of fresh vanilla coffee that Madison made on Tuesdays filled the room.

"Well, that's the front lawn, the back lawn, the side lawn, and that patch of overgrown grass down at the end of the drive all mowed and trimmed." Caleb announced sitting down at the table.

Jason rubbed a hand over his face and yawned.

"Yep, all the chores are done and just in time! We're gonna get some rain. I just hope it doesn't ruin the crop, we need to bring in the harvest but we can deal with some of that tomorrow. Saturday, Sean and the boys are coming out here to help."

Caleb thanked his wife with a warm smile as she handed him a steaming cup of coffee.

"Caleb, have you seen the kids?" Emma asked, her deep chocolate brown eyes filled with worry.

"No, why?"

"Dad, Sean and I can't find any of the boys." Aubrey said as she came into the kitchen from the back door.

It had started to rain outside and her hair was damp. She glanced at her father, her heart in her eyes, begging him to solve their problem.

Caleb's fingers tightened around his mug, "Where's Sean?"

"I'm here," Sean stomped in, shaking his head like a wet dog.

"You didn't find them?" Emma asked concerned, her eyes filled with tears when he shook his head.

Outside, thunder crackled and lightning streaked the darkening sky. Aubrey wrung her hands, "The boys got done early with Sean at the garage. They wanted to show Reese, Jade and Hunter something."

Jason went over and pulled her into a hug "We'll find them, honey. Don't you worry."

Oh Bryce! Where are you and Ivar? Aubrey pressed her lips into a thin line as she glanced out the window at the storm which was blowing in.

The sky's had darkened making it feel like midnight, rather than just after midday.

Another flash of light from outside made Emma jump.

Caleb took her hand, "Don't worry, Ivar and Bryce will look after Hunter and the girls. They've both got a good head on their shoulders."

Jason disappeared into the washroom. He came back holding a torch and several blankets. "Sean, Caleb you two come with me. Maddie; you, Aubrey and Emma stay here and-"

"-Oh no," Madison interjected, pulling on her own jacket. "We're coming too."

Jason glanced at his son and Caleb nodded at his unspoken question.

"Okay then, ladies stick close." Jacob pulled his own rain coat on and grabbed a flask, filling it with hot coffee.

"Sean, any idea where the boys were heading?"

Sean scratched his chin and rumpled his hair. He shifted his cap from hand to hand.

"Well Jason, your farm is a couple miles outta town and you got a lot of land and the Davis family farm backs right up against the base of Pike's Peak. I heard Bryce mention something about a great stream that ran along the back of your property near Pike's Peak."

Emma and Aubrey groaned almost simultaneously.

Jason nodded and headed for the door while screwing the cap of the flask on, "Okay, no use yakking. Let's get a move on."

~

"I want Mommy!" Hunter wailed.

Reese bit her bottom lip and huddled up next to Ivar, pulling Hunter into her lap. "It's okay Hunter, Mom and Dad will be looking for us."

"Yeah, buddy," Ivar said trying to sound encouraging, "and I'm sure Uncle Sean and Auntie Aubrey are searchin' right along with them and Grandma and Grandpa."

Jade pushed her wet hair back, water droplets dripped from the tree branches above them.

"Bryce, please, for the sake of my sanity, stop pacing." Her voice sounded tired.

Bryce glanced at them; his brother and three cousins huddled at the base of a large Rocky Mountain juniper.

The rain was coming down in large sheets of pelting droplets. The mid-afternoon sky was as black as night, thick storm clouds covered every inch of the vista.

"Bro," Ivar said, "stop pacing and come help me think."

"I am thinking."

"You're pacing." Reese said.

Jade nodded, "And you look like a Labrador who's just been dunked in a lake." She said.

Bryce stared at her, then looked up towards the strands of wet blond hair that stuck to his forehead.

"You don't look like a beauty queen at the moment yourself, Jadey,"

Jade's eyes narrowed, "I told you not to call me that Brycey-boy."

The childhood nickname stopped Bryce in his tracks. He turned and faced his cousin. Ivar watched as emotion after emotion flashed across the bright green eyes of his brother.

"Jade-" Bryce's voice rose.

Ivar cut him of, "Okay, that's enough you two. Jade don't call Bryce that and Bryce don't call Jade that."

"Only Dad and my brothers can call me that." Bryce mumbled.

Jade sat back as Bryce resumed his pacing.

"Bryce, pacing is not gonna get us home." Reese murmured quietly. Bryce kicked at a rock and watched as it smacked against the side of a tree, bounced off and fell into the stream.

Bryce dropped down by the edge of the water, "This is useless. Can't we just start walking?"

Ivar shook his head, he pulled off his jumper and wrapped it around Hunter.

"No, Bryce,"

"Why not?"

"Look at Hunter," Ivar said. "He's tuckered out and in this rain it might take an hour or two to walk back to the farm."

"Why did Grandpa have to own such a big chunk of land?" Jade sniffed and rubbed her eyes.

Bryce felt his heart tug, he crouched down next to his cousin holding out his denim jacket, "Here."

Jade smiled her thanks as Bryce wrapped it around her shoulders.

Hunter squirmed in Reese's lap. Ivar reached out and took him, "Are wou scared of the rain, Ivar?" Hunter's lower lip stuck out.

Ivar smiled, "I'm not, why?" He asked half-laughing.

"Wou don't want to go as its raining," Hunter scrunched his little face up. Bryce laughed along with his brother. Ivar shook his head, "No, Hunter, it's just too far for you to walk in this weather."

"Oh, can't wou carry me?"

Ivar let out a long breath, "The fields will be swamped with all the water running down from Pike's Peak, so even if I did we wouldn't get very far." A weary smile tugged the corners of his lips.

Hunter's chin quivered.

"Hey, don't cry buddy. They'll find us," Ivar glanced at the sky as Hunter nestled into his chest.

"And let them find us soon, God." Bryce whispered, adding onto the silent prayer that he saw in his brothers eyes.

~

Mud splattered out from under the wheels of the four by four. Jason spun the wheel as the truck swivelled in the dirt.

Sean clung on as he gripped the sides of the truck and Aubrey's eyes darted from left to right. Emma sat inside the truck's cab with Madison and Caleb.

"I-var! Bry-yce!" Sean hollered.

Emma wound down the window, "Ja-ade, Ree-eese!"

"Hun-ter!" Caleb yelled.

Jason turned down a dirt track.

"Dad, where are we going? The main track is back that way." Caleb said, gesturing in the other direction.

Jason nodded, "I know, Son" He never took his eyes of the road.

"Then why?"

"It's a shortcut, trust me." He gave a wry smile and his voice aged, whilst he leaned on the car door. "I was brought up here, I brought you up here, and my grandkids are partly being brought up here. Don't you think I know every nook and cranny of this place?" He asked.

~Chapter Ten~
'Rejoice with me; I have found my lost sheep.' Luke 15:6

"Mommy!" Hunter wailed.

Ivar flinched and held the boy closer while flipping his wrist to see his watch.

It blinked 16:00 at him.

He said that it was almost evening when Reese asked the time.

Jade was soaked to the skin, so Bryce pulled his coat off and wrapped that around her as well as his denim jacket, then he rested back against a tree.

He closed his eyes for a brief moment struggling to hold back the tears that burned behind his eyelids. *It's been raining since 12:45, surely they would be looking for us by now.*

He blinked open his eyes and stared up into the torrential downpour, his jaw clenched as the raindrops pelted his face and slid down his cheeks and through his hair.

He allowed the sharp wind to pummel its strong, freezing fist against his chest. *Where are you? This is all my fault,* he thought.

When Reese sat up suddenly, Ivar squinted with one eye to stare at her. "What is it Reese?" He shouted over the rain.

Reese frowned and pointed vaguely to somewhere out of sight.

"I think I saw headlights." She said, close enough to Ivar for him to hear.

Ivar shoved back his wet hair and rolled onto his ankles staring into the murkiness, holding Hunter against his chest. He yelped as bright white lights flashed in his eyes.

He fell back on the seat of his pants, gripping Hunter tightly as to not let him fall on the muddy ground.

"Ivar!"

Ivar blinked as his name was called and shielded his eyes with his hand.

"Dad?" He shouted back.

Bryce watched it all happen in a blur of rain, arms circling him, voices, and warm rugs.

Before he had time to think, Bryce was holding a thick warm blanket around his shoulders with a rain coat thrown over it. Ivar was seated next to him as was his dad and uncle in the back of the truck as it rolled through the drizzling rain.

Reese and Jade sat with Hunter and the women inside the truck's cab.

Jason kept the truck moving slowly so his grandsons wouldn't get splattered with mud.

Bryce watched as the dark clouds pulled back from the sky to reveal a pale blue sky.

Peach-coloured wispy clouds tinted the blue mass. The last few drops of rain fell and the scent of wet grass and hay filled the air. Mud squelched under the tires as field after field rolled past. "What time is it?"

Caleb raised an eyebrow and checked his phone,

"Mmm, 16:25, why?"

"Just wonderin'" Bryce said.

Bryce's eyes met his dad's. Emerald green against emerald green, staring one another down.

"You okay?" Sean asked.

"Yeah," Bryce said and took a deep breath, letting it out again after a moment's hold.

"Well, at least we found the stream by Pike's Peak."

Ivar shot him a look, bordering on a glare.

"We're soaked, and all you're thinking about is how we found the stream."

"Hey, that was a neat stream,"

"I'm sure it was!" Sean said quickly, seeing Ivar's mouth open as if he was ready for a verbal fight.

"Well, the most important thing is that you're all safe and that we get Hunter and the girls warmed up." Caleb said, his forehead creased with concern.

~

"Well, Hunter's asleep and the girls have retreated to Maddie's and my room for a movie night with Grandma." Jason said, entering the large open-plan kitchen diner, "Well, thank you, Father that none of them shall catch a cold or anything because of being soaked to the skin."

Jason prayed while drying his greying hair with the towel Madison had given him before he came down.

"Amen," Caleb murmured from where he sat at the Davis family table. The Walkers sat opposite Caleb and Emma. Sean nodded and inhaled the steam that arose from his coffee mug.

Jason watched his grandson trace the rim of his mug with his index finger. "You okay, kiddo?" He asked, pulling up a chair next to Ivar.

"Huh," Ivar looked up, snapping from his dazed stupor. "Oh yeah," he gave a watery smile. "I'm fine, Grandpa."

"You sure?"

Ivar nodded slowly.

Aubrey rubbed his arm, "Hey, if something is bothering you," she smiled affectionately and ran her hand through his damp hair.

Ivar rubbed his face, "I don't know," he said, "I'm fine, I just.." He shook his head.

The room fell silent, Caleb and Emma held hands under the table and watched their nephew with silent love and compassion in their eyes.

Sean rocked onto the back legs of his chair, his hand resting on Ivar's knee. Aubrey sat on the other side of Jason and Bryce leaned over the back of his uncle's chair watching the whole scene with wide eyes.

"What if something had happened to the girls, or to Hunter?" Ivar asked suddenly, he pressed his hands onto the tables smooth wooden surface. "It would have been my fault, if anything had happened and I-I don't think I could bear it."

"Ivar," Emma breathed, "everyone makes mistakes. It's okay, you didn't know it would storm like that when you left and you did the right thing in keeping everyone still and together." She smiled warmly and Ivar returned the smile.

"Besides, if I had been in charge, I would've had them all marching through the mud." Bryce grinned.

"Well, then remind me never to let you be in charge of them alone." Sean snickered, sending a dish cloth flying towards his son's face.

Bryce laughed behind it, peeled it from his face and blinked several times. "But seriously bro', it's not your fault, it was my idea to go see the stream anyway."

Ivar nodded slowly, several moments passed before the tight tension in his face relaxed, replaced by relief and a spark of mischief. "So this was all your fault, was it?" He said slyly, turning to face his brother.

Bryce's eyes widened in surprise, his eyebrows flew up and his mouth curved downwards.

"Hey now, I didn't say nothin' like that."

Ivar smiled at him.

Later as the two stood on the porch tugging their coats on before heading home, Bryce said half-heartedly. "So if anything had happened to me you would have been fine and dandy about it?"

"What?" Ivar stared at him.

"Well, you said that if anything had happened to the girls or Hunter you couldn't bear it. So I was askin', does that mean you would have been fine if something had happened to me?" Bryce stuffed his arm into the coat's sleeve.

Ivar straightened and started to button up his jacket, he cast Bryce a side glance.

"Seriously?"

"Well yeah," Bryce bent at the waist and started to tie his boot laces so his brother couldn't see the laughter in his eyes.

He found himself suddenly gasping for breath as Ivar launched at him, pinning him to the ground, Ivar wrestled his brother, the two boys rolled on the ground at the base of the porch steps.

 "And the purpose of that was what, exactly?" Bryce said brushing himself off once the scuffle had ended.

Ivar grinned, grabbed the side of the truck and jumped in as his parents gunned the engine.

Bryce got in next to him.

"I couldn't live without you brother." Ivar said in a husky voice after a while. "And you know it."

Bryce stared at him for a moment before looking down at his shoes. He pushed his hair back and traced a finger along his jawline.

"Well," he spoke after a few moments, "I'm glad. 'Cause you're stuck with me."

Ivar glanced at him, studying his brother's face. Bryce's features were handsome, with high cheekbones and a strong-edged jawline. His green eyes brought out his blond hair.

"Good." He said simply.

~Chapter Eleven~

*'My son, pay attention to my words;
incline your ear to my sayings.'
Proverbs 4:20*

The novel snapped shut and Jason breathed deeply. He placed the book on his bedside table and glanced across at his sleeping wife.

He reached across to turn his reading lamp off, and as he did so, his fingertips brushed across the cover of his leather-bound Bible.

Slowly, he gripped it and pulled it into his lap.

A smile, tainted with fondness, stretched across his lips as he watched page after well-loved page fly past his eyes. Highlighted paragraphs and verses filled his vision.

The smell of rain, mingled with hay and horses floated through the window that Madison had left ajar.

Jason stopped on the page that was marked with the well-frayed ribbon.

The book of Proverbs stared up at him. Chapter four stood out and Jason ran his finger down the page until he hit the right passage.

"My son, pay attention to my words; incline your ear to my sayings. Do not lose sight of them, keep them in the depths of your heart. For they are life to those who find them, and health to the whole body."

Jason breathed in as he scrambled in the bedside table's drawer until he found a pen. He circled it in red.

"I should show this to Aubrey tomorrow." He said, with another smile. He scribbled the verse on a piece of paper and placed it and his Bible back on the bedside table.

He let out a satisfied breath as he lay back against the pillows, "Well God, you did it again, you watched over my bunch." He chuckled softly, "Thank you Lord for protecting them. Those kids are as sturdy as rocks but, boy, do they need constant watching. Especially that young Bryce. Though he's as mischievous as a groundhog, there's a quietness about him. I see it when he plays that fiddle or when he's talking about you. A well, how would you put it?"

Jason scratched his chin and stared at the roof as if it held his answer, "Ah yes, almost like a sacred quietness that he likes to keep between you and himself. There's a verse in the book of Psalms, well, you know that says 'be still and know that I am God'."

Jason blinked and smiled to himself, he laughed quietly "Well, of course you know it, it was you sayin' it."

He grinned, "Well anyway, I think Bryce does that more than we know. I think he thinks about you an awful lot. Now, Aubrey on the other hand Lord, she needs to keep her guard up, Father."

Jason shook his head, "It's in our weakest moments that we need you the most and, well, like the bank, we can't withdraw money unless we put money in first. Aubrey can't withdraw the word of God from her heart and stand on it unless she puts it in there first. Now, that's not to say she doesn't spend time with you, Lord, but like I was saying to Maddie the other day, it's also a lot like my field. I've got to plant the seed and cultivate it before I can expect a harvest. It's the same with your word, Lord. Gotta plant it like a seed in your heart, then water it, give it sunlight, and then watch it grow. But caring for a harvest is a daily thing, gotta keep cultivating it so it will flourish!"

Jason yawned, "I think it's lights out now for me Lord, I may still be active, but boy, those grandkids take it out of me."

He laughed, turned off the lamp and pulled the blankets over him.

Suddenly Jason sat up in the darkness, "Uh Lord, just to clarify, I meant that the grandkids take it out of you in a good way, by the way." He said, his eyes closing slowly.

"But then," he yawned and lay down again, "you know that too." He fell asleep with a smile on his lips.

$\sim$

"I love Wednesday's." Reese pulled out a handful of straw and let it rain down from where she sat amongst the barn rafters.

"Why's that then?" Bryce swung his legs and stared down from their high perch.

"Well, during term time it's when I have cross country." Reese let another handful of straw fall.

Bryce tilted his head, raising a eyebrow at her.

"Okay, and Wednesday is a funny word."

Bryce laughed heartily.

He leaned over and ruffed her hair, "so I guess you sitting up in the barn rafters with me means I'm forgiven?"

It was Reese's turn to tilt her head and raise an eyebrow now. "What did you do wrong?"

"Uh let's see, led you all on a hours long trek just to see a stream, got us all stuck by the side of the stream for several hours in the pouring rain, got you all soaked to the skin." Bryce counted them all off on his fingers.

Reese laughed, "don't worry about it. As scary as it was in the moment, now I think about it, it was actually quite fun!"

Bryce smiled at her weakly, he dragged his fingers through his messy blond hair and blew at a rebellious strand that hung over his eyes, tickling his nose.

He went to speak but Reese shushed him.

"Look," she mouthed and pointed downwards.

Voices floated up towards them as Aubrey walked into the barn with Madison and Caleb.

A spark of mischief filled Bryce's eyes.

"Get two handfuls of straw," he whispered, wiggling back a couple inches.

He rested his hands on the edge of the rafters.

Holding up one hand he counted down, "three, two, one," he mouthed.

Reese and Bryce let the straw rain down on them.

Reese almost cracked up with laughter.

Bryce threw himself onto her, clamping a hand over her mouth to stop her squeaks from being heard.

Down below Aubrey was shaking straw off her.

"Bryce Andrew Walker! Get your backside down here."

For a moment Bryce thought she was mad. But then he heard her laughing and he grinned.

~Chapter Twelve~

"Wouldn't live any other place than here."

Sean waved as his wife pulled out the driveway.

Aubrey waved back out of the window as she turned at the end of the road and drove out of sight heading out for a meeting at the church café.

"Okay boys," Sean said, turning around and walking back into the house, "both of you go and jump into the back of the pickup truck. The buyer should be coming by later for the red truck and we need to go clean up at the garage before he gets here."

Ivar nodded and hopped down from the stool at the breakfast bar. He discarded his bowl of cereal in the sink and went to find his jumper.

Sean glanced around the kitchen-diner, "Hey Ivar, where's your brother?"

Ivar cocked his head to the side, a faint, knowing smile spreading across his face.

Sean's brow furrowed, then the muscles in his jaw relaxed as the sound of country folk music floated down from the bedroom at the end of the hallway.

Whilst Ivar headed out of the bungalow towards the truck, Sean walked briskly towards the end bedroom. Smiling slightly he tapped on the door, "Hey Bryce," The fiddle music stopped and the door swung open.

"Yeah?" Bryce stood in the doorway, dressed in jeans, a shirt and denim jacket.

His tousled blond hair hung down below his ears, almost touching his shoulders and he shoved it out of his eyes with a quick movement.

Sean grinned, "That getting too long for ya?"

"What my hair?" Bryce laughed, and shook his head again, flicking more out of his eyes, "Nah, it's good."

Sean chuckled he slapped the door frame, "Well then, put that fiddle away, we need to get down to the garage."

Bryce nodded, he turned back into his room, setting the well used instrument in its case, "Oh, er Dad?"

"Yeah?" Sean turned back and came to the door.

"Uh, my legs been hurtin' somethin' awful this morning." Bryce clicked the clasp's on the case shut.

Sean frowned, "Is it still painful, or is it wearing off?"

"Its still painful, but it's a little better, I think."

"Okay," Sean said, "just take it easy today okay? We can always call Mom for advice if it gets worse."

Bryce nodded "Yessir,"

Ivar was waiting in the back of the pickup when the two walked out, "Come on!" He hit the side of the truck, the sound echoing in the clear air. "The day is getting late,"

Sean slipped into the front of the truck, pushed the keys into the ignition and smiled like a kid at Christmas as the engine roared to life.

"Dad's sure proud of his truck ain't he?" Bryce commented as he jumped up next to his brother wincing slightly when his pain shot up his leg when his right foot hit the floor.

Ivar nodded as they pulled out, "Yeah, he cleans it like twice a week."

"That's not too bad," Bryce said, his voice slightly muffled as the wind swept both boys' hair back as they drove through town.

"You know Randy? Well his dad bought a new truck the other week. Randy was tellin' me that he gets it cleaned like four times a week."

"No kiddin'! That's obsessive! He hand wash it?" Ivar asked.

"Ha," Bryce choked on laughter, "I don't think Randy's dad has ever touched a cleaning product. He uses the carwash downtown."

"Ah," Ivar watched as the row of trees on his left passed and Pike's Peak came into view. The large mountains stood magnificently against the blue sky.

They rose up from the landscape like guardians of the city of woodland park Colorado, the most populous city in the teller county.

Bryce breathed in the air deeply, "Wouldn't live any other place than here." He murmured, running his hand over the trucks exterior.

Ivar agreed, smiled and waved slightly as they passed Savannah who was just coming out of the grocery store. Bryce elbowed him in the rib cage once she was out of view.

Ivar wrinkled his nose up slightly, "What?"

Bryce shook his head and chuckled "No-othing, just that Savannah's pretty cute."

Ivar rolled his eyes, "Hey, you keep your nose outta this okay?" he lifted his chin, "'sides, you wouldn't understand, little brother."

"Little brother indeed," Bryce said his pride slightly injured, "says the boy only two years older than me."

Ivar glanced at him and smirked.

~

"Spanner? Thanks. Wrench please? Thanks. Yeah, and spanner again please? Uh that's not a spanner, Bryce." Sean crawled out from under the truck and put the hammer on the workbench. He stood in front of his son and waved a hand in front of his face, "Earth to Bryce."

Sean frowned, Bryce's eyes were clouded over, his forehead creased as if he was thinking deeply.

"Come in Bryce, Brycey-boy." Sean snapped his fingers close to Bryce's ear.

"Huh? Oh yeah what?" Bryce looked up, his voice pulled tight.

"You okay, son? The leg still playing up?" Sean squatted down in front of him.

"Huh," Bryce blinked and shook his head, "Uh yeah, I'm fine why?"

"You like literally zoned out. You gave Dad a hammer instead of a spanner," Ivar noted from the other side of the truck. He came around and crouched next to his brother, "Everything okay?"

Bryce nodded and stood up, "Yeah I'm fine," he grabbed the spanner off the bench. "Just a bit tired I guess."

Sean stood up, stretching his back as he did so. Bryce held out the spanner.

"Thanks, you say if anything's bothering you, okay?"

"Yessir," Bryce flickered a smile at him.

Sean nodded again, removed his cap and messed up the blond curls that stuck to his forehead with sweat like honey to a knife. He glanced across at Ivar for a moment before slapping his cap back down on his head and crawling back under the vehicle.

~

"Hey Dad, Mr Holler is here." Bryce walked past the truck, he bent down and stuck his head under, "The buyer."

Bryce moved back as his dad crawled out.

"Good, we finished this thing just in time, then," Sean glanced at Bryce, "You okay now, kiddo?" He asked.

Bryce nodded.

"Sean Walker!" A large man wearing grease-covered overalls and tattoos up his arm walked in. He grinned broadly and pumped Sean's hand up and down as if it were a lever.

"Bob Holler," Sean pried his hand from the firm grasp, "It's good to see you again. This is the truck," he guided the bearded man over to where the red flatbed was parked.

"Hey Ivar," Bryce pushed his hair back as he stood up. His green eyes were unusually bright and a slight flush had crept into his cheeks.

"Yeah?" Ivar who was watching his dad and Bob Holler closely, didn't notice the slight wobble in his brother's voice.

"I'm gonna go sit down inside the garage storeroom for a bit," Bryce said grabbing hold of the door that led into the back.

Ivar looked up, "Yeah sure, everything okay?"

"Yeah," Bryce skimmed his eyes over Pike's Peak through the open garage door, "Just feel a little off. It's probably this August heat."

Ivar nodded, "Sure."

Bryce breathed only once he could feel the cool air of the air-con in the store room envelop him.

Flopping down instantly on the cold stone floor he rubbed his right leg just above the knee. "Aww, that's sore." He moaned slightly.

Bryce glanced at his watch, *11:30 am* He groaned inwardly. *I wonder how long Bob Holler will talk today.*

He thought. *Last time he talked for a half-hour straight just on the right type of gas to put in the truck.*

His thoughts were interrupted by a spasm of pain shooting through his leg.

~Chapter Thirteen~

'Do not be anxious about anything, but in every situation by prayer and petition, with thanksgiving, present your requests to God and the peace of God which transcends all understanding, will guard your hearts and minds in Christ Jesus.' Philippians 4:6-7

"I'm back." Aubrey paused with her hand on the doorframe and tilted her head slightly, listening to the quietness of her home. "Sean? Ivar? Bryce?"

Aubrey placed her car keys and bag on the kitchen counter, "Hon'?" Her brow furrowed as she went through each room, "Anyone?" Aubrey glanced out the window, it looked as if the world were on fire as the sun went down.

Where on earth are they? Aubrey placed her hands on her hips and bit down on her lip, her meeting at the church had gone well and she was in a sprightly mood.

Bouncing slightly on her toes she went across to the coffee pot that had been set to boil.

"Sean?" She called as she grabbed a mug from the cupboard.

"Mom?" Ivar's tall frame appeared in the back door.

Aubrey let out a long breath and walked around the breakfast bar to give him a tight hug, she laughed slightly slightly, smiling, "I thought no one was home. Are your dad and Bryce outside as well?"'

She looked over his shoulder and out the back door towards the empty backyard.

"Mom," Ivar's voice wavered slightly.

"What?" Aubrey swept the yard once more with her eyes before turning them onto her son.

She searched his face, "Ivar, what's wrong?" Her voice firmed as she saw the panicked look on her sons face.

Ivar's lips moved as if he wanted to speak but no words came out. Finally, he stuttered

"M-mom,"

Aubrey took him by the shoulders and moved him over to the couch, "Here, sit down."

Getting back up she went to the kitchen and grabbed an extra mug, filling it with hot coffee, going back to sit next to Ivar she gave him the drink and said, "Now, tell me what's going on."

Ivar's back was ridged, but Aubrey saw the slight tremor in his shoulders as he swallowed the lump in his throat, "Mom, Dad's taken B-Bryce to t-the-" Ivar shook his head and he blew out all his breath.

He covered his face with his hands his fingers trembled.

"Shhh," Aubrey whispered as a slight sliver of fear took root in her heart.

What's going on with Bryce and Sean? She reached over and pulled Ivar's hands away from his face and covered his hand in between both of hers. "Tell me slowly what's going on." Ivar sat up and ran a hand over his eyes, breathing deeply for several seconds.

"Bryce has gone to the ER."

Aubrey's heart fluttered, "ER, why? Why didn't Dad call me?"

"You have no signal near the church. Anyway, Bryce has been in a lot of pain with his right leg all day. This afternoon when we got back from the garage it got worse. He said it was like a brand of fire had snapped beneath his skin. Dad called the emergency line and they said he should take Bryce in."

Aubrey stared at the floorboards, she pressed a hand against her forehead, groaning. Her heart pounded in her ears.

Ivar watched fear fall like a curtain over her face. "Mom, is he going to be okay?"

Aubrey shook herself, shivers running up and down her back. She went to speak but then stared past him towards the front door, Sean stood in the doorway, holding Bryce in his arms.

"Sean!" Aubrey flew towards him.

Ivar got stiffly to his feet, his eyes glued on Bryce's flushed face.

"Oh Bryce," Aubrey gently stroked the hair back from his forehead. "What's wrong with him?" She asked, looking up at Sean as they walked towards his room.

Ivar followed slowly behind as his dad said, "They're not a hundred percent sure. They wanted to keep him in overnight and run some tests, but he didn't want to." Sean helped Aubrey lay Bryce on his bed.

The boy's eyes fluttered open,

"Hey Mom." He said.

"Hey you, what you doing going and visiting the hospital?" Aubrey pushed his damp hair back, stroking his cheek with the back of her fingers.

Bryce smiled weakly, his eyes filled with pain. "Any chance of some painkillers, please Mom?"

"I've got it." Ivar said turning and heading down the hall, grateful for something to do.

Bryce breathed out, his chest rising and falling as his breathing picked up pace. Aubrey looked up at Sean, tears and desperation filling her eyes.

Sean crouched down next to her and cupped her chin in his palm. "It's going to be okay," he whispered leaning forward so that their foreheads touched. "I promise." He said with a slight tremor in his voice.

Bryce smiled despite himself, a slight laugh passed his lips, "You two mind doing all the mushy stuff somewhere else?"

Sean gave a watery laugh, "Just close your eyes for a moment."

As Bryce did, Sean ran a hand briefly over his eyes before kissing his wife.

~

The sounds around him blurred in and out as Bryce drifted between sleep and consciousness.

His mind was a flurry of confusion. He didn't know what was happening and the pain in his leg burned. He was vaguely aware of someone leaving his room, the door left ajar, letting in a strip of light.

A slow tear crawled out the corner of his eye and down his cheek before dropping off his chin and onto the pillow. *Lord, I'm so scared, I don't know what's happening to me.* He felt warm all over and his head ached horribly.

He slipped into a restless sleep before waking up to the sound of his brothers voice. "I come bearin' painkillers."

Bryce opened his eyes to see Ivar standing over him.

His brother held two white tablets in his palm whilst holding a glass in the other hand.

"Thanks," Bryce whispered. He tried to push himself up, his leg moved and pain ripped up and down it.

Tears sprang to his eyes, he drew a sharp breath in between his teeth and clenched his jaw.

Ivar quickly put the glass and pills down. He looped his arms around his brother and lifted him into a sitting position.

"Thanks," Bryce breathed. "Where's Mom and Dad?" He added once he had swallowed down the painkillers.

"You dozed off about a half-hour ago. Mom's out on the porch with Dad." Ivar reached for the door, "you want me to get them?"

"No, it's okay." Bryce slid down the bed. Wincing in pain he closed his eyes before opening them again and staring at the roof. Tears blurred his vision.

"Ivar?"

"I'm here." Ivar perched on the edge of his bed.

"Can you play my fiddle?" Bryce asked.

Ivar studied his brother's face. The normally luminous green eyes were filled with pain and his cheeks flushed with fever.

"Uh," Ivar fought back the fear that rose in his throat, threatening to choke him, "I can try."

The corner of Bryce's mouth tweaked.

Ivar stilled his shaking hands before picking up the well-loved instrument. He swallowed and paused, his fingers trembled. Bryce managed a small smile, Ivar returned the weak gesture and set the bow to the strings.

He bit down hard on his lower lip as music started to spill from the fiddle. After a while he put it down, "It sounds much better when you play."

Bryce murmured softly, "That's because you gave up playing a few years back."

Ivar nodded and shoved his hair back. Standing, he placed his hands on his knees and stared at the floor.

"Yeah," he said, "I did, it's strange. I can't remember why."

Bryce opened his eyes and looked longingly at his fiddle, "I think it was because you took up the guitar instead."

Ivar nodded, "Yeah maybe. Hey Bryce?"

"Yeah,"

"Are you scared?"

Bryce smiled now, he looked down towards his leg, "A little, but I've got peace."

"Peace?" Ivar squinted.

"Yeah," Bryce coughed, "Here pass me my Bible."

Ivar handed it over, Bryce winced and shifted slightly.

He gave a slight gasp of breath as he pushed himself into a more comfortable position.

"Are you okay?" Ivar asked, concerned.

Bryce nodded, "Yeah, it just hurts to move." He flipped his Bible open and moved the pages, "See, here, in Philippians 4:6-7, it says uh."

Bryce trailed his finger down the page, "Do not be anxious about anything, but in every situation by prayer and petition, with thanksgiving, present your requests to God and the peace of God which transcends all understanding, will guard your hearts and minds in Christ Jesus."

"When did you find that?" Ivar asked, taking the Bible and re-reading the verse.

"Reese showed it to me on Tuesday."

Ivar nodded, "It's a good one, a real keeper, the bit about having peace that transcends all understanding. You know what that means?"

"It means to go beyond. I guess it means that the peace God gives us is so unthinkable, it goes past of knowledge to the human mind, like we cant comprehend how such peace is real and liveable." Bryce said, closing his eyes. "Bookmark it for me, would ya?"

Ivar nodded and picked up one of the many bookmarks that littered Bryce's desktop. He slid it into the page before closing the Bible.

~

Sean's arm was around Aubrey's shoulder as they sat on the porch, watching the stars peek out from behind the curtain of clouds.

"He'll be ok. Won't he Sean?" Aubrey bit her lip, her life, family, it had all seemed so effortless and beautiful a few days ago. Now it felt like everything was falling to pieces.

Sean sighed and pulled her closer, "I hope so." He closed his eyes for a brief moment, when he opened them he looked down to see Aubrey leaning against his chest.

"He'll be ok love." He whispered.

"Your sure?" She looked up at him, her eyes pleading.

Please let him be ok! She prayed inside.

Sean wrapped his jacket around Aubrey as a unusually cold breeze ran through the night.

"The kids have just got their summer hols and it already feels like winter is on its way." Aubrey shifted slightly on the porch steps.

"A whole month to go before September. Then we get autumn."

Aubrey shivered and huddled under the jacket, Sean felt her shiver and asked, "What's wrong?"

Her voice came out small and weak, "What if Bryce isn't here to see the autumn…or to see the snow settle across woodland park." She sniffed and brushed at a tear that crawled down her face.

Sean shook his head, "Aubrey, stop that right now. Bryce isn't going to die."

"Sean-he's in *so* much pain. He can't even stand. I'm so scared." Aubrey balled her hand into a fist and thumped it against the steps. "So, so scared."

"I know." Sean said slowly, "I know."

~

Ivar laid awake for hours.

His parents voices wee raised and urgent throughout the night. Bryce's pain-filled voice caused Ivar's heart to wrench. Through the gap in the door, he saw his brother kneeling just inside the bathroom door.

He heard his dad's hushed voice as the walked past his door. "Aubrey, he needs to go back, he can't even walk to the bathroom. He had to crawl it was so painful for him."

Ivar clenched his eyes shut as tears burned when he heard his moms strangled sobs.

~Chapter Fourteen~
In the mighty name of Jesus...

"Phone for wou, Grandpa," Hunter's blue eyes were wide and his hair stuck out as if he had just woken up.

"Thanks buddy. Now you go and see your momma about your hair, okay? You look as if you have been dragged through a hedge backwards." Jason grinned crookedly and took the phone, patting his grandson gently on the backside as he toddled out the barn.

Jason leaned on the spade he had been using and lifted the phone up, "You have reached the Davis family farm, Jason Davis speaking."

He tilted the straw hat Jade and Hunter had made him slightly and stuffed his free hand into the side pocket of his jeans.

The blade of straw he had been chewing on was pushed to the side of his mouth as he concentrated on the call, "Ah, yes, hello. Uh huh, sure. Mmhm,"

Jason continued to dig with his spade single-handedly as he spoke into the phone. "Yes sir, I can get that to you by the end of next week."

He stared out towards the fields of flourishing corn, "Yes sir, a mighty good harvest this year."

Jason pushed his hat back and ran a hand through his hair as the phone call continued, "Uh huh Mr Shaw, yessir. My grandson's and I will bring your order by next Saturday after we finish bringing the harvest in, yessir, thank you. Okay, yes, good day now."

Jason let out a long whistle as he pocketed the phone, hanging the spade up on the peg by the back wall he headed towards the house.

"Maddie! Caleb, Emma! Guess what, Mr Shaw just placed an order for half our harvest once we bring it in."

He shut the screen door behind him and wiped the mud off his boots as he came into the kitchen. "I'm gonna ask Cameron and Ivar to take the load over with me next Saturday. Cam comes home on Thursday and he said he'd help me haul the next load he was around-"

The strong smell of burning filled his nostrils as he entered the kitchen, but that wasn't what made him stop mid-sentence. Madison stood next to the range cooker, a pan boiling dry on the stove, the home phone dangling limp from her hand.

"Madison?" Jason advanced towards her as she lifted her deep brown eyes towards him.

They brimmed with tears that spilled over and rolled in large drops down her face.

"Maddie? What's wrong?"

Jason disposed of the burning pan, filling it with cool water and putting it outside the kitchen door before turning towards his wife. Taking the phone from her, he checked no one was still on the line and placed it back in its cradle on the wall by the refrigerator and pulled out a chair.

He guided his stunned wife into the seat and knelt in-front of her, taking her hands in his. "Madison, love, what's wrong?"

Madison blinked and broke into a fresh flood of tears.

Jason took her lovingly into his arms and held her there for a while. "Shh, tell me what's wrong and I'll see if this old man can make it right."

Madison drew a long shuddering breath and wiped her eyes.

"Aubrey just called, she, Sean and Ivar are taking Bryce to the hospital. They are on their way at the moment."

Jason rocked back onto his heels and shoved his hands through his greying hair.

"Why?" He asked.

Madison hugged herself. "Bryce has been in agony over his right leg since yesterday mornin'. Last night it got so bad he couldn't even stand, let alone walk across the room."

Jason who had taken up pacing - a trait Bryce had picked up - came back over and hugged her.

"What else did our daughter say?"

Madison rubbed her face, "She asked if we could pray and said they'd call if they need us there. She said to go on with the harvest as planned, and she'd send Ivar up as soon as they leave the hospital." Jason swallowed the lump in his throat. *My baby girl and grandson need me and all I can do is harvest some wheat! Oh God, let Aubrey lean on your strength.*

"Well, pray we can. Go get Emma and Caleb whilst I round up the youngsters." he said, his voice thick with emotion.

~

Caleb shifted from foot to foot, his natural instinct told him to jump in the car and race down to the hospital to be with his sister and nephew. But instead Emma had advised him to wait until after they had prayed.

Caleb listened as his dad's voice rose and fell with each word he said. "Lord, we come to you right now knowing you are Bryce's healer. Isaiah 53 says that you bore our infirmities and by your stripes we are healed. Father God, we refuse to go by what we see, hear, or feel. Right now we choose to walk by faith and not by sight."

Jason's voice rose and his grip of Caleb and Madison's hands tightened. "And right now Lord, we call our grandson, cousin, nephew, Bryce. We call him healed, whole, and strong. Whatever it is that is trying to attack his body right now, in the name of Jesus we take authority over it and command it to get out, get off, and get lost! In the mighty name of Jesus."

~Chapter Fifteen~

"Have I not commanded you? Be strong and courageous. Do not be afraid; do not be discouraged, for the Lord your God will be with you wherever you go."
Joshua 1:9

The doors swung open, Sean stared down at the hospital bed then up as the doctor walked in.

"Well?" Aubrey sat next to Bryce, perched on the edge of his bed. Ivar hovered at the end of his bed, his hands clasping and unclasping behind his back.

The doctor looked at the family, his grey eyes full of determination, mingled with pity.

"Mr and Mrs Walker, I'm sorry, but we have to take Bryce into theatre now."

It felt as if the whole world had slowed down, then sped up again into a flurry of emotions, jerked to a stop and shattered into a thousand pieces. Each piece of their lives and dreams lay like broken glass on the floor.

Aubrey felt as if all the oxygen had been sucked out of her lungs. She stared unseeingly at the doctor, "Theatre," she echoed incredulously, barely breathing.

The doctor nodded as he flitted around the room, "Yes Ma'am, if you want your son to survive we need to take him in right now for operation."

Ivar fell back into a vacant chair, he put his head into his hands, groaning.

Sean pulled Aubrey into his arms and cried with her.

"Ma'am, Sir? I need to take your son in." The doctor urged.

Sean glanced at the doctor cautiously. Getting to his feet shakily, he went over to Bryce's bedside. "Bryce, can you hear me?"

Bryce's eyelids fluttered, "Yes,"

"They need to take you in to have an operation. We will all be right here when you come out, okay?"

Bryce's eyes widened slightly, his chin quivering.

Ivar watched between his fingers, he swallowed as he saw the fear fill his brother's eyes. He stood and made his way over to him. Gently he placed his hands on Bryce's shoulders and leaned in so that only Bryce could hear him.

"Bryce, you hear me?"

A quiet groan confirmed he could.

"You told me once, about a year ago; remember when we heard from Cameron's work that he was MIA, missing in action? You told me to be strong and very courageous, not to be terrified, for the Lord our God will be with us wherever we go."

"Joshua 1:9," Bryce breathed.

Ivar swallowed. "Be strong and very courageous, Bryce, the Lord our God is with you wherever you go."

He drew back as the doctor stepped forward to take Bryce to theatre. Ivar kept eye contact with his brother as he was whisked away.

Aubrey stood and pulled her son into a hug, "It's okay," she whispered, rocking him back and forth as Ivar cried into his mom's shoulder. Sean joined them, circling them both with his arms.

"God," he whispered, sounding like a broken man. "I-I don't know what to do. Right now, we need a miracle. We need a miracle." He swallowed, "I-I know that the doctors' report is not the last and final decision." He continued, finding his voice, "There is always a second opinion. And that's what your word says. And your word says he's healed." He ended in a choked voice.

Ivar dug his knuckles into his eyes, "God, perfect love casts out fear." He said, "Right now I'm scared for Bryce's life. But you love him more than any of us. And you're a good, good Father. And you only want good things for your children and well, God, this isn't a good thing so I know it's not what you want for my little brother. Your love for my brother is perfect and that casts out all fear."

Aubrey buried her face in Sean's shoulder.

Her fingers gripped his shirt. She tried to speak but all that came out was a half-sobbed squeak.

~

Light after light passed overhead.

Bright white pulsating lights passed before Bryce's eyes as he was whisked down the hallway. Closing his eyes against the glare, he focused on what he heard around him.

A doctor was murmuring to a nurse on his right.

"You think he will pull through?" The nurse asked, while the doctor breathed heavily, pushing the bed through the theatre doors.

"We will do everything we can."

Bryce's eyes opened, he took in the room.

Its ceiling was high and another light hung low in front of his eyes. He lifted a hand to shade his face as the white sterile walls seemed to close in on him. A doctor came up and Bryce warily eyed the large, protruding needle he held. The doctor, seeing the apprehension in his patient's eyes, tried to calm Bryce's nerves.

"It's just going to make you fall asleep so we can perform the operation." He raised an eyebrow, "Okay?"

Bryce closed his eyes for a brief moment. *Ooh, Lord please, anything but a needle. Aside from small spaces, spiders, crocs and snakes that's the one thing I really hate!*

He opened his eyes again and glanced at the doctor. *Even a needle must be worth it to get rid of this pain.* Bryce winced; his leg throbbed with a burning sensation that made all the nerves in his body race with agony.

He glanced towards the clear metal cabinet across from him and saw his reflection. His hair was damp and stuck to his forehead and his cheeks reddened with fever.

"Okay," he relented finally.

A nurse pulled his left arm out, rubbing a numbing cream onto his skin. It tingled for a moment and Bryce clenched his jaw as he saw the doctor place the needle tip against his arm, he felt it against his skin for a moment before the feeling became a cold, quick, numb stab as the needle went in.

Bryce breathed deeply for a moment; the doctors glancing from him to the needle.

Bryce could feel his whole body giving into the anaesthetic that was being put into him.

For a moment every part of his mind screamed for him to fight it. Not give in to it.

The doctor at his side put a hand on his shoulder as he tried to sit up, "Lay back and relax." He said.

Bryce drew a short breath, he fought the anaesthetic for a moment longer, scared of what might happen. Then his eyes started to close and his muscles relaxed. Everything around him grew darker.

He briefly saw the surgeon pulling gloves on, walking over, taking a long breath, and picking something up off a silver tray, the surgeon looked at Bryce for a moment, as he leaned over him. A hand hovering over Bryce's right leg, waiting for him to fall under the anaesthetic.

Bryce allowed sleep to wash over him. The last thing he knew was the pain ripping up and down his leg, and the still, small voice that spoke peace to his innermost being.

I am with you, fear not.

~

"It's going to be okay Ivar," Savannah's voice crackled over the phone line.

Ivar rubbed his forehead, "Yeah, thanks Sav," he stared at the cup of takeaway coffee he was holding and took a long drink, tracing patterns on the hospital floor with the side of his trainer.

"You okay?" Savannah's voice was soft.

Ivar smiled gently, "Not really, but I'll make it." He gave a watery laugh.

"Please tell me you'll take care of yourself,"

"I will, I promise. Have a good trip yeah?"

"Yeah, thanks Ivar, I'll be praying for your family."

Ivar drained his coffee, "thank you Sav. I'll see you when you get back, yeah?"

"Yes, okay. Dad's calling, bye Ivar!"

"Bye Sav," Ivar hung up and stared at his phone.

Despite everything, a silly boyish grin spread across his mouth.

~Chapter Sixteen~

"For those who believe, 'impossible' is not a word."

Lights.
Voices.
Dull pain throbbing in his leg.

Bryce's eyes fluttered open, he glanced down at his leg. It was bent at the knee because stretching it out caused too much pain. He noticed orange-coloured antiseptic covering his leg around the thick white bandage.

For a moment he struggled to remember where he was. Then, like a flood let loose, it all came rushing back.

Hospital.
Operation.
Pain.

Ugh. Bryce groaned slightly.

At his voice, a tall figure bounded across the room to his side, her red hair hanging like a curtain around her face.

"Bryce, honey."

"Hey Mom," he whispered.

Aubrey hugged him to herself and Bryce could feel her tears against his neck. Bryce - with the help of his mom - pushed himself up into a sitting position.

"How do you feel?" Aubrey gently stroked the hair back from his forehead.

Bryce's eyes skirted around the room.

"Like a circus act. Why's everyone watching me?" He asked. Reese, who was sitting next to him, picked up his left hand and held it against her wet cheek. The 13-year-old whimpered. "We didn't know if we would see you again."

Bryce smiled weakly and brushed her cheek with his hand before lifting her chin with the crook of his finger.

"You're stuck with me, sorry."

A choking sound came from behind him. Tilting his head back, Bryce saw Ivar quickly wipe his eyes and look away.

A slightly wobbly laugh came from his uncle, "Bryce is made of steel, of course he was gonna make it."

All the same, his eyes teared up.

"Does *everyone* have to keep looking at me?" Bryce chuckled slightly.

"Get used to it, hon'," Emma smiled gently. Reese squeezed his hand, Bryce glanced at her as her eyes filled with tears.

"Hey," Bryce breathed while patting her shoulder. "Don't cry, I'll be up and around in no time." He sniggered, "And I'm gonna throw you in the lake again."

Reese laughed through the tears that coursed down her face. The door opened and the smell of chocolate mixed with butter and sugar drifted into the room.

"Hey Bryce," Maddison walked in with Jade, bearing a tray of tempting-looking cookies. "Jade and I killed time by baking up a storm back at the farm." She laid the tray down next to his hospital bed.

Bryce smiled at his cousin, "Thanks Grandma, thanks Jade." Jade nodded, her eyes red and swollen from crying. For all their arguments, the two loved each other deeply and Jade would have hated for anything to have happened to him.

Caleb coughed and everyone turned looked at him, he blinked several times and turned to face the wall. He held a hand up, "Just got something in my eye, that's all."

Jade's mouthed curved at the corners, as she whispered, "He's crying."

Emma stood next to him, wrapping him in a hug.

Aubrey sighed and leaned her head against her son's.

He reached out and took her hand, giving it a loving squeeze.

The door swung open and before anyone could do a thing, a bundle of energy had thrown itself onto Bryce's lap. Hunter's face was puckered and the ice cream he held lopsided. Bryce winced in pain as Hunter landed in his lap.

"I bringed wou ice!" He exclaimed, proudly giving Bryce the melting treat.

Bryce laughed slightly, still feeling bleary and not quite with it straight after his operation. He glanced around the recovery room for a tissue as the ice cream dripped on his hands.

"Hold it Hunter, give the boy some room." Jason removed the small boy from Bryce's lap.

"Hang in there, kiddo." He winked at Bryce.

"Hey Grandpa," Bryce's eyes clouded over, "what day is it?"

"Saturday, and don't worry, I know what you're thinking. Ivar, your uncle and I are going to start bringing the harvest in on Monday. You just rest up and get better, yeah?"

Bryce smiled weakly, "Okay."

Someone cleared their throat in the doorway, "I'm sorry to break up the reunion but the young man needs to rest now before we put him back onto the ward."

A serious faced doctor came in with Sean.

Aubrey took one look at her husband's face, it was strained and his eyes wet. Her grip on Bryce's hand tightened.

"Aubrey," Sean said, "Dr. Wilson wants to speak with us outside." Aubrey waited until everyone had left before she kissed Bryce on the forehead and followed her husband and the doctor out of the room.

~

Dr. Wilson ushered them into a small office and sat down on the edge of his desk and took a long breath.

"Your son has osteomyelitis."

Sean leaned forward his brow furrowed, "And that is what exactly?"

Dr. Wilson picked up a piece of paper, "It's a deep bone infection. It's very rare and only a very few children in the world get it. Unfortunately, your son is one of those children. What type of osteomyelitis it is, we haven't identified quite yet, so we need your son to stay in hospital until we can identify it. We have removed the infection from the bone but he needs plenty of time to recover." He cleared his throat. "The outcome still isn't clear, to be perfectly honest, there's still a chance he might not make it. He could lose his leg, or at the very least, have to learn to walk again."

Sean sat back in his chair, sweeping his hand across the day-old stubble. "Oh. That's what it is."

A choking sound came from next to him, he turned slightly and Aubrey buried her face in his chest.

"I'll give you a minute," the doctor said, standing.

Sean nodded his thanks and watched while he walked out.

"Aubrey," Sean stroked her hair, "Aubrey hon', look at me," he lifted her chin up so he could look her in the eye.

"It's. Going. To. Be. Okay." Every word was punctuated with a breath.

"But Sean, he just said that Bryce could-" Aubrey whimpered she closed her eyes as more tears leaked out from under her eyelashes and down her face.

Sean shook his head firmly, "You know that what the doctors say isn't always the last word. There is always a second opinion, always another verdict. Remember, faith can move mountains."

"But it seems impossible, I'm so scared Sean. So, so scared!" Aubrey sniffed, Sean cupped her face with his hands. "I know, hon', I know. But it doesn't matter what we have heard the doctors say. For those who believe, 'impossible' is not a word." He smiled and brushed her lips in a kiss.

"Remember what is impossible with man, is possible for the Lord. Remember the doctors' word isn't the last word on the matter. Now, you go be with Bryce and I'll drop Ivar off at the farm."

"Dad's not going to bring the harvest in till Monday now." Aubrey murmured, unable to process everything.

Sean nodded, "I know, but I just want him out of here. He's clammed up and whenever I look at him he's crying. I want him to be with his cousins in the fresh air."

He glanced down at her, "In fact I want you both out in the air, Bryce won't get better with us all moping around him."

Aubrey nodded slowly, "You should stay in hospital with Bryce."

"Yeah, I thought about that. Ivar needs you at home and with Cameron coming home on Tuesday-" He didn't finish, but glanced around.

Aubrey dried her face, and sighed heavily, "You're right. I'll take Ivar over to Dad's. I want to speak with him anyway."

Sean nodded.

Aubrey took a deep breath and rubbed a hand over her face, she gave Sean a brave smile, which he returned with a encouraging squeeze of the hand.

She then got up and crossed the hall to the recovery room, Aubrey knew Sean was watching from the office doorway as she went across to Bryce's bed, hugging him goodbye and promising to be back the next day.

~Chapter Seventeen~

"What if, when you look up, all you see is darkness and the storm you're walking through?"

Monday morning brought the heat and Ivar to the farm. Jason glanced towards his grandson as he toiled alongside him. He then looked over to where his son, Caleb, was starting up the combine harvester so they could harvest the wheat crops.

Jason moved a hay bale from the barn's back wall and threw it across the rom. It landed with a thud against the right side wall. He noticed Ivar's far-off look as he pulled hay bale after hay able off the stack and threw it with an aggressive passion. Jason climbed the tall stack of bales and once at the top he stared down at his grandson.

The boy's head was bowed as he worked, keeping his eyes on the floor. Once the back wall was clear they could store all the wheat. Jason pulled an armful of hay loose and let it rain down on Ivar.

"Uh, hey! Grandpa!" Ivar said, protesting loudly, he shook his head and brushed at his shirt and jeans.

"Look up,"

Ivar looked towards his grandpa, expecting another rain of hay. "Huh?"

"Look up."

"Why?"

"Because when you look down all you see is where your feet have been. Not where they can take you." Jason called.

Ivar pursed his lips and stared into the hay, "What if, when you look up, all you see is darkness and the storm you're walking through?"

Jason sat down on the top bale. He kicked free a bunch of hay and chuckled softly as Ivar grunted and shook the straw off himself.

He ran both hands through his hair. "Ivar."

Ivar looked up towards him.

"You know the quote Reese likes? When it rains look for rainbows, when it's dark look for stars? Well, you know what?"

"What?" Ivar asked after starting to ascend the stack of bales. He sat down next to his grandpa, Jason smiled slightly, "To do that, you have to look up."

He put a hand under Ivar's chin and tilted his head back. Ivar stared through a gap in the wooden roofing.

Overhead, an eagle soared effortlessly in a sky that was as blue as his grandpa's eyes. It was a clear, bright reflection of the ocean when the sun bounces off it, making it look like polished crystal.

The eagle dipped and soared on the air currents.

~

Reese pulled the dish out of the oven, the smell of double chocolate fudge brownies filling the farmhouse kitchen. She bit her lip as she set it on the side.

"You okay sweetie?" Caleb pushed his hat back and straddled a chair.

Reese smiled at her dad, "Yeah, I guess so." She dug a knife into the brownies soft gooey centre and cutting a slice, she placed it in palm of her hand, offering it to her dad.

Caleb bit into it, his hand cupped underneath to catch any falling crumbs.

"Mmm, Rweese, wis is weally gwood!" He nodded in approval, speaking around the chocolate dessert in his mouth. Reese smiled weakly, placing the rest of her bake into a tin and closing the lid.

Caleb swallowed the rest of his brownie, he stood up and brushed the crumbs off his hands by wiping them on his jeans.

"Hey, baby girl. What's wrong?"

Reese sniffed a tear rolling off her cheek and hitting the brownies tin. "I'm scared for Bryce."

"Aw, Reese," Caleb pulled his youngest daughter towards himself, hugging her.

"It's going to be okay Reese, Bryce will pull through this, okay."

Reese nodded her hot face buried in his shirt, Caleb stroked her hair gently. Rocking her back and forth, Reese glanced up at her dad, his blue eyes twinkled reassuringly down at her from under his mass of blond curls.

He kissed her forehead.

"Everything will be okay."

Reese swallowed and nodded, hugging him tighter.

~

Jason looked up, he wiped the sweat from his forehead. Ivar and Caleb where harvesting the crops from the far fields. The sound of the combine harvester rumbled through the air.

Aubrey's Land Rover pulled up in the driveway.

Jason hung out the combine harvesters door, he waved the blue bandana he kept in his back pocket.

He saw Aubrey get out the car and wave back. He noticed that she didn't going into the house, but headed towards him.

She walked over the freshly harvested side of the field, stopping as she reached the rest of the wheat.

Jason glanced towards Caleb and Ivar who were working in the far back field. Their forms small dark silhouettes against the bright sky.

Jason cut the engine on the harvester. He swung the door open a little wider and dropped down.

He waded through waist high wheat towards his daughter. They were meant to talk Saturday evening a few hours after Bryce's operation, but a call from Sean saying Bryce needed her had sent Aubrey racing back to the hospital.

So. The talk had been set for today.

When he reached her, Jason hugged his daughter tightly. "How's my girl doing?"

Aubrey rubbed her face, she hadn't slept since Bryce went into hospital. Her cheeks were pale and dark circle surrounded her eyes which looked unnaturally large today.

"Hi dad." Aubrey said. She returned his hug.

"How are you?" He asked again.

Aubrey breathed out, "I don't know dad." She stared out towards the mass of golden wheat.

Her eyes seemed to catch sight of the young man working in one of the fields. She watched Ivar for a long moment. The young man worked with precision, his movements tight with the tension that constricted his muscles. Aubrey inclined her head, noticing how many times he stopped and stared up into the sky.

"I just don't know, I can't deal with everything everyone is saying about Bryce. It's, just so!" She gritted her teeth, "stressful!" Aubrey pulled at her hair. "Do you know what they say Dad? They say he might die, loose his leg or at the least have to learn to walk again."

She paused, her chin wobbling, "My Bryce."

Jason put a arm around her shoulders and guided her towards the wheat field.

"He's a miracle working God, Aubrey and the doctor's word isn't the final say on the matter."

"I know dad, I just don't think I have enough faith for that right now. I'm so busy it's like I've run dry." Aubrey buried her face in her hands.

Jason nodded, "Mhm, I had noticed that."

"Want to know what's worse?" Aubrey lifted her head to look at him, "The Lord told me to press into him, right before this all happened. But I didn't listen, I was to caught up with everything. At the moment I should have been walking strong with the Lord, I wasn't."

Jason pursed his lips, "C'mon hon. Let your old Pa show you somethin'"

Taking her arm he led her towards the field, "listen hon, I know how it feels to feel dry, when I was your age I went through a spiritual drought."

"A what?"

Jason removed his hat and ransacked his hair.

"I forgot about the Rosetta Stone."

Aubrey's strawberry blond eyebrows bobbed up and down. "Isn't that the stone covered in hieroglyphics, that they used to understand Egyptian writing?"

"Uh, yes, but this is a different type."

"How so?"

"Hon see our fields, ripe and ready to be harvested?"

Aubrey nodded.

"To have a harvest, you have to plant seeds. It's the natural way things work. To have a spiritual harvest you have the plant spiritual seeds, the word and cultivate them the same way you would cultivate a field."

Jason plucked a ear of wheat and rubbed it between his hands.

"Just like you can't throw out seed the day before harvest and expect it to grow, you can't put the word of God before your eyes at the very moment you need it. You need to plant those seeds and continually water them. So that when you need a harvest your crops will be ready."

Aubrey groaned, "I need a harvest right now, but I've missed it. I let my field go dry."

"It's not to late sweetie," Jason placed a hand on her shoulder, "it's never to late until you don't need it."

"Dad."

"Yup,"

"Why did you say the Rosetta Stone?"

"Well see, it's the parable of the sower from the Bible. That parable is like the Rosetta Stone of the Bible. For everything else that his word says to work in your life you have to allow this teaching sink into your heart. You have to plant the seeds and let them grow so you can revive a blooming harvest."

Jason smiled and let the handful of wheat be carried away on the wind.

"You need a harvest right now honey and all you need to do is plant the seeds so you can see it flourish. Bryce needs a harvest, y'all do."

He rubbed her shoulder affectionately and stared at the sea of golden wheat.

"It's osteomyelitis dad, the rarest form. Often it's fatal." Aubrey's voice was strained and her words forced.

Jason took a few deep breaths, he closed his eyes and breathed in the scent of the fields and trees. The smell of freshly cut hay lay heavy in the air.

"That's right, it's Osteomyelitis Aubrey, that's all it is, a word a name of something. Why is that so scary?"

Aubrey turned and stared at him incredulous.

"Dad-how-didn't you hear me? It's often fatal!"

Jason grabbed both of her shoulder and faced her, he stared into her eyes.

"And don't you think that our God is bigger than that?"

Like a slap to the face, or a punch in the stomach, those words hit Aubrey with such force that she stepped back a few paces.

"Don't you think that the Lord who rose from the death and conquered all is bigger than a name. Than a word, than a illness? Don't you think he is bigger than it all?"

Another mental slap.

Aubrey glanced upwards towards the sky.

"Aubrey,"

Jason cupped her face, "He is bigger. With man it may be impossible, but with God nothing is impossible. Nothing Aubrey, nothing! The doctor does not have the final say."

Aubrey sniffed, tears slid out from under her eyelids. Gently Jason brushed them away.

"It's. Going. To. Be. Okay." He whispered.

Aubrey swallowed, "Sean said those exact same words." She breathed, her eyes brimming.

"I always knew he was good for you," he pulled her into a tight hug, "now, go plant those seeds and watch your harvest grow."

~Chapter Eighteen~
The doctors' word is never the final report.

That night Aubrey stared up at the ceiling.

Her vision blurred as tears stung her eyes and spilled over down her cheeks. She glanced at the empty bed space next to her, missing Sean and wishing he was there, but thankful he was staying in hospital with Bryce.

Choked sobs caught in her throat. Throwing the covers off, Aubrey slipped out of bed. In the darkness, she found her dressing gown and pulled it on over her pyjamas. She walked down the hallway, the house was in eerie silence; the dark hush that filled the home was suffocating.

Walking into the kitchen, Aubrey set the kettle to boil, her face now soaked with the tears that wouldn't stop flowing. Her phone blinked with a new voicemail.

Picking it up, she listened, "Hey honey, it's Dad."

Jason's voice came over the line.

"I know it's late, but I was up praying for you all so I thought I'd drop you a line. I hope you find this in the morning which means you're asleep. I wanted to remind you, honey, of what we talked about this morning. Remember it's only too late to plant seeds once you don't need them, and right now you need a whole harvest. It's not too late to plant those seeds, Aubrey. Just like our field, if you plant those seeds and cultivate them, they will grow a produce the harvest that you need. The harvest may come a little late, as those seeds need to grow. But with attention and care, those seeds will grow and produce the harvest you need. Get planting and never stop cultivating, honey. Mom and I are here any time you need something, and so is the Lord, hon'. You know he's a healing God. Plant those seeds and see the miraculous happen."

The voice message ended.

Aubrey brushed away tears, "Thanks, Dad."

She took her coffee to the sofa and sat down, curling her legs up underneath her. She fixed her eyes on the Bible laying on the coffee table underneath the doctor's letter she had been given.

The doctors' word is never the final report.

The words of her dad and Sean echoed in her mind.

"Okay God, they say that the doctors' report isn't the only report there is." Aubrey swallowed the lump in her throat. "He's so sick, Father, my boy is lying in a hospital bed so sick they say he might die."

Picking up the letter she scrunched it up in her hand. Aubrey drew a long breath.

Plant the seeds. The Holy Spirit seemed to whisper.

"Father-" she choked up.

Slipping off the sofa and onto her knees, Aubrey buried her face in her arms. She gripped her bible until her fingers hurt. *I'm so scared Lord. So, so scared.*

"The doctors say he might die, but you, God, say right here in Psalm 118:17 that I shall not die, but live, and declare the works of the Lord."

Aubrey looked up, her eyes staring out through the window, past the front gate and up at the stars.

"I claim that for my son, God. I claim that for him. Bryce Walker shall live and not die. He will declare the works of the Lord in Jesus' name."

Aubrey flipped the pages of her Bible, coloured highlights flying past her eyes. One caught her attention and she moved the pages back.

She got up off the floor and sat on the edge of the sofa. Aubrey stared down at the verse, "But those who wait on the Lord shall renew their strength; they shall mount up with wings like eagles, they shall run and not be weary. They shall walk and not grow faint."

Aubrey felt something switch on inside her; she glanced at the letter laying open on the table and her spirits dipped. "No!"

She stood up abruptly, snatched up the letter and shredded it. More tears slipped rapidly down her pale face. Grabbing the Bible, she started to pace back and forth along the front window.

She paused, threw it open and welcomed the night's cool breeze and country air. Her finger trailed down the page until she found the verse again.

Aubrey breathed deeply. "The doctors say Bryce may have to lose his right leg, but you, God, say that those who wait on the Lord shall renew their strength; they shall mount up with wings like eagles, they shall run and not be weary. They shall walk and not grow faint. I claim that for my son in Jesus' name. I claim that for him! He shall walk and not grow weary. He shall run and not grow faint. In the name of Jesus, I call my son healed."

Take away my fears Father God. Take away my fear.

Aubrey opened her eyes and her gaze fell on the bible verse calendar that hung up by the fridge.

The monthly verse seemed to stick out at her.

For this is the way the holy women of the past who put their hope in God used to make themselves beautiful. They were submissive to their own husbands, Like Sarah, who obeyed Abraham and called him her Master. You are her daughters if you do what is right and do not give way to fear.
1 Peter 3:5-6

An amused smile played on Aubrey's lips.

I'm not sure what Sean would think of me calling him master. She thought. *But I do like that part about being a daughter of Sarah if I do not give in to fear.*

She bit her lip, wondering if she would be able to not give into fear, but to walk by faith.

"It's so hard." She whispered, "So hard. But it will be worth it."

~Chapter Nineteen~
"Don't give into fear, okay?"

Sean pushed Bryce's wheelchair outside into the hospital's community garden. Bryce took a deep breath.

 It wasn't the family farm, but at least he wasn't staring at bricks and mortar.

"How is it Bryce?" Aubrey placed a hand on the side of his pale face. Bryce leaned forward in his chair, gripping the arm rest until his fingers turned white.

"It's not Pike's Peak, but at least it's something." His lips tweaked.

Aubrey sat on a bench underneath a tree, "Yes, at least it's something," she echoed.

"And out in the air," Sean added. He parked the wheelchair next to the bench and sat down, stretching out his long limbs. Bryce stared longingly at the stone walkway and the tall tree his mom was leaning against.

"I'll climb you yet," he said under his breath, firm resolution forming in his eyes. Aubrey heard his quiet muttering and glanced up into the leaves.

Ivar had told her what Jason had said about looking up and not down. The wind rustled the leaves and she caught a glimpse of the bright blue sky. A faint smile played on her lips. A gentle sigh came from next to her, she looked down at her hand as Sean took it in his and intertwined his fingers with hers. She lifted her eyes and smiled at him.

Sean smiled back.

Bryce glanced at them, he shook his head and smiled. Tucking both hands under his chin, he leaned forward on his elbows. "Say, Dad, ain't you supposed to be collecting Cameron from the station?"

Sean tipped his cap back, "Huh?"

"Cameron? The station?" Bryce raised both eyebrows. Sean blinked, then jumped up. "Oh wow, I'm late picking up my own son!" He called while sprinting from the garden.

Aubrey laughed and stood up, "I need to get you back inside, they want to do some blood tests."

Bryce groaned as he was wheeled back into the hospital.

"I loathe blood tests with a passion." He said as his mom pushed the wheelchair into the elevator and hit the level three button.

"Well, what would you prefer? Tight spaces or a blood test?" Bryce blinked several times, "Uh, blood tests." He shuddered, "I hate small tight spaces."

Aubrey laughed quietly.

Bryce fell quiet for the rest of the elevator ride, staring at his reflection in the large mirror-panelled wall. He had lost a little weight in the four days he had been there. His face was slightly thinner, making his high cheekbones more prominent. His green eyes were unnaturally large and bright in his almost sheet white face.

Bryce shuddered again and looked away.

Aubrey leaned over and placed a gentle kiss on his forehead. "You still look handsome," she whispered comfortingly whilst running a hand over his blond hair.

"Thanks mom," Bryce said as the lift doors parted and he was pushed out into the ward. A sour-faced lady walked up. "I'm Nurse Cheryl. If you will follow me I'll be taking your blood tests."

Bryce made a face once her back was turned and Aubrey swatted him on the back of his head.

"Be nice," she warned, her voice close to his ear. Bryce motioned his mom closer as they followed her down a long white sterile hallway. "Her face froze,"

"What?" Aubrey asked.

"Well ya know, when we frowned, Dad used to say 'careful, if the weather changes your face may stay stuck.'" Bryce nodded towards the nurse they where following. "I think the weather changed and her face froze."

"Bryce!" Aubrey hissed.

Bryce grinned impishly and Audrey smiled in spite of herself. The smile soon vanished as they turned into a small room and Bryce saw the needle and blood test tubes waiting for him. Aubrey helped lift Bryce onto the examination table, the nurse was still frowning as she pulled his right arm out and rubbed a small wipe over his skin.

Bryce squeezed his eyes shut as she pressed the needle into his arm. He winced visibly as she repeated this several times.

"This is torturous." He groaned.

Aubrey's eyes softened, "It will be over soon."

Ten minutes dragged slowly on, Bryce started to count how many she had done. *Six blood tests. Seriously!* Aubrey studied her son's face after a little while.

He looked tired, worn out by even this.

"Okay," Aubrey stood up, "Nurse Cheryl, can we finish this tomorrow or another day? Bryce is worn out."

The woman curled her lips, "Fine." She stood up and cleared away her equipment, "There are only a few more. However, yes, fine. We can save them for another day."

~

Bryce flopped back with an exhausted breath. His eyes closed almost instantly once his head hit the pillow.

Aubrey sat on the edge of his bed and rubbed his hands. "You okay Bryce?"

His eyes fluttered open. "Just—tired." He whispered, his eyes closing again.

"They're gonna start getting you to straighten your leg this week." Aubrey brushed his hair back, her hand rested on his forehead for a long time as she fought back the tears burning behind her eyelids.

"Do they have to? It hurts when I try."

"I know," Aubrey comforted, "but it will help in the long run."

Bryce nodded, "Can Cameron and Ivar come soon? Please." His eyes filled as he glanced to the window on the other side of the children's ward.

"Sure, sure they can."

Bryce smiled weakly, "I-I'm scared Mom." A tear slid down his face.

Wiping it away, his mom nodded, "I know, I know baby. But it's-I'm sure everything will be just fine. Okay, God loves you more than even I do. And he won't let you go, your gonna get through this Bryce. He's a healing God who will work a miracle in your life." She gave his hand a gentle squeeze, "Don't give into fear, okay?"

Bryce closed his eyes and more tears slid down his face, his lips quivered, "Okay."

Aubrey waited by his side until sleep claimed him.

~Chapter Twenty
"I forgave you ages ago…"

"Okay, just try and straighten your leg for me now, Mr Walker."

Bryce did as the physiotherapist asked.

His heart skipped a beat as his leg loudly protested against being straightened by sending pain through him.

"You have been with us a week now, young man, and we want to start you on crutches, but first you need to straighten your leg." The woman said as she peered at him over the glasses perched on the end of her nose.

Bryce nodded, gritting his teeth and trying to ignore the pain in his leg as he forced it to straighten, unable to bare the pain, Bryce allowed his leg to bend back again, shivering he shook his head, "I can't do it."

The physiotherapist sighed, "Maybe if I do it Mr Walker. It's really important that we get your leg to stay straight."

The door to the ward swung open as the lady took hold of Bryce's right leg, she put a hand above his knee and another one on his ankle, pulling his leg straight and holding it there. Bryce gasped in pain, and a tear trickled down his face.

"Stop that! You're hurting him." Ivar's eyes blazed as he crossed the room towards to them in several long strides. The lady looked up at Ivar. She frowned and looked over his head towards the three adults coming over.

Sean placed both hands on Ivar's shoulders, "She's helping to get him to straighten his leg, Ivar."

The lady nodded, "As it hurts him too much to do it, I'm going to put a brace around his knee and a little way up the thigh where he had the operation. It will force the leg to remain straight."

A slightly nervous laugh came from the man standing next to Aubrey. "Brace yourself for it, Bryce."

Bryce raised his eyebrows at him.

"Yeah that was an awfully-timed joke," The man rubbed the back of his neck as he walked towards Bryce.

Bryce looked him over; the reddish brown hair and soft coloured eyes. He looked him up and down, the man was stronger than he remembered, muscles rippled down his arms and his chest looked as solid as iron. He also walked with purpose. Last time he had seen him, the man had walked with an angry thud in his step.

The man laughed at Bryce's visual search. "C'mon Bryce you remember me, don't you?"

Bryce stared at him for what seemed like an eternity. *No way that's Cam,* he thought, *last time I saw him before he went off to train with the fire service he was as thin as a whip. He's filled out and toned up. No way that's Cameron.*

The man arched an eyebrow, "You do remember me right, Bryce-boy? A year isn't that long."

Yep, that's definitely Cameron. Bryce's face broke out into a broad grin,

"Yeah, I remember you." He sniggered and wiped away the tear that still rested on his cheek, "How could I forget? You plague my phone all the time."

"Aside from when you and Ivar are plaguing mine." Cameron's mouth twitched as he sat next to his younger brother.

Ivar looked up and cast an accusing eye on Cameron. "Hey, Bryce plagues your phone the most."

He protested, a slight smile tugged at his lips and he perched on the bed next to Bryce.

"I wouldn't call it plaguing per se." Bryce rubbed a hand over his face.

"Dad was saying you've been here a week now. You gonna be a boarder or you planning on coming home soon?" Cameron tried to make his voice sound light, but his words couldn't mask the pain in his eyes.

Aubrey touched Bryce's shoulder, "Dad and I will let you boys have a moment."

Bryce watched as they walked away with the physiotherapist.

Cameron's voice was wobbly as he spoke. "Bryce. I'm so sorry I couldn't be there. I'm sorry that the moment you needed me most to be here I couldn't be."

Cameron didn't look up, keeping his eyes on the floor. Bryce choked, he rubbed his eyes and placed a hand on Cameron's shoulder, "Hey, it's okay." He wiped his eyes, "Did you, uh, save any lives?"

Cameron looked up, his eyes wet, "What?"

Bryce smiled a little, "Did you save anyone's life? At work I mean."

Cameron inclined his head, "Did none of my voice messages reach you?"

Bryce's brow furrowed.

Cameron stared at Ivar, "No?"

Ivar shook his head, "Only some voicemails from a guy called Jack,"

"What did Jack say?" Cameron asked, he scrunched his nose up and tried to tidy his messed up hair.

"Uh, that he knew you from the station and that you had asked him to relay a message but that he couldn't remember what it was." Ivar rubbed his jaw.

"Jaaaack," Cameron groaned, he shook off his denim jacket and jammed a navy blue baseball cap down on his head. He tucked both fists under his chin and stared at the floor.

"What was it you wanted us to know?" Bryce asked quietly. Cameron opened his mouth to speak, "Bryce, I-I was injured in the last fire. I had to stay back a while-" he looked up, "I was scared...scared of seeing you after all this time. I know we've messaged and stuff. But it's not the same,"

He shifted his chair closer to Bryce's bed. "When I left last year for the station, you and I didn't get on."

Bryce nodded slowly, "I never knew why you acted as if you hated me." Underneath the blanket that was pulled up to his shoulders, Bryce found the wooden cross his dad had given him around his neck.

Cameron swallowed, "A few months before I left, I had a call out from the station near home. I had to go into a block of apartments. Bryce, I saved a boy that day who looked like you did when you were seven. He survived but he was burnt up bad. Every time I saw you I saw that day. I worked it into my mind that if you were around me then you'd get hurt some way or another. So I pushed you away."

He scrubbed a hand through his hair. "I guess I hurt you even more, but the fact that I couldn't forget that day made me angry, and I guess I took it out on you."

Cameron choked on his words. "And I'm so sorry. A month or two ago, I got right with God and now I want to get right with you. I'm so sorry, can you forgive me?"

Bryce reached out a trembling hand and touched the tip of his fingers against Cameron's shoulder, "I forgave you ages ago Cam."

His laugh was watery. "Now what was this injury that delayed my brother?"

Cameron smiled weakly and went to speak but before he could, the door at the end of the ward swung open and the physiotherapist walked back in with Aubrey and Sean.

Cameron pulled his cap down further and tugged the ends of his shirt's sleeves over his hands, shoving his hands in between his knees.

Aubrey smiled gently at her eldest, she pushed back his cap slightly and ran the back of her finger gently over his cheek. She winked at him. Cameron smiled back.

The physiotherapist walked forward holding a bundle of folded blue fabric.

"Brace." She said holding it up.

"Yeah?" Bryce looked at her.

The lady smiled and shook her head, "No I mean, I've got the brace. Not Bryce as in your name."

"Ah, oh right." Bryce felt his cheeks flush.

Sean hovered over him, "Okay, she's gonna put the brace on now to support your leg okay?"

Bryce nodded and clenched his eyes shut. He gasped slightly as his leg was pulled straight.

"Brace yourself." Cameron whispered close to his ear. Bryce opened both eyes and glared at him.

Cameron chuckled slightly. Aubrey could feel Bryce's grip on her hand tighten as the physiotherapist fitted the brace and strapped it on. "It's okay, honey." She said calmly. The lady patted his leg slightly and said, "It's fitted, all done."

"Good, can I take it off now?" Bryce gasped.

The physiotherapist smiled sadly, "Sorry, young man. No, you got to keep it on now until you're all healed up."

Bryce groaned.

"Can ya do that for me?" The lady asked, pushing her dark hair back behind her ear.

"Yes Ma'am." Bryce managed to push the words out with great effort.

Aubrey smiled and stroked back his hair.

"I'm proud of you, hon'."

~Chapter Twenty-One~
"You look stunning, you always do,"

"Well, it's Saturday." Jason sat on the porch and breathed in the scent of his coffee.

Caleb nodded and took a sip of his own, "You sure you don't want me to help make the drop at Mr Shaw's?"

Jason shook his head as he wrapped his hands around his mug, "No thanks, son. I appreciate the offer but I want to chat with my grandsons, with Cameron and Ivar."

"Ivar's tagging along?" Caleb glanced across at his two nephews who were working hard to bring in the last few crops.

"Yeah, Bryce is having tests all day and being around so much sickness depresses Ivar. In fact," Jason got up and placed his mug down on the porch banister he arched his back, "the hospital itself is depressing. If you want to get better you should out here in the countryside where you can be close to God's creation and soak in his word."

"Amen," Caleb murmured.

He drained his own coffee and set it down on the top step, Caleb pulled his boots back on and stood. "Speaking of that, Emma and I were talking with Mom this morning. What if we could start bringing Bryce out here for a few hours each day? He'd be back on the ward in time for treatment and stuff."

"Hmm," Jason rubbed the side of his forehead, "it would do him good, maybe we can get that fiddle back into his hands."

Caleb nodded, "I'll ring Sean while you guys make the drop at the Shaw Estate."

Jason nodded, "Okay, thanks Caleb," He placed a hand on his son's shoulder and smiled at him. A lifetime of love and appreciation flowed between the two without a word in that one glance.

Jason called into the house, "Honey! The boys and I are gonna head out to the Shaws' now."

"Okay," Madison appeared in the doorway, holding Hunter who was asleep on her hip. She squinted out towards the sky line.

Jason breathed deep, he mounted the steps suddenly and kissed her. "You look stunning." He whispered, his mouth close to her ear. "You always do," he looked her over, a glimmer in his eyes. "Even in work clothes."

He grinned and pushed her silvery-blond hair out of her eyes. Madison laughed softly and smiled shyly. For a moment Caleb blinked and it was as if he saw his parents when they were younger. Both his mom and dad standing on the porch holding each other, a small blond baby boy in his mom's arms. Caleb grinned and blinked.

Then the moment was gone.

"Be quick with your delivery," Madison said, "the clouds are darkening. I think it's going to rain."

Jason nodded, "I'll be quick." He kissed her cheek before bounding back down the steps and towards the truck where Ivar and Cameron where loading sheaths of wheat into the trucks flatbed. "Throw a tarpaulin over the wheat Ivar, would ya. Your grandma said it might rain."

A loud sound came from the barn where the horses were housed. Ivar looked up, frowning as he fastened the tarpaulins straps down. "I'll go check on them, they can probably smell the rain."

Ivar trudged up the path towards the barn, he swung the six bar gate open and walked into the area where the barns where. He passed the workshop and hay barn on his left and the small barn where Daisy the cow lived. The horses were housed in the largest barn just ahead.

Ivar pushed the large red doors open, "Hey you." He stepped into the barn and walked over to one of the stalls. Reaching over he stroked the mare's soft golden coat. "What's up girl?" He smiled and gently patted her back. "There you go, Charis," he laid an armful of hay in her stall.

Turning, he raised his eyebrows as four more pairs of eyes stared at him. "What?" He asked.

A horse with the colouring of dark marble tossed its pitch-black mane.

"Listen y'all, just quieten down okay? A little rain never hurt no one and now the crops are harvested, the water will do the ground good."

Charis whined behind him.

Ivar turned, he reached back over the stall and stroked her neck, "Shhh, there we go girl." He gently ran his fingers through her mane, "I know, I know you're Bryce's horse. I know you miss him. I miss him also, but hey, we got a good God who's in the healing business. You're gonna be riding through those fields with Bryce on your back in no time I promise you that."

Golden eyes framed in thick lashes looked at him mournfully. Ivar closed his eyes for a moment and leaned his head against the horses.

Slowly, tears started to roll down Ivar's face. "I miss him too girl, I miss him too." He said quietly and patted her back.

The marble-coloured horse snorted and ran against his stall door.

"Hey, you stop that right now you wild thing." Ivar rolled his eyes and went over to the horse. Dark black eyes stared him down.

"Listen if you want a ride, you have to wait for my dad. You're his horse and thank the Lord for that. You're as wild as a bear. How he controls you, only heaven knows." He tapped his finger on the horse's nose. "Now be quiet, Chilli,"

Ivar looked around the barn, the horse tack was hung up on hooks by the back door, several saddles where stacked by a water trough next to what looked like an empty stall. "Carson?" Ivar leaned over the empty stall.

He tilted his head and smiled, "Ya know Carson, when you lay down you make your stall look empty."

He glanced around and spotted a barrel of fresh ripe apples. Picking up one, Ivar waved it close to Carson's nose, "Come on boy,"

He grinned as his horse got to his feet and trotted over, eating the apple straight from Ivar's open palm. "There's a good boy," he stroked Caron's nose allowing the long smooth strokes to go down his neck then back up and over his ears. Ivar smiled slightly, he turned and headed out the barn.

As he walked past Charis in her stall he saw something colourful behind her.

Ivar lifted the latch and entered her stall, closing the gate firmly behind himself.

Ivar ran a hand along Charis's side as he walked to the back. A thick woollen blanket was folded over a square object. Sitting down cross-legged, Ivar pulled back the covering.

Tears immediately sprung to his eyes.

Underneath the blanket was a wooden picture board, covered in photos of the three brothers. Each of their names had been made out of wood and stuck at the top.

Underneath the names were snapshots of Bryce and Ivar riding, Cameron and Bryce before Cameron left to join the fire service and Bryce and Ivar messing around in the yard. The memories went on.

With each one, a fresh stab of pain drove through Ivar's heart. He peered at a recent photo at the bottom of the board.

It was from the week before, a few days before Bryce fell ill. In the photo Ivar and Bryce were wading out of the lake, both soaked from head to foot after Bryce had the idea to ride down the hill in a wagon. Flipping the board over, Ivar read the words, *Bryce's Memory Board* on the back.

Choked sobs started to rise in Ivar's throat as he realised his brother had made this. He hugged it close and leaned back against the stall's wall.

He hid his face in his arms and wept. He lost time of how long he sat there and just let the tears course down his face.

~Chapter Twenty-Two~
"Never be ashamed of your tears, boy."

"Where is he?" Cameron leaned over the back of the truck, he raised both eyebrows.

"Hmm," Jason bit his lip and looked towards the barns. "I'll go see if he's okay."

He tapped the truck's exterior as he walked past.

Jason checked his watch as he walked; *12:30 pm.*

I need to have that order at the Shaws' before 2, where's my grandson?

The barn door opened with a groan, Jason stood in the doorway, hands firmly planted on his hips.

"Ivar?"

He stepped in a few feet, the sun shining on his back as his shadow filled the doorway.

"Ivar?"

Jason walked towards Carson's stall, but a soft muffled whimpering made him turn around.

He found Ivar with his face buried in Charis's mane sobbing. He glanced at the photo board leaning against the wall in the corner and immediately knew what was wrong. Stepping into the stall, Jason gently pulled Ivar away from the horse.

The 18-year-old lost it instantly. Ivar buried his face in his grandpa's shirt and wept.

Jason's eyes filled as he rubbed the young man's back with a strong steady hand. He glanced up towards the barn rafters. *God,* he cried out silently from deep within his heart, *I believe you for a miracle. But this is so hard. Please, please help me stay strong for them.* Leaning his own head on Ivar's shoulder he let his tears fall alongside his grandson's.

After a while he pulled back and cupped Ivar's face, "Never ever be ashamed of your tears, boy. Never."

Ivar sniffed but nodded, his face stained with tears.

~

Cameron glanced back over his shoulder as the truck turned down a lane and onto a country road which led to the Shaw Estate. Ivar had stuck his head out the open window and allowed the wind to whip his hair back from his face.

"So, Cam, you gonna tell Ivar why you couldn't come and why Jack was to relay your messages?"

Jason leaned one arm on his open window, his hand resting lightly on the wheel. Ivar pulled his head back in and stared at his older brother, one eyebrow arched.

Cameron laughed slightly, "You really don't act like a young adult, Ivar."

Ivar rolled his eyes upward, trying to see what had happened. Dark brown hair stuck out everywhere.

Ivar shrugged, pulled his brother's cap off and shoved it down on top of his own head. "There, better." He said, folding his arms over his checkered shirt and sitting back in his seat.

"Working with Dad in the garage and on the farm really helped fill you out, kiddo," Cameron smiled nervously.

Ivar raised his eyebrows and glanced down at himself, his shirt sleeves were rolled up to reveal strong tanned arms. He looked back at his brother, "Mm hmm."

Jason sighed and stared at his grandson, "Cameron. Stop changing the subject."

Cameron let out a long breath and stared out the window at the passing fields.

"Cam, why didn't you come when Dad first called you about Bryce? I know you and Bryce have had a rough patch but I thought you were doing pretty well since last Easter?"

Ivar leaned forward, tucking his fists under his chin, a position that all the Walker boys adopted.

Cameron hesitated and glanced at him in the rearview mirror. Finally, after a long breath he said, "Believe me when I say I wanted to, Ivar. I really, really did."

"Are you scared to tell me?" Ivar asked his normally soft eyes darkening with fear.

Cameron and his grandfather shared a look.

"Okay, so Grandpa knows, so I'm guessing Mom and Dad do too." Ivar leaned back in his seat.

Jason nodded, "They do."

Ivar tipped the cap back, "C'mon, Cam, tell me. It can't be that bad."

Jason shifted in his seat and slowed down at an intersection. "Ivar, Cameron knows you're going through a lot at the moment. He was going to tell you but your mom advised him not to tell you straight away," He pulled away from the intersection.

"Is something wrong, Cam? Are you sick, too?" Ivar's eyes widened.

Cameron inclined his head to the side, "I-," he stopped and grabbed the wheel throwing the car to the right.

Ivar flew forward and smacked his head on the back of his grandpa's headrest.

"Cameron, what on earth?" Jason pulled the car straight.

"Sorry there was a bird in the road."

"Seriously? A bird won over my forehead?" Ivar rubbed his forehead.

"Sorry," Cameron said again simply, shrugging.

Ivar put the cap back on pulling it low to cover the bruise blossoming on his forehead.

"So keep talking." He said.

Jason stared at Cameron, "Go on, he should know."

"Okay Ivar, I'll shoot straight. When I came down from New Orleans I came straight from the ER." Cameron focused on a spot outside the car.

"Okay…" Ivar said slowly.

Cameron pulled the sleeve of his shirt up, a white bandage covered his entire upper arm. Cameron rolled the bandage back just enough to for his brother to see the large burn mark.

"A fire," Ivar realised.

"Yeah,"

"Were you the only one injured?" Ivar asked quietly, his eyes glued to the burn mark.

Cameron covered it up, blinking hard,

"No, the other firefighter got worse burns up and down his leg," he shook his head. "They kept me back at the ER for a day because of how deep the burn went."

"How did you get it?" Ivar asked, watching transfixed as his brother rolled his sleeve back down.

"By shielding a boy from falling debris."

Ivar nodded slowly. "Did he survive?"

"Yeah, we got him out." Cameron had a satisfied look in his eyes.

"He alright?" Ivar fiddled with the corner of his shirt.

"Uh, yeah I think so. The last thing I saw was him with his sister outside before I blacked out."

Ivar grabbed his good arm, "You blacked out with a burn?" His voice was strained.

"To much smoke inhalation." Cameron grinned.

Ivar shook his head and let go of his brother's arm.

"So you're a bit of a hero?"

"Maybe to that boy and his sister, but I'd always rather be the one who's there for his own brothers." Cameron rubbed his forehead. "I'm sorry I didn't tell you sooner, Ivar. I just thought you had enough on your plate at the moment."

Ivar was silent for a long time.

They pulled up at the Shaw Estate and all three of them started to unload the wheat.

Cameron and Ivar were carrying a large crate of wheat into the main barn on the Shaw property when Ivar said, "Thank you."

"For what?" Cameron grunted as they lifted the heavy load onto a large storage unit.

"For waiting until I was ready to hear your news, and for giving me time to process it afterwards." Ivar smiled softly.

"You're not upset I didn't tell you earlier?"

"My life, no, I was trying to stop myself from freaking out about the fact you're hurt and Bryce's in hospital." Ivar tilted his head.

Cameron smiled, "Well, I'm here now."

~Chapter Twenty-Three~
The thought hurt like a punch to the gut.

"Nine days of seeing only the inside of a hospital, and now, I get to see the sky, the birds, Charis and everyone!" Bryce allowed his window to wind all the way down.

He breathed in the country air.

Sean glanced across at him and saw a hint of colour creep back into Bryce's cheeks.

"Well, we have until four o'clock at the farm." Sean said, whilst turning the car up the dirt track leading towards the farm. Bryce grinned as his grandparents' fields, now fully harvested, rolled past. He pulled his eyes away from the window to smile at his dad.

"And I can use the crutches right?" He urged, fed up with the wheelchair.

"Only for a little while, okay? Mom and I don't want you getting tired out." Bryce chewed the inside of his cheek and glanced downwards. The August heat beat down harshly, causing heat waves to appear on the road ahead.

Bryce's denim shorts gave a clear view of the blue brace still supporting his leg. His scowl was interrupted by a gentle hand on his shoulder. Sean grinned and pointed out the window towards the field they were driving next to. Bryce glanced up, his brow furrowed.

"Bryce! Bryce!"

Bryce peered out the window, Ivar was riding Carson as close to the fence line as possible.

Ivar narrowed his eyes and pushed his horse faster as the car moved ahead.

"Bryce!" Ivar waved his right hand , keeping hold of the horses reins with the other hand.

Bryce grinned and waved back.

Sean laughed as he pulled the car to a stop in front of the farmhouse. Ivar came up behind them at a gallop, slowing quickly to a canter and then a trot. Sean got out of the car and came around to Bryce's side.

Ivar had dismounted and ran quickly into the house.

"Mom! Grandma, Cameron, guys! Bryce is here." He just stopped himself from squeaking with excitement.

The next few hours moved in almost slow motion for Bryce as his family swarmed around him. His mom couldn't stop crying and Madison had to take her into the kitchen and sit her down with a hot drink to calm her down.

Cameron and Jade kept trying to keep Hunter from jumping on Bryce whilst Reese and Ivar just stared at him and grinned. Jason and Caleb came in a little later from the fields.

"So who's up for a spot of fishing? The lake's full of fish that are just begging to be caught and eaten."

Cameron and Ivar were on their feet along with Sean in a matter of moments.

Bryce sat up straight, "I am-" He slowed down as he remembered he was sitting on the sofa with crutches next to him "-am going to have to sit this one out," he slumped back. Jason glanced at Caleb, he ran a hand over his hair before slapping his straw hat back down.

"Well, actually," he inclined his head towards the rest of the guys.

Cameron and Ivar were grinning like madmen.

"What?" Bryce squinted at his brothers, Aubrey laughed, "Just tell him already. Can't you see the suspense on his face?" She sat behind Bryce, a hand resting on his arm. Madison smiled and said, "Well, if you guys won't I will." She placed a hand onto of Bryce's blond head.

"Ivar is gonna ride Charis down to the lake, and you're going to ride behind him. Cameron is going to ride Pepper next to you guys just in case."

Bryce felt tears prick his eyes, "As in I can go?"

Aubrey nodded and wiped away the tears in her own eyes.

"Yeah, you can go." She whispered, running a finger across his cheek.

"And when you get back," Caleb added, "you can play this old thing." He held out Bryce's fiddle.

Reaching out Bryce touched it lovingly, the look in his eyes like that of a lost child returning home.

He looked across at Ivar, "Do you have your guitar with you?"

Ivar nodded slowly, "Yeah, I do. It's in the washroom."

"I'll play, if you play."

Ivar swallowed the lump in his throat and fought the urge to cry, "Sure thing." He whispered.

Cameron grinned, "Well, come on then. The fish won't catch themselves."

"Ready Bryce-boy?" Sean asked, standing in front of his son. Bryce nodded and put an arm around his dad's shoulder as he was lifted up off the sofa.

Sean carried Bryce up to the barn where Ivar emerged on Charis's back.

"Hey girl!" Bryce chirped, he reached out a shaky hand and gently stroked the animal's nose, "Ready," he confirmed. Sean moved over to stand by Charis's side.

Bryce clenched his jaw and nodded. Ivar held out an arm and Bryce grabbed hold of it as his dad helped him onto Charis's back.

"Hold on now." He warned.

Bryce nodded and clung onto his brother's shoulders.

"She's a good girl, isn't she?" Bryce whispered as Ivar started down the hill.

"Yep, and faithful," Ivar commented, keeping Charis at a slow trot. Sean, Caleb and Jason were walking just ahead of them holding the fishing gear. Cameron rode just a little to their right on Pepper, their uncle's horse.

Bryce chuckled softly and tossed his messy hair back out of his eyes, "It's hard to find a girl like that, hey Ivar."

Ivar shot him a look of his shoulder, "Would you be referring to the horse?"

"Mmm," Bryce's lips tweaked, "or Savannah."

Ivar's eyes narrowed slightly and his mouth pulled up into a lopsided smile.

"If I wasn't so intent on keeping you on the horse I would have knocked you off for that."

Bryce laughed, "Yeah sure you would."

~

Cameron tied the two horses to a tree near the lake.

Ivar dismounted Charis and asked Bryce, "You want me to get dad?"

Cameron laughed, "Aw, c'mon Ivar, why not piggyback your brother?"

Ivar choked, "Me? Carry him on my back?" He toyed with the idea, "How heavy are you again?"

Bryce shrugged, "Lighter than I was before I went into hospital."

Ivar flinched, he looked away and ran both hands through his hair. "Okay fine, just don't flatten me." He rolled the sleeves of his shirt up and stood with his back to Bryce.

Cameron helped Bryce swing his right leg over the side of the horse so he was sitting side saddle on Charis's back.

"One, two, three." He helped lift Bryce onto Ivar's back.

"Uh man." Ivar staggered slightly.

Bryce shook his head, "I do *not* weigh that much."

Ivar smirked at him before turning to face Cameron. Cameron saw the raw pain in his brother's eyes. *He's lighter than Ivar's admitting.* The thought hurt like a punch to the gut.

"Okay," Ivar shifted and started towards where their dad, uncle and grandpa were. Caleb looked up from hooking some bait on his line and laughed, "Don't look now Sean, but Ivar's put you out of a job."

Sean tilted his cap back. He grinned at his sons, "If your nurse could see you now she would have a fit."

"Yeaah." Bryce drawled, "But she can't see me so she won't know." He groaned a little as he was set down on the soft grass next to his dad. Ivar sat next to him and took the offered pole.

"Okay," Jason said, standing up to get Bryce a pole, "first fish caught gets double the dessert later."

"What's Mom making?" Caleb asked, a hopeful look on his face.

Sean shook his head, "Apple pie and custard."

Cameron made a face, "I'll let you guys get the first bite."

"Still can't stand the taste of custard can you son?"

"Nope, and don't plan to." Cameron grinned.

"Well, I love custard and pie so you guys are on." Bryce said, throwing his line out. Ivar glanced at him and smiled slightly, colour had filled Bryce's cheeks again and the usual spark had filled his eyes.

~Chapter Twenty-Four~

"I had to take the truths in the Bible, plant them in my heart and keep them there in my heart."

Aubrey leaned over her steaming cup, she sifted through the pages of healing scriptures in front of her.

"Found some more," Cameron dumped another stack of pages in front of her on the dining table.

Aubrey smiled up at him, "Thank you. You want a drink?" Cameron nodded and pulled up a seat, "Thanks," he took the mug his mom held out to him.

"How long has it been now?" Cameron took a long drink. Aubrey was quiet for a long time and Cameron took the time to study her face. She seemed to have aged ten years with the stress of everything. She was still lean and in good health, but her mouth was nearly always tilted in a focused, determined look, her eyes set like those of a runner before a race. "Just coming up to the end of his second week there." She said at length, sitting back down at the table with a tired sigh. She closed her eyes for a moment, her head bowed over her coffee cup.

Cameron reached across the table and covered his mom's hand with his own, "Mom,"

He waited until she looked at him. "It's going to be okay. Bryce is strong and we serve a God who is stronger."

Aubrey smiled through the tears that glistened in her eyes. She reached out and placed a hand on the side of his face, "When did you become so confident in him, Cam? When you left to go to serve at the station in New Orleans your dad and I were so worried you would walk away from the Lord."

A contented sigh passed Cameron's lips as he leaned into his mom's hand.

"I know, I almost did." He closed his eyes as if remembering. "I got a letter one day from Grandpa," Cameron laughed, "he doesn't like emails, does he?"

"No, not if it's a sentimental letter. He'd rather write it by hand. It also means just that little bit more to the person receiving it."

"Yeah," Cameron blinked open his eyes, "He told me that God had great plans for my life and asked me never to lose sight of that. He also said that just like my work took time, hard work and effort so did my relationship with the Lord," His eyes brimmed and he leaned into his mom's hand again. The sound of Ivar's guitar came from down the hallway. Cameron went on, "He told me how my heart was like a field and that I had to cultivate the seeds I planted in it. Bad seeds would produce a bad harvest, but good seeds planted would produce a good harvest. He said that if I wanted to see effective change, that was the word of God producing fruit in my life, I had to start spending more time in fellowship with the Lord through the word. I had to take the truths in the Bible, plant them in my heart and keep them there in my heart."

"Your grandpa also taught me that when Bryce first went into hospital. Why did it change you?" Aubrey brushed his reddish-brown fringe back from his forehead.

"The morning I got that, I had a call out to a fire at a retail park. Several houses had gone up in flames and several workers were still inside. I was one of the first men on the scene and I was sent inside to find and rescue them."

Cameron swallowed and stared out the window. "I had been in such a rush that I had stuffed Grandpa's letter in my pocket before suiting up. Before I went inside I had this overwhelming sense of fear that I wouldn't survive this one. That I'd get caught out or something would collapse on top of me."

He closed his eyes and fought back the tears, "I had to fight that fear a lot before that day. It would consume my thoughts day and night. But when it came to the punch I just had to get my head down and do it afraid. But that time when I felt that fear while headin' into the building," he shook his head, "I hadn't felt fear that strong before."

Cameron quickly drained his coffee.

He spread his fingers out on the table. "When I felt it, I remembered what Grandpa said about the law of sowing and reaping. You plant a seed, you reap a harvest. I was constantly feeding my heart and mind with thoughts of fear, dwelling on the thought that I would die in this fire, or the next one, or the next. Every time I faced a fire I knew it would be my last one. Inside those buildings, I kept thinking that every breath I took would be my last. I was heading into the fire terrified."

Cameron stopped and took a breath, he curled his fingers around the mug, inhailing the smell of coffee mixed with hot chocolate.

"But that one time I stopped just as I walked through the doors. I stopped for a second to get my bearings of the building and then I knew it. Every time I dwelt on that death-oriented fear, I was sowing the wrong type of seeds into my heart. It was as I went into a fire-filled room, that it was as if saw that Bible story of those three guys who walked through the fire. Ya know the one you used to tell us as kids. About

Shadrach, Meshach and that Abednego-dude. I realised that for them to do that with so much strength and faith in the Lord, they must have had to have a harvest of faith and trust in their hearts. I knew I couldn't go on going through fire after fire afraid. I was scared I might die and the harvest of those seeds might catch up with me one day."

Cameron stared at the plate of blueberry muffins on the table. He picked one up and started to peel back the case.

"I made the conscious decision there and then that I wasn't going to allow fear to consume my every thought and every breath anymore. I wasn't going to do it afraid."

He looked up at his mom and saw that her eyes were filled with tears that spilled over and down her cheeks. He reached out and gently wiped them away with his thumb.

"It says in 1 Peter 5:7; cast all your cares unto the Lord for he cares for you. It hit me, if He cares enough for me that his Son would die for me, then He would take care of me in that fire. Being afraid was just stupid."

He grinned and wiped away another tear that trailed Aubrey's cheek.

"Aw Mom, don't cry. I went into that fire that day, planting seeds of faith and courage with each step I took. Yeah, of course fear tried to rise up and get me to think about it all again. But you know what? All I had to do was set my focus on the Lord and remember that verse in Joshua 1:9 which says fear not, for the Lord your God goes with you wherever you go. Since then, every fire I've gone into, I've done it knowing that because I live in the shelter of the Most High, I will find rest in the shadow of the Almighty. I will declare about the Lord, He alone is my refuge, my place of safety. He is my God and I trust in Him. For He will rescue me from every trap and protect me from deadly disease. He will cover me with His feathers and under His wings I will take refuge. His faithful promises are my armour and protection."

Aubrey blinked back tears as he finished quietly, "Thank you Cameron."

Cameron sat back, his eyebrows drawn together in confusion, "For what?"

"For teaching me what I should have put into practice years ago. That I don't need to fear, for my God is with me." Aubrey covered her face with her hands and started to cry. Cameron got up walked around her side of the table. "Aw, Mom," was all he could say as he wrapped her in a hug and held her there for a long time.

~Chapter Twenty-Five~

"He's awesome in that way. Really he is and he died because he loves me. Because he loves us."

When Ivar heard the phone fall from his mom's hands in the hallway he knew something wasn't right.

He stood up and glanced across at Cameron who was playing around with his guitar. Cameron raised both eyebrows and stood quickly.

Aubrey appeared in the doorway, her hands shaking as she grabbed the door frame, "Ivar, Cam, that was your grandpa. He's at the hospital with Dad."

Seeing his mom's face was almost as white as a sheet, Cameron got up quickly and went over to her. "What's wrong?"

"It's Bryce, isn't it?" Ivar looked as white as his mom now. Aubrey nodded slowly, "Yes,"

"What's wrong with him?" Ivar asked quietly.

He walked towards his mom and brother with slow steps as if his feet were weighed down with blocks of cement.

"He's gone downhill. They're having to put a dripline through his shoulder and into his bloodstream so they can pump antibiotics into him. They're gonna sedate him."

The last word ended on a high squeak as Aubrey crumpled. Cameron knelt in front of her and Ivar joined them.

Cameron cupped his mom's face, "It's going to be okay."

"They say he may die still!" Aubrey sobbed, holding onto Cameron's shirt, "They say he may still die…"

"Remember Mom," Ivar fought to keep his voice under control. "Remember what Grandpa said, what Dad said. What the doctors say *isn't* the last word on the matter."

Aubrey pulled them both close and hid her face between their shoulders.

"Cam, Ivar, he's not with it."

"Who? Who isn't?" Ivar forced his mouth to voice words.

"Bryce, he's not with it."

"Ohhhh," Cameron groaned and pulled her into a tight embrace. He looked at Ivar over the top of her head.

Their brother.

Their little brother who brought the joy and music to the home was practically lying at death's door in the hospital.

"He's-he's" Aubrey couldn't finish. She didn't need to, they knew what she meant.

"And we are powerless to do anything." She whimpered. Cameron held his mom at arm's length, "Don't say that!" He said firmly.

"Mom," Ivar touched her arm gently. "We can do more than you think,"

Aubrey blinked and stared at them, "What?" She wiped away her tears, thinking how much Cameron's character took after Sean's and how strong Ivar had become in his spirit and faith.

Ivar laughed through his tears, "Pray, Mom. We can reach further in prayer than we ever could with our hands. You know something, Mom. Jesus didn't say climb your mountain, he said *speak* to your mountain and it will move and be cast into the sea."

Cameron took her hand, "And when you pray, pray in faith that it will be done for you by our Father in heaven."

He paused and rubbed away his own tears. "Faith, Mom, it's the substance of things hoped for; the substance of things not seen. We may not see Bryce well right now, but he will be. It's coming."

~

Sean gripped Jason's shoulder as he watched the nurse put his son under sedation. He closed his eyes and looked away, fighting the terror that was locked in his chest.

Jason blinked back his own tears, but smiled through them as he heard Bryce's drowsy voice.

"He's awesome, he really is, he walked on the water, he gave the blind man sight. Raised the dead. Restored a woman who had been rejected by society. He healed a group of lepers; He's awesome in that way. Really he is and he died be-because he loves me. Because he loves us." Bryce's voice slowed down until he wasn't speaking anymore. He couldn't. The nurse turned to face Sean and Jason.

"They say that when a child goes under sedation, it's what is in their heart that comes out." Her own eyes were wet, "And it's clear that what's in your son's heart is something more beautiful than anything. It obviously means the world to him. You have a good son, Mr Walker and an amazing grandson, Mr Davis." She smiled gently and walked out of the room, patting Bryce's leg on the way out.

Sean pulled up a chair next to his son and took his hand. "God, w-we-" He didn't get any further before breaking down. Jason placed a hand on his son-in-law's shoulder and another on his grandson's head. He picked up the broken prayer.

"God, we take your word right now and claim it for Bryce. We speak your healing word over his life right now in the name of Jesus." The only sound in the room aside from Bryce's quiet breathing was the sobbing coming from Sean.

~Chapter Twenty-Six~
We go by faith, not by sight.

It was late and outside, clouds hid the stars from view. The darkness matched Ivar's mood almost exactly. The warmth of the August day had dissolved into an unusually bitter night. Ivar swallowed the lump in his throat pulling his coat around himself and stepping out of the car. He normally rode with his dad but today, at this moment, he needed to do this alone, so he had driven.

The hospital building looked sinister and large as he walked towards it, terrified of what he would find inside.

Fear, like a large dark fist gripped his heart and squeezed it, threatening to squeeze all hope from inside. His throat constricted and tears stung his eyes as he stepped into the waiting room.

Cameron's words before Ivar had left echoed in his head. *Fear not, Ivar, we go by faith. Not by sight.*

Ivar breathed deeply and looked around. The room was air-conditioned and a vending machine buzzed in the corner. Men and women in crisp white and blue uniforms flitted about. Ivar stood stone-still in the middle of it all, watching in slow motion as a door swung open at the end of the hall. Two doctors and a nurse pushed a trolley bed towards him and as they passed Ivar looked down.

A small boy with remarkable likeness to Bryce was asleep under a blanket. His thumb had found its home in his mouth and his arm was curled around a teddy bear.

Ivar swallowed and looked away, this shouldn't be happening. Not to him. Not to his family. Not to his brother.

We go by faith, not by sight.

Ivar could almost see his older brother, standing with his hands on his hips looking at him while saying those words.

"Can I help you, Sir?"

Ivar was snapped out of his trance by the voice of a nurse. He blinked and stared at her.

"Can I help you?" She repeated.

Ivar shook himself and drew himself up to his full height, "Uh, yeah, I'm Ivar Walker. I'm here to see my brother, Bryce Walker."

The nurse nodded and ran her tongue along her bottom teeth while she consulted a list in her hands.

"Walker, Walker, Walker." She muttered tapping her pen against each listed name. "Ah yes, Bryce Andrew Walker, isolation room four, level three. At the end of the children's ward."

"I-isolation?" Ivar stuttered, feeling all the blood drain from his face.

"Mmhmm," The nurse nodded and pressed her lips together, "He was moved there last night after the doctors and surgeon discovered how dangerous and rare his bone infection was."

"What do you mean?" Ivar asked.

The nurse smiled and tilted her head slightly, "How old are you, son?"

"Eighteen," Ivar replied, wondering why that made a difference.

"Okay," the nurse smiled reassuringly. "Your brother has one of the rarest forms of osteomyelitis, a deep bone infection." She said. Ivar felt mixed emotions swirl through his mind. The nurse was speaking, "As we told your parents, one of three things will happen."

Ivar blinked and focused back on her, "Whats that?"

"Either we will lose him, he will lose his right leg, or at the very least he will have to learn how to walk again. But honestly, son, we are doing all we can to help him get through this."

Ivar glanced down at the nurse's pass he had been given; he had fifteen minutes with him. The nurse smiled gently, squeezed his shoulder and hurried off.

He's going to die, and there is nothing you can do about it, a dark voice spoke in the back of his mind.

Ivar swallowed and for a fleeting moment he was tempted to give in and believe the voice.

He squeezed his eyes shut and clenched his fists. "No, he's not. He won't die, get out of my head, devil. You're nothing but a liar-" His sentence was finished on a choked sob.

Ivar pushed away the taunting voice and forced his legs to carry him towards the lifts.

The ride up to the third floor was a constant raging battle of the will. The thought that Bryce would die kept creeping up into his mind.

He gripped the railing and squeezed his eyes shut.

Stop. His head screamed, *in the name of Jesus I cast you down! It says-* he choked on his sobs, *it says in the word to take every thought captive and right now I take captive these thoughts and say that Bryce will live and not die!*

A large knot had formed in the centre of his chest by the time the lift doors slid open.

A doctor came towards him, "Can I help you, son?"

Ivar nodded, "Uh yeah, I'm here to see my brother Bryce Walker. He's in isolation. I have a nurse's pass."

The doctor looked at the slip of paper and nodded, "He's right through there." He pointed towards a door at the end of the ward.

Ivar swallowed, nodded his thanks and pushed his hands through his hair, drawing a long breath.

He walked towards the end of the ward, passing several children in hospital beds, but his focus remained on the one young man in the end isolation room.

"God," he paused and prayed, placing a hand on the doorknob, after rinsing them with anti-bacterial gel.

"I don't know what I'm going to see, I don't know what I'm going to hear or feel. But right now, right here, I choose to believe your word and what you say. I walk by faith and not by what I see, in the name of Jesus, my brother-" his voice faltered, "is healed." He pushed the door open.

As he stepped into the room he closed his eyes reflexively. "Jesus," he breathed, "your name is higher than any other and at your name every knee must bow." Ivar breathed deeply and opened his eyes.

The room's white walls reflected the clouded moonlight coming through the window.

Just like Bryce, he thought, *always wanting to see the sky.*

His mind instantly went back to that day in the barn with his grandpa a week ago.

They had been moving hay bales when his grandpa had told him, "Look up. When you look down all you see is where your feet have been, not where they can take you." He had then tilted Ivar's head back so he could see the cloudless blue sky through a gap in the rafters. Ivar blinked and shook himself from his thoughts.

A fluid bag was suspended on a rack next to the hospital bed. Ivar followed the intravenous line with his eyes down from the bag and into Bryce's right shoulder.

Bryce.

Ivar swallowed and smiled weakly.

Bryce was lying in the hospital bed, the blanket drawn up to his chest. His tousled blond hair was plastered to his forehead. His eyes were closed, his face pale, cheeks sunken and slightly thinner from where he had lost weight during his stay. Headphones were playing something in his ears, they were plugged into his phone which was lying on his stomach.

Ivar walked up to the bed. He picked up his brother's phone and turned it on. Staring at the screen, a smile flickered.

Even now in this state, Bryce was pumping the healing word of God into himself.

"Hey, Bryce," Ivar perched on the end of the bed and placed a hand gently on his arm. "You awake?" He watched the rise and fall of his brother's chest for a moment. "Bryce? You awake?"

Bryce didn't respond, his eyes remaining closed and his breathing shallow.

"You know, just by looking at you, you wouldn't know how painful this was for you." Ivar glanced down at the end of the bed. Under the blanket Bryce's right leg was straightened out with the brace, it being too painful for him to straighten it without support.

He kept his eyes on his brother's face. "Lord, I choose t-to believe your words and not those of the p-people around me-" Ivar couldn't even finish. Sobs choked him.

~

Ivar stared at the car's steering wheel.

 He sat there, in the hospital car park for ages, tears pouring down his face like a river.

 "Ugh!" He smashed the palm of his hand again the wheel, "God!" He cried, "Help me remember that it's what *you* say that counts. It's what you say that is true." He dashed at the tears trailing his face, "It would be so easy for me, Lord, to throw a pity party and curl up and cry. It would be so easy for me to mourn over him, but what's that going to do? Nothing, nothing! Fear isn't going to save him, I could stop right now and let fear grab a hold of me. While my brother lies there dying, I could die on the inside alongside him, b-but no! I refuse to walk in fear."

Ivar gripped the wheel until his knuckles turned white. "We go by faith, Lord, and not by sight. Father, you say to cast all our cares onto you because you care for us. I cast my fear onto you and choose to believe, no, I choose to *know* he is healed."

Ivar breathed deeply and thought back to his brother, wearing headphones, listening to the healing power of God allowing it to flow into his body.

Ivar's phone beeped. Picking it up, he saw a message from his grandfather.

Remember Ivar, it read, ***Isaiah 53:5 says 'but he was wounded for our transgressions, he was bruised for our iniquities; the chastisement for our peace was upon him,***

and by his stripes we are healed.' Remember the chastisement for Bryce's peace was upon him and by his stripes, Bryce is healed. I love you, Ivar.

Ivar sniffed, dried his eyes, put the car into reverse and backed out of the car park as a slow, tired smile formed on his lips.

~Chapter Twenty-Seven~

*'When all around was shifting sand,
You raised me up and made me stand.'*

Bryce turned slightly and stared into the darkness.

The words coming through his headphones started to fade as his thoughts became the focus of his attention.

Lord, he prayed silently, *I know this isn't what you have in store for me. I know that what the doctors say isn't what you say. I mean, come on, I'd much rather be wrestling my brothers, or be riding Charis, or playing the fiddle. And Lord, I believe I will. I believe you have a perfect plan and will for my life.*

Bryce shifted, he squeezed his eyes shut and two tear drops slid out from under his eyelashes as pain throbbed through him. He blinked away the tears and looked across at the needle in his shoulder. He pressed his lips tightly together and closed his eyes again. His heart burned within him. *I'm scared Lord, please help me,* he whispered.

Bryce lifted a hand and rubbed his eyes. He stared out of the window as several stars peeked out from behind the clouds. The moon shot beams of light into his room, falling across his face and highlighting his light hair with a silvery tint.

~

*"Looking back on all you've done, the miracles,
How far we have come.
The story of your faithfulness, I won't forget.*

When all around was shifting sand,
You raised me up and made me stand.
I'm anchored in your perfect love. I will not fear.
Yet I'll say, arise, arise my soul and sing.
Remember all the greater things that he has done,
What's yet to come."

Aubrey turned the volume up on the car's radio and listened intently as the song lyrics filled the car.

She pulled over as the radio announcer called out the artist's name. Aubrey typed the name into her phone, found the song and downloaded it. Connecting her phone into the car's bluetooth she put the song's album on. After a while she started to drum the music's tune on the car wheel. Then she started to sing along, "We are free indeed, no longer slaves but daughters and sons. We are free indeed, no longer chained, but held in your love. Ransomed."

Aubrey was still singing when she pulled up into the car park of the local superstore. She stopped the car's engine and left the music playing. Whilst listening, she sent a message around to her family.

At the store, does anyone need anything?

Cameron got back first with a message asking for anything that had sugar in. Aubrey laughed and sent back a 'no' in block capitals followed by a laughing emoji. Ivar sent a text saying he was good.

When Sean's message came in Aubrey felt her heart constrict.

Milkshakes, it's the only thing Bryce will eat/drink at the moment.

Aubrey let out a long breath and sat back in the seat. She rubbed both hands over her face, "Okay God, I need strength to remember not to fear."

Aubrey fumbled for her phone, she slid her finger down her contact list until she hit her dad's number. Aubrey waited as it rung; he wasn't the best at answering his phone. The call cut through to his voicemail.

"Hey Dad, it's Aubrey." Aubrey stared at the storefront through the car's windshield as she spoke. "I just needed to talk. Bryce is only eating, or rather, drinking milkshakes at the moment. Nothing much else, the doctor just says he's getting worse." Her voice was tight and strained. "I'm reminding myself constantly to remember what you and Cameron said but it's so hard when I feel so helpless." She let the message run out.

Aubrey got out the car and headed into the store, snatching up a basket on her way through the doors.

"Mornin' Ma'am." The store clerk chirped cheerfully and waved her hand.

"Good morning." Aubrey smiled gently and went down an aisle. Consulting her list, she found the frozen meat section and picked up several packets of chicken pieces.

Her basket filled as she went around in a daze, her mind on Bryce. She had been to see him almost every single day over the last two and a half weeks.

She was holding a salad bag in her hand when the store clerk came around the corner. Her brown eyes were soft as she came towards Aubrey.

"Ma'am?" The girl was obviously younger than her.

"Yes?" Aubrey turned to face her, the salad bag still in her hand.

"You're Aubrey Walker, aren't you? Madison's daughter?"

Aubrey nodded, "I am,"

The young lady grinned, "I'm Sarah Foster. Madison comes in here often and she was telling me about your boy. Bryce, is it?"

Aubrey blinked, she stared at Sarah as if in a daze and shook herself suddenly.

"I'm sorry," she said running a hand across her eyes. "Yes, Bryce Walker, that's my son."

Sarah grinned, "Your Mama was telling me about him," her voice held the familiar strong Colorado accent which Aubrey loved.

"Oh? What did she say?"

Sarah grinned and took the basket from Aubrey. She walked over to the counter and started to scan the items in the basket.

"She said that your son is going through a lot right now, being in hospital and all and that y'all needed a lot of prayer and love."

Aubrey nodded numbly, "He got better then went back downhill." She placed her hands on the countertop and stared down at her fingers. She looked at her wedding ring, remembering back to the day she and Sean had found out they were expecting their third boy.

"Cameron, Ivar, kitchen please!"
Sean was grinning proudly as his two sons walked in.

Seven year old Cameron came in the room hanging from Grandpa Jason's back. Three year old Ivar came to the back door, his face red and he was pulling on the rope around Daisy the cows neck.

"Mommy, Daisy not want-a-come in!" *He protested loudly, his eyes large and wet with unshed tears. Aubrey laughed and went across to him. She picked him up and swung him around the kitchen laughing the whole time. Madison came in and leaned against her husband as he put Cameron down.*

"What's the news, sweetie?" *Jason looked at his beaming daughter and son-in-law. Aubrey giggled and blushed as she slipped her hand into Sean's and smiled shyly. Sean pushed his cap back and messed up his wavy blond hair, grinning,*

"We are having another baby." *He announced proudly. Madison clapped her hands together.* "Praise the Lord! The blessings never cease!"

Jason tried to untangle Ivar and Cameron who where wrestling on the floorboards.

"Did you two ragamuffins hear your Momma? You're gonna have a baby brother or sister."

Cameron sat up and stared at his mom's stomach area. He pointed and said to Ivar rather matter of factly.

"The baby is going to be in her tummy, just like you!"

Ivar's face puckered. "No! I not there!"

Sean scooped him up, rocking him gently, "Hey, hey, Cam, you came from there as well."

Cameron screwed his face up, "Ew."

Ivar stuck his tongue out and pointed his small finger in his big brother's face. "Wou came from Mommy's tummy!"

Madison went over to her daughter "Do you know what you're having?"

"A boy," she said softly, "he's gonna be called Bryce."

Ivar looked at her, "I protect my Bwyce." He whispered loudly in her ear.

Cameron lifted his chin, "And I will protect my Bryce and Ivar."

~Chapter Twenty-Eight~

"Remember, faith is the substance of things hoped for, the substance of things not seen."

Aubrey smiled as the memory faded.

"Mrs Walker? Cooee!" Sarah leaned over the countertop.

"Huh? Oh, I'm sorry my mind was somewhere else." Aubrey gave Sarah a weak smile.

"I bet," Sarah commented. She fiddled with something behind the countertop before passing Aubrey's grocery bag across the counter to her.

"Oh, I haven't paid for that yet. Just let me find my purse-" Aubrey paused as Sarah shook her head and held up a hand.

"No need, it's already paid for."

A strawberry-blond eyebrow arched. "But I didn't-"

Sarah laughed and shook her hair out of her face, "It's paid for Mrs Walker. Enjoy your day and rest assured I'm praying for y'all."

Aubrey studied the young woman across the counter for a moment. Sarah was beautiful in a word, with light brown skin and deep, soft chocolate-coloured eyes that spoke of a deep unearthly love. Her dark wavy hair was pulled back into a ponytail that bounced across her shoulders when she moved and when she smiled it was as if the sun shined down from heaven.

Her smile was one of pure joy that knew no end. Aubrey reached across the countertop and enclosed her hand over Sarah's. She smiled and said, "Thank you Sarah, I needed to hear that today."

"Aw, you're welcome into my family's store anytime, Mrs Walker!" Sarah tilted her head and the curly ponytail swung across her back.

"I'll be back, trust me, and I'll bring my son Bryce with me so you can meet him." Aubrey hooked the grocery bag over her arm.

"That's the way to think, Mrs Walker, and when you bring your boy he *will* walk through those doors. Remember, faith is the substance of things hoped for, the substance of things not seen." Sarah winked and smiled showing a row of perfectly straight white teeth.

Aubrey paused and tucked a loose strand of hair back behind her ear. "You know my oldest said that to me not a few days ago."

Another grin lit up the younger girls eyes. "Well, then maybe it's just what the good Lord wanted ya to hear."

"Yes, maybe it was. Thanks again, Sarah." Aubrey pushed the door to the store open and stepped out in the mid-morning heat. She put her groceries in the back of her car, went to get in the front seat, but had second thoughts.

Leaving her car in the grocery store parking lot, she walked through the town.

Several folks she knew smiled or stopped to ask about her family's health. As she walked she past Sean's garage, she was surprised to find it open and the doors flung open wide to welcome in the weather.

I thought Sean and Ivar were with Bryce.

Aubrey knocked gently on the door. A noise like metal hitting to the ground came from inside the garage.

Someone spoke, "Uh, one moment please."

Aubrey laughed and walked inside. She found a large blue truck parked inside the work area. The lower portion of a young man stuck out from the underside of the truck near the engine. Aubrey tapped the truck's exterior and said,

"So, who's the hard worker?"

There was a bang and a groan, the young man pushed out from under the truck and sat up rubbing his forehead. Grease covered his face, "Mom? You half-scared the wits outta me." Aubrey laughed, "Cam, when was the last time you fixed a car?"

Cameron chewed on his cheek and squinted at the roof. "Uh, days that go back at least seven years. Bearing in mind I was thirteen then." He chuckled and crawled back under his car.

Aubrey leaned on it, "I mean, is it broken?"

"Nah, just needs a little adjusting. Dad said I was free to use the garage to fix it up." His voice came from under the truck. He pushed back out and grinned, "Did you bring me something with sugar?"

Aubrey laughed and shook her head.

"No, but your dad always keeps the small mini fridge stocked up just through there in the store room." She nodded towards the door at the back. Cameron rolled onto his knees and rubbed his hands together

"Awesome." A glint of hunger and mirth lingered in his eyes as Aubrey chuckled.

* * *

When Aubrey got back into her car, her phone rang. "Hello, this is Aubrey Walker speaking."

"Aubrey it's Dad."

Aubrey felt relief wash over her like a wave.

"You okay, sweetie?"

"I guess," Aubrey rubbed her face, "I, uh, did you get my voicemail?"

There was a long pause and the sound of a cow mooing. At long last, Jason's voice came across the line.

"That I did, and it seems to me that you need to stay in prayer."

Aubrey put the phone on loudspeaker and laid it on the seat next to her as she started to back out of the parking lot.

"Dad, I have a family, I can't spend all day praying, as much as I want to." There was a trace of longing in her voice.

Jason chuckled, "You know what, sweetie, when your brother was a small boy he fell ill with the flu, serious flu. Your mom and I set up an hourly prayer watch even through the night. Every hour an alarm went off and we would get up and pray for him."

Aubrey stopped at the traffic lights and rubbed her forehead with her thumb and finger. She breathed out, "Even through the night," awe lingered in her voice, "I don't remember Caleb being ill."

"Yeah, you were very young. But, hon', that's love, devotion and doing *all* you can, even to your own hurt. Yes, we lost a lot of sleep but yes your brother was healed. We raised you and Caleb to know how powerful prayer is Aubrey. It can reach further than we ever could with our hands."

Aubrey thought for a long moment, "Thanks, Dad. I'm going to do that,"

"Remember what I told you about the Rosetta Stone? The parable of the sower shows us how to plant and reap our harvest; once you have knowledge on that story, you can unlock the secrets of every other parable! It shows us how to keep his word. Our hearts are like flower beds, or fields, sweetie. The soil is there, ready and waiting, and when we plant seeds of life, love and faith into the soil, beautiful things grow up. But when we plant those seeds, we can't just wander off and leave them to fend for themselves. No, we have to take daily care of the seeds and plants. Watering them. Giving them light. Treating them right. Caring for them. When we plant what is right in our hearts, we have to keep that seed strong and protected. We can't let other things come and grow around it, ready to uproot our beautiful flowers. Our flower bed is small, but out of it will grow beautiful things. Your seed may be small, but when you let it grow, take care of it and nurture it. Aubrey, amazing things will happen and show in your life. So, take care of the seeds you plant in your heart. Don't let the crows come and peck them up."

Aubrey bit her bottom lip as she listened, "Where do you learn all this, Dad?" She sniffed and wiped at the lone tear that had slid down her cheek.

"Time, experience, and plenty of planting." Jason's voice was soft as it vibrated through the phone.

"I think my field is pretty barren." Aubrey commented wryly. Jason clicked his tongue, "It's never too late until you don't need it. Go plant and watch the harvest flourish."

"Okay Dad, I'll try."

"No, hon'. There is no try with God, just like there can be no try with your boy. You can't *try* it's either life or death here, Aubrey. It's either do or don't."

Aubrey hadn't heard her dad's voice so firm in years. "Okay. I'll do it then dad."

"Good girl. Mom and I will be praying right alongside you."

"Thanks Dad." Aubrey hung up as she pulled into the driveway outside her family's home.

~

A scream filled the night air. Ivar sat bolt upright in bed, grabbed the bedside table firmly and swallowed the rest of the screams back down.

A light came on in the hallway, footsteps padded up to the door and it swung open slowly. Cameron stuck his head around the door, his eyes half closed.

"Laws-a-mercy Ivar. Why're ya screaming like a cat that's been dunked in a pond?" He rubbed his eyes and crept closer.

"I heard an alarm or somethin', real loud. It scared me out of my wits." Ivar huddled into his quilt.

More footsteps echoed in the hall. Aubrey came in the room holding her phone.

"I'm sorry, I forgot to turn my alarm down before I went back to sleep."

Ivar's heart was racing.

He closed his eyes, gave his mom a small smile and tried to get his breathing back to normal.

"The alarm didn't help my dreams," he tried to sound lighthearted, but failed.

Cam yawned, "Eh, I've heard enough alarms in my life to know the difference between a fire alarm and a phone alarm."

Aubrey sat next to Ivar and took his hand. "What do you mean, your dreams?"

Ivar ran his free hand over his mouth, frowning, "Just a bad dream about Bryce."

"Wanna talk about it?" Aubrey put an arm around his shoulders. Cameron had fallen asleep on the end of the bed. Ivar chewed his lower lip thoughtfully.

"I just had the same, short recurring dream, that Bryce didn't get better and that we lost him." He shuddered and hugged himself, feeling less and less like the young adult he was and more like a scared little boy.

"Oh, Ivar." Aubrey wrapped him in a tight hug and the two sat there for a long moment. After a while Aubrey pulled away and held him at arm's length.

"Listen, that's just fear trying to get ahold of you." She placed a hand on his chest right over where his heart was. "Listen here, Ivar, you and I both know the truth. That Bryce shall live and not die. You told me about how fear tried to get a hold of you when you went to see Bryce just after he had gone downhill. Remember what you told me?"

Ivar nodded and slowly, he could see the burning strength in his mom's eyes. "I took every fear and thought captive and cast it down."

Aubrey smiled, "That's right," she reached out and brushed his hair back. Ivar suddenly threw his arms around her neck impulsively and hugged her.

"Thank you," he whispered close to her ear.

"For what?" Aubrey laughed slightly rubbing his back.

"For not only walking through this time with Bryce, but also with me, you've been there. Like my rock. I know you're not perfect and we have all had to rally our strength but thank you for being my pillar. And for loving me." Ivar hugged his mom tighter. "I love you,"

"I love you too." Aubrey whispered, tears buried in her eyes.

~Chapter Twenty-Nine~

*'Arise, arise my soul and sing, remember all the greater
things that he has done, what's yet to come.'*

Bryce was vaguely aware of the sound of voices, of the brush of clothing as people walked past him, of the shaky touch of his dad's hand upon his arm.

A man's voice cut through the fog in his mind.

"I'm sorry," was all Bryce could make out.

There was the sound of a door opening and closing as someone left the isolation room.

Bryce drew a long breath and tried to open his eyes. His body was too tired, too weak and worn out to do so. He tried to hear what was being said.

"It doesn't look good," came another voice, then the sound of that person leaving the room.

Then silence.

Stifling silence.

So quiet a pin could have dropped and been a rude interruption.

Then his mom's quavering voice broke the silence. It sounded as if she was trying her best not to cry. A sob caught up her throat as she said, "Sean."

Her voice broke and Bryce heard his dad pull his wife towards him. "Remember, Aubrey."

His mom laughed a little, it sounded watery. "I know. It's going to be okay, I know, Sean." There was the sound of clothes brushing against clothes and Bryce guessed his mom had buried her face in his dad's chest.

"Shh, shh, it's okay. What's the song you have been listening to non-stop recently?"

Aubrey sniffed, and sung brokenly, "Looking back on all you've done, the miracles, how far we have come. The story of your faithfulness, I won't forget. When all around was shifting sand, you raised me up and made me stand. I'm anchored in your perfect love, I will not fear. Yet I'll say, arise, arise my soul and sing, remember all the greater things that he has done, what's yet to come. Arise, arise my soul and sing. Give praise to the risen king."

Bryce loved the sound of his mom's voice, he wished he could tell her how beautiful she sounded, even though her voice shook.

Bryce heard his dad kiss his mom and say. "That's right, think of all the greater things. Remember the miracles, what he's done and what's yet to come. Don't fear."

He wished his body would corporate so he could look at his parents and tell them how much he loved them. Smile and tell them he was going to be ok.

His body wouldn't relent though and he sunk back into oblivion.

~

Aubrey's voice was less strained the next time Bryce heard it. He had fallen asleep and now woke up to her coming close to his bedside.

"Bryce? Honey,"

Bryce forced his body to obey his wishes.

His eyes cracked open, and his mom's face filled his vision with her sweet smile. "Hey there, baby boy." Aubrey reached out and pushed back several strands of his longish blond hair. Bryce's lips tilted slightly in a half-smile.

"I've got to go now, okay honey? Before Ivar and Cameron utterly destroy the kitchen."

Bryce blinked slowly as an acknowledgement. Aubrey ran her fingers along the side of his cheek, she leaned in and kissed his forehead.

"Say hi to Ivar and Cam for me." He croaked in a broken whisper.

Aubrey nodded "Will do," she watched as Bryce's eyes closed again. *By his stripes, Bryce is healed.* The words ran through her head, faith fitted itself into the broken part of her heart. Taking Bryce's limp hand into her own, she brought it up to her mouth and kissed his fingers.

"It's going to be ok Bryce." She spoke to herself just as much to her son. "It's going to be ok. Daddy God has you." She swallowed and said once again, "Daddy God has you."

For a few more minutes, she waited by his bedside, watching the rhythmic rise and fall of his chest. His face pale aside for the bright red fever marks on his cheeks.

And I have you also Aubrey.

The whisper was soft. Tender. Loving.

Pressing her cheek against Bryce's hand, Aubrey started to cry, not fear riddled tears, but tears that showed a understanding for a greater love than she had for Bryce.

A love that said.

This is not my best. This is not my will. I am willing, he will be made whole. I will heal my son. I will watch over my son. And I will protect my daughter.

A love that went to the cross and bled so that not only could they be forgiven but healed.

~

The smell of burnt food hit Aubrey as soon as she entered the house. Walking into the open plan kitchen-diner, she found the floor covered in the cushions off the couch.

"What's going on in here?" She asked skeptically, trying to hide her yawn.

Ivar crawled out from underneath a stack of cushions. "Huh?"

Cameron walked in holding a large fun-sized box of chocolates "Ivar do you think another box is too drastic?"

He paused when he saw his mom and grinned sheepishly.

"What's going on?" Aubrey asked again, putting her bag down on the table and walking over to inspect the cushions and blankets over the floor.

"We didn't want to spend the night alone again." Ivar said. Both young men sat down on the floor. A large chocolate box half-empty lay in the centre of the room.

"And Ivar kept burning the food." Cameron added, nodding towards the kitchen sink piled high with pans. Aubrey didn't know whether to laugh or cry. She chose to laugh slightly, "Give me a minute." Aubrey walked down the hall towards her room.

Ivar raised his eyebrows as he looked at his brother. "Caramel?" He offered, holding out the box.

Cameron rummaged through the mix of chocolates and wrappers, "Aw, you ate the last coffee one, Ivar."

Ivar just shrugged, distracted.

Aubrey came in, dressed in her pyjamas with a quilt wrapped around her shoulders like a large cloak.

"Okay, move over boys." She sat down in between her sons. Ivar pulled his knees up to his chest and pulled on the fabric of his own pyjamas. He pushed his hair out of his eyes. Cameron manoeuvred over stacks of pillows, grabbed the TV remote off the cabinet and moved back next to his mom and brother.

The boys flicked through the TV channels.

After a while Cameron dropped off, his head tilted back against the cream coloured leather sofa behind him. Ivar rubbed the back of his neck and pulled the lid back from the second box of chocolates. He glanced at the clock then did a double take. "Mom, it's past midnight,"

Aubrey nodded, her eyes glassy. "I'm not tired."

"Good, neither am I." Ivar rested his head against her shoulder. "Is it me or is this TV program slightly weird?" He scrunched up his nose and stared at the movie.

Aubrey blinked and looked towards the TV.

"What even is it?"

Ivar suppressed a yawn, he squinted at the screen.

"It's about a colour changing uh-" He tilted his head. "-what *is* that?"

Aubrey rubbed her eyes and leaned forward.

"I think it's a chameleon."

"Oh, and that would be great if I knew what a chameleon was." Ivar sat back, his eyebrows drawn together.

Aubrey glanced at him, "You don't know what a chameleon is?"

"It's a reptile, right?" Ivar pinched the bridge of his nose with his thumb and forefinger.

Aubrey shook her head in disbelief.

Ivar raised an eyebrow, "It's not?"

Aubrey rubbed her forehead, "No it is, what did you learn at school exactly?"

Ivar opened his mouth to try and defend his education, "I-" he blinked and pursed his lips, "Absolutely nothing worth remembering." He grinned and then frowned, "But a Chameleon is a reptile right?"

Aubrey shook her head, "I don't know anymore, Ivar. I'm so tired, but can't sleep. I keep thinking of Bryce."

Ivar hooked her arm around his, "I know what you mean, I keep wondering how he's doing." Ivar sniffed and looked away, blinking back tears. Reaching out, Aubrey put a hand under his chin and brought his head back around so he would look at her.

"Listen to me, Ivar Benjamin Walker, Bryce is going to be okay. Do you hear me? He is going to be fine and he is going to be running around causing havoc again quicker than you know it."

Aubrey's hands trembled, Ivar sealed them between his own. "He's going to be okay."

~Chapter Thirty~
"Don't you dare give in."

Jason stared at the doctor in front of him.

Madison tensed and Sean's face became like flint.

"I'm sorry," the doctor held his hands out, "but the infection has grown back in your son's bone. We have discovered just how dangerous it is and we need to take him down to theatre for another operation now."

Jason put an arm around Madison as he heard a weak breath escape her. Sean stared at the doctor levelly.

"Are you sure?"

The man nodded, years of experience in his eyes, "I'm sorry, yes, and if we don't get him down there soon to do the operation," He hesitated.

"What?" Sean moved to the edge of his seat, his eyes like thunder as he looked the doctor in the eyes.

"What is it?"

The doctor ran a hand over his slick black hair.

"He will probably die."

Time stopped.

Sean sat back in the chair feeling utterly broken. He could feel the blood draining from his head leaving him almost as white as the hospital walls. He swallowed, blinked hard and looked back at the doctor. "Can I have a few minutes to call me wife, please." His voice nothing but a weak whisper.

The doctor nodded, "Yes, I'll be just outside. I'm so sorry, Sir."

Once the doctor had left, Jason stood in front of his son-in-law. "Sean, listen to me, don't let this bring you down." Sean's lips trembled with the painstaking emotion that flowed through him. He covered his eyes with his hand for a moment and hung his head. Then he ran his hand through his hair, knocking his cap sideways. Jason leaned forward and placed both hands on Sean's shoulders.

"Sean. Look at me."

Sean swallowed again and looked up into the deep, compassionate blue eyes of his father-in-law. "Don't you *dare* give in, Sean Walker. Don't you dare give in."

Madison reached over and placed a hand on his arm, "Sean," she said slowly. "Jason's right. I know this is the worst news any father can get but you can't give up. You can't let it shake you."

Sean rubbed both hands over his face. When he pulled them away, both his palms and cheeks were wet with tears.

"I-I just feel so-so-"

Madison stood up and hugged him, "Shh there." She patted his back slowly as he cried.

Madison glanced across at Bryce who was laying still. So still.

In the hospital bed, the blanket covering him hardly moved with each breath he took. Bryce's face looked almost lifeless save the feverish flush that crept over his skin.

Madison held Sean close as if he were her own child.

"Oh God, we know you have a perfect will and plan for Bryce's life, a destiny and a purpose. It doesn't end here. No, Lord, it doesn't end here." Madison closed her eyes as tears of her own fell. Jason leaned against the wall and shifted Sean's cap between his hands.

"Listen, we need to call Aubrey."

Sean pulled away and dried his eyes. "Yeah, I need to call her." His voice was husky. He took the phone Jason held out, Aubrey's number was already up. Taking a deep breath he pressed the call button.

"Hello?" At the sound of her voice Sean felt his heart tear in half. Stepping close to Bryce, Sean took his son's hand. He could practically feel the heat from his fever radiating from him.

"Hey babe, uh I need to talk with you."

Aubrey could sense the strain in his voice. "What's wrong with Bryce?"

Sean felt his stomach clench at the panic in her voice.

"They say they have to take Bryce down for a second operation or he may not make it."

Sean looked down at Bryce's face. His eyes were closed and strands of hair trailed across his forehead and cheek. As gently as he could with trembling fingers, Sean reached out and brushed back the blond strands.

He heard the air on the end of the phone go still.

Nerves fluttered in the pit on his stomach and pain twisted in his chest. Across the phone, there was the sound of a choking sob filled with pain.

"Aubrey, baby, shh, it's okay." Sean gripped the phone with both hands, trying to comfort his wife as best as possible.

The sobs continued, each one gasping for breath and uncontrollably filled with pure, terrifying agony.

"Babe," Sean said softly into the phone. "Honey," Sean banished his own tears, rubbing at his eyes furiously. He reached out and laid a hand a hand on Bryce's cheek. His chest constricted as he heard his wife's sobbing and stared down at his sons flushed and feverish face.

Pulling his attention back to comforting Aubrey, Sean said, "Aubrey, listen to me, girl."

He kept his voice as steady as possible, fighting the turmoil inside him. "Listen my girl, you have to calm down, okay? Everything is going to be okay."

Her voice came across in a small squeak, "Please don't let them do anything until I have time to pray about this."

Sean nodded, then remembered she couldn't see him nodding.

"Sure," he whispered. "I need to tell them soon so let's take the next half hour to pray about it."

"Okay," Aubrey said, a tremor in her voice.

Sean hung up and turned towards Jason and Madison.

"Aubrey's gonna pray now with the gang at home, we also need to pray right now." His voice shook slightly as he started, but as he went to pray, his voice grew in strength.

"We need to seek God's wisdom on this second surgery."

~

Ivar rubbed the back of his neck. "Thanks Savannah."

He crossed his ankles and glanced across the café's table at his friend. Savannah smiled weakly and tucked a strand of hair back behind her ear.

"I'm sorry this has all happened to your family, I really am." She swirled the spoon in her coffee mug. "Is there anything I can do?" She lifted her face to look at him, her brown eyes large and sober.

Ivar felt a slight smile tug at his lips despite the emotional battle raging in his heart.

He glanced out the café's store-front window. The sky was a marmalade colour and the sun was just visible as it had almost come to the end of its decent. A full moon was clear in the sky above Pike's Peak. "That's sweet of you Savannah. And we appreciate it," Ivar looked at her and smiled.

"What?" Savannah pushed back another rebellious strand of hair that had escaped her braid.

Ivar shook his head as a slight laugh passed his lips. "*What?*" Savannah scrunched up her nose.

Ivar grinned boyishly, he loved it when she did that. Savannah's family owed the café. Her dad, Peter van Dyke, was a Scandinavian cook and the owner of the café. Savannah's mom served over the countertop where she could keep an eye on her daughter and Ivar.

He studied Savannah for a moment. Her thick reddish brown hair hung in a fishtail braid over her left shoulder. Her dark eyes were framed by thick long eyelashes that rested on her cheeks every time she closed her eyes or blinked. A splash of freckles covered her nose. Ivar loved it when she scrunched up her freckled nose.

It's cute, he often thought. *It makes her look so young and innocent.*

"Ivar," Savannahs voice was light and airy. "Why are you staring at me like that?" The girls brow furrowed as she stared at her friend.

Ivar shook himself out of his daze, "Sorry," he said before sucking a mouthful of his chocolate banana milkshake through the straw.

As the sweet foamy liquid filled his mouth Ivar froze.

He looked down at his drink and his hands tightened around the glass. His eyes teared up as he realised that, almost without thinking about it, he had ordered Bryce's favourite milkshake flavour.

Ivar choked on it, almost spitting it back out. He gripped the table edge and clenched his eyes shut, forcing himself to swallow and breath again.

He was vaguely aware of Savannah jumping up out of her seat. Semi-aware of the yellow shirt she wore with her denim skirt. Her hand rested on his arm but Ivar didn't seem to register it. Almost as if he couldn't feel anything other than the remorse flowing through him.

Savannah's voice broke through the haze in his mind. "Ivar, are you okay?" Her hand gently touched the side of his face. Ivar kept his eyes closed trying to swallow the liquid in his mouth. *Finally.* His body and emotions relented and he swallowed, then gasped for breath.

He started up when his phone rang, but not sure he was able to answer he waved it away. Savannah's eyes searched Ivar's face. When the phone rang again she picked up.

"Hello?"

Ivar rubbed a hand over his face, all the muscles in his jaw were tight. He glanced at Savannah slightly, hearing her speaking on his phone.

"Yes, Mrs Walker he's here. Why didn't he pick up?" Savannah looked up at her friend, her eyes filling with the softest caress Ivar had ever seen. "He was choking on his milkshake I think." Her eyes danced now and she laughed a little. "Yes, Mrs Walker. He's okay now. Yep, I'll pass you over to him." Savannah held the phone out to Ivar. She tilted her head to the side as he took it.

"Hey Mom? Yeah I'm fine, yeah-" Ivar listened to his mom go on about how Savannah was such a sweet girl. He smiled at her slightly, before staring back down at the table. He could tell by the controlled tone of voice his mom used that something wasn't right.

"Mom, what's wrong?" His voice quavered ever so slightly.

~Chapter Thirty-One~
Three words. A promise. Life.

The glass fell sideways off the table, milkshake spilling over the wooden café table and onto the floor, pooling on the white laminate.

Ivar's phone hit the table's surface, his eyes vacant.

Savannah didn't pay attention to the mess that was forming on the floor or to the stares they received from other people in the café. The look of pure horror on Ivar's face made her skin crawl.

"Ivar?" She ventured quietly. "Is everything okay?" Savannah crouched down next to his seat, putting a hand on his own to stop it from trembling. His fingers closed around her hand as tears started to form in his eyes, spill over and run down his face.

"Bryce," he choked, the name slipping out in a half whisper.

"What's wrong with Bryce, how is he?" Savannah asked anxiously. The pain that was in Ivar's eyes made her want to put her arms around him and tell him it would be okay.

"I'm sorry, Sav," Ivar pushed back his chair and stood up abruptly, his feet landing in the puddle of chocolate and banana milkshake.

He froze and stared down at it, his mouth forming a thin grim line.

"Ivar, it's okay. I'll sort it out, now tell me what's wrong." Savannah stood up and took both of his hands.

Ivar lifted his face towards her, "They want to take Bryce down for a second operation. Or-" he stopped and pulled his hands away from Savannah, clenching them into fists.

"Um, they don't think he will pull through otherwise. I really need to go." Ivar looked at Savannah for a long moment.

He brushed a strand of hair back from her face. "I'm sorry." Savannah smiled gently, "It's okay, I understand. I'll be praying for Bryce and for you."

Ivar caught the gentle love in those words, he gave her a quick hug, before hurrying out from the Café.

~

Aubrey had been at the farm when Sean had called.

Now she sat at the kitchen table with Reese, Jade, Emma, Hunter and Caleb.

Jason and Madison were still at the hospital with Sean. The screen door opened, slamming against the wall in the hallway. Ivar's hurried footfalls sounded as he pushed the kitchen door open and came in at a half run. "Mom?"

Aubrey got up and went over, holding him tightly.

"Where's Cam?" He asked, scanning the room over her shoulder as he hugged her.

Aubrey rubbed away tears, "He's letting out some pent-up energy on a stack of logs in the yard."

Ivar nodded slowly.

He sat down next to his mom, putting an arm protectively around her shoulders as if to protect her from everything that was going on. He felt as if he had aged several years in the twenty minute drive over from the café. He felt more like fifty than he did eighteen.

Caleb who was standing next to his sister's chair, started to rub her shoulders. "Sitting here worrying isn't gonna save his life, now is it Aubrey."

Ivar was glad his uncle was taking charge.

"You told Sean you would pray for Bryce so let's do just that."

Aubrey wrapped an arm around Ivar as he rested his head wearily against his mom. Reese crept over towards her cousin. She pulled a stool up and sat next to him, holding onto his arm. Hunter was crying into his mom's dress, whilst Jade sat quietly on the countertop.

While Caleb prayed for God's wisdom on what should be done, Aubrey watched little Hunter with love in her eyes. Emma must have sensed that her sister-in-law was remembering when Bryce was a youngster because she got up and placed Hunter in Aubrey's lap.

Caleb held Emma close and looked down, watching Aubrey interact with her nephew.

Hunter's large blue eyes were filled with tears as he hugged his aunt. "Bwyce haws to get better." He wailed, his face puckering up as if he had just eaten a lemon.

Aubrey ran a hand over his soft blond curls.

"Shhh, shh," she bounced him slightly on her knee, not bothering to wipe away her own tears. Reese reached over and touched his cheek.

"He will, Hunter, Bryce is made of strong stuff."

"And we serve a God who is stronger than osteomyelitis." Emma observed leaning into Caleb's warm embrace. Aubrey nodded slowly and allowed Hunter to grip her two forefingers.

Then, as if she had just been thrown forwards in time Aubrey felt a jolt.

She closed her eyes and in her mind's eye saw it all stretching out before her.

Bryce. Her heart whispered, *Bryce, turning eighteen.*
Bryce riding Charis,
Bryce playing music.
Bryce running after Hunter, laughing as the wind rushed through his hair.
Bryce helping out on the farm,
Bryce waiting at the front of a church, nervously twisting his fingers together.
Bryce walking arm in arm with his wife,
Bryce as a father.
Bryce throwing his baby daughter in the air and catching her, with pure delight on his face,
Bryce, well, strong, healed, alive!

Aubrey resisted the urge to open her eyes, allowing Hunter's arms to close around her neck in a hug, letting the images flood her mind.

Then she heard it, *That still, small voice.*
The voice of her Creator, Father and King.
The words were simple, yet direct.
Gentle, but leaving no room for argument.
Loving and strong.
Full of power.

No more surgery.

Three words.

A promise.
Life.

~Chapter Thirty-Two~

"Tomorrow is a new day, who knows what it will bring."

Bryce blinked open his eyes to see his dad leaving the room with a doctor. His grandparents were no longer there.

Bryce followed his dad with his eyes as he walked out. "Dad," he whispered.

Sean stopped, turned, saw him and hurried over, leaving the doctor in the doorway.

"Bryce?" Sean placed a hand on the side of his face, standing over his son. "Are you okay?"

Bryce let his eyes slide shut. It felt as if the fever running through his body was boiling him. Eating him alive. Pain throbbed in his leg. Sean hovered nervously next to him. "Brycey-boy?" Gently he took his son's hot hand and rubbed it between his own.

"Where're you going, Dad?" He said quietly, gripping his dad's hand with every bit of fragile strength he had left inside of him.

"It's okay, I'm just stepping outside to speak with Dr. Martin, okay? I'll be right back, I promise."

Bryce's eyes brimmed. He felt hot all over, he felt ill, sick and nauseous and his leg hurt like nothing he had felt before. He didn't want his dad to go out of sight and leave him alone. *Bryce!* He sternly told himself. *You're sixteen years old! Laws-a-mercy, boy, pull yourself together, there is no need to cry.* Out loud though, he murmured, "Okay."

Sean squeezed his hand gently, "That's my boy."

Bryce closed his eyes tightly as he felt his dad's hand leave his own. Heard the door close. Heard voices murmuring out in the hallway. Bryce tried to push himself up into a sitting position. He failed, flopping back into the pillows.

Bryce turned over slightly, gasping with pain. He stared out the window. The sky was a mix of blues, purples, and reds as the sun said farewell and the moon came into view.

Talking voices rose, then dropped in the hallway. *That means they don't want me to hear.*

Bryce lifted a hand and ran it through his damp hair. Sleep was trying to claim him, to drag him into the unknown and relief. Bryce fought it, not wanting to close his eyes and give in.

Not yet.

Not ever.

He was a Walker.

And Walkers don't give up, he told himself mentally. *Walkers are strong, we don't let anything stop us.* Determined to show his body who was boss, Bryce gritted his teeth against the pain and pushed himself up into a sitting position. *Lord, I, I choose to believe that you say I am healed.*

He clenched his jaw. Leaning back into the pillow behind him, Bryce looked around the room for the first time properly. *When did those get here?* He stared at the bedside table covered in get well soon cards and smiled at the coloured cards, blue, green and orange crayon-scribble covered the front of it.

Hunter.

Bryce looked around again. He fumbled with the top button of his shirt and pulled the wooden cross out from underneath.

"Because we all need a reminder every now and then that He will never leave us." He murmured quietly.

The faintest of smiles turned up the corners of his lips and he closed his eyes and leaned back into the pillows.

"You never leave. Never forsake. Never go back on your promises."

Cracking open his eyes, he glanced towards the window. Outside, the sky had turned black with night, the light from his room reflected in it.

He saw his reflection clearly in the window. Bryce peered at himself closely, then jumped at what he saw. He almost didn't recognise himself. His face was flushed and thin.

His eyes were unnaturally large, his cheeks slightly sunken in. His blond hair had grown a little, and hung down in damp clumps around his neck.

It's not supposed to get that long...

The hospital gown he had changed for his own clothes a good week ago, hung on him, his red and blue checkered shirt officially to big for him now.

Before coming into hospital, Bryce had been a well-formed, strongly-built young man, with strong arms.

Now, staring at himself he noticed how thin and weak he was. He groaned and sat back, closing his eyes against the image. *How did I get so weak, so quickly.*

∼

When Sean came back in, closing the door behind him, his face showed his weariness and the pressure he had just been put under. Bryce was half-asleep when Sean went over towards him.

Bryce was still fighting to stay awake and not give into to the absolute exhaustion that was trying to claim him. Sean sat next to him. Leaning his head back against the wall, he took Bryce's hand in his own.

"Is everything okay?"

Bryce's voice jerked Sean awake. "Bryce, oh, I thought you were asleep."

Bryce felt his lips tilt up in a slight smile. "No, no, I'm not. Is everything okay?" He asked, his voice tired.

Sean nodded, "Everything will be fine." He smoothed a hand over Bryce's hair, "Tomorrow is a new day, who knows what it will bring."

~Chapter Thirty-Three~
"If He said that then I know everything will be okay."

The axe whistled through the air. It hit its target and wood chips flew everywhere. The motion repeated itself in long, slow, precise movements. Reese stood watching, shadowed by the door frame and the night.

A gentle breeze took the edge off the summer night's heat. She heard her cousin's heavy breathing, his grunting as he lifted the axe and watched as wood flew in all directions.

The axe was put down and Reese watched his shadowed form carrying an armful of chopped wood to the log pile by the porch. Then he went back to chopping wood.

The thud, thud, thud, smack, crack sound filled the air. Reese breathed out and pulled her hair back behind her shoulder, tugging it into a ponytail and then persuading it into a low-set bun. She walked over towards him, "Give me a whack?" She said, holding a hand out.

Cameron taken by surprise, almost dropped the heavy axe on his foot. "Reese, how long have you been there?"

Reese didn't answer, her eyes on Cameron's bare arm. His shirt sleeves where rolled up showing the bandage on his arm. The same one he had shown Ivar.

Cameron saw Reese staring. He tugged his shirt sleeve down and flicked a smile at her. "It's nothing to worry about." He reassured. He straightened and held out the axe, the handle extended towards her, "You asked for a go?"

Reese nodded and took it.

She grabbed it; one hand at the base and the other near the top by the axe head. Reese let it swing, her top hand sliding down half way as the axe struck against the wood.

Cameron ducked and covered his face with his arms as the splintered wood flew everywhere.

"Whoa," Cameron straightened again and took the axe from his cousin, resting it against the porch. Reese picked up the log she had split and tossed it onto the pile. Suddenly she whirled around and stared at Cameron.

"Why are you out here splitting wood instead of being inside and praying for your brother?" Like a slap to the face, Cameron felt her words.

"Reese," Cameron opened his mouth to speak but closed it again when Reese's eyes flashed.

"Aunt Aubrey told Mom about what you told her, about fear and all that."

Cameron took the axe back up again and placed a log of the ground. He hefted the axe up over his shoulder, ready to whack at the wood. Reese's next words were shot out like a bullet from a gun.

"Throwing a pity party ain't gonna help no one. Yes, you can feel upset, and concerned but wasn't it you that said to cast all your cares on him for he cares for you?"

Cameron swallowed, the axe going slack in his hands.

"Yes," he said.

"Well then, act on it." Reese took the axe from him, a tired breath passed her lips as she split a few more logs before she handed the axe back to him and placed the logs onto the pile. She stood watching as he split wood, her eyes still smouldering.

Cameron watched her out the corner of his eye.

She was drawn tight, her body tense.

"Reese are you oka-"

He was cut off as she suddenly threw herself at Cameron, hugging him as she let her tears soak his shirt.

Cameron stood still for a moment, startled, then rubbed her back in large, relaxing circles. "Hey, Reese," he bent his head down towards hers. "It's okay, you're right. I do need to act on it. Practice what I preach, hm?" He cupped her chin with his hand and brushed away tears with his thumb.

Gently he planted a kiss on top of her hair. "Hey, hey, don't cry." He whispered. He ran the crook of his finger across her cheek. "Hey, little cousin."

Reese sniffed and rubbed her eyes.

"I'm thirteen." She objected, "I'm not that little."

Cameron laughed, "I stand corrected."

Reese sniffed again and dashed at her tears.

"I'm sorry, I shouldn't have been so forceful." She whispered. Standing back, a slight embarrassed flush started in her neck and crept up into her cheeks.

"No, I deserved that." Cameron ruffled his hair, flicking his reddish brown fringe out the way. He put the axe down and leaned against the porch.

Reese smiled a little, "Yeah, you kinda did." She grinned then blinked, a thought coming to her, "Why *are* you chopping wood in the middle of the summer anyway?"

Cameron stared at the pile of wood.

"Uh, well, I, uh, yeah I don't know." He shrugged and stuffed his hands into his jeans' pockets. "Is stocking up for winter a good enough excuse?"

"Mmm," Reese said, letting it slide.

"Good then." Cameron stared out towards the patch of trees at the back of the farm. Reese rubbed her forehead staring up at the few stars that blinked down at her. She shrieked as Cameron ran at her, he grabbed her around the waist and swung her onto his back, fireman style, before running around the dark yard. Reese screamed,

"Cam!" She thumped his back in protest, "Put me down!"

~

Emma came to stand next to her sister-in-law and they stood together, watching Cameron and Reese, "She really loves her cousins." Emma said.

Aubrey nodded, "All the boys love your girls. I'm glad they're so close. They watch out for them as if they were their own sisters." She rested her chin in her hand and leaned on the windowsill.

Emma placed a hand on her shoulder, "We are all praying honey, and Bryce will be okay."

Aubrey nodded, and sat up, "The Lord is the one who told me no more surgery. If He said that then I know everything will be okay." She smiled weakly, then looked around. "Where's Ivar?"

Emma smiled, "Jade and Hunter are wrestling him in the family room."

~Chapter Thirty-Four~

Suddenly an unexplainable urge to pull a face at the camera came over him.

When Bryce woke up the next morning, he remembered it was the day marking halfway through his third week in hospital. As he shifted in bed, he felt an immediate difference in his body. His skin felt cool to touch and the throbbing pain in his leg was gone. He felt as if a cool wave had washed over him, renewing his strength and filling him with new life.

For the first time in two weeks, he felt hungry.

Pushing himself up into a sitting position, Bryce pushed back the hospital blankets. He stared down at his leg, a slight smile tilting his mouth.

He glanced across at the small camera in the corner of the room. He knew that the nurses could see him through the camera from the nurses' station.

Suddenly an unexplainable urge to pull a face at the camera came over him.

No, I couldn't. I shouldn't, Bryce chided himself. But slowly a grin spread across his face. Glancing down at his checkered shirt, Bryce rolled the sleeves up to his elbows. He ran his hands through his hair trying to control its unruliness. He glanced at the camera again.

A song his mom liked popped into mind and Bryce couldn't help himself, he pulled a face at the camera and started singing, laughing, "I'm a survivor, I'm gonna make it! Not gonna give up, keep on surviving." Bryce laughed, then flopped back onto the bed and closed his eyes as a satisfied smile filled his face.

The door opened and Sean walked in.

He froze in the doorway, "Bryce?"

"Mornin'" Bryce chirped. Sean walked over and placed a hand on his forehead.

"Praise be to God." He breathed.

"Mr Walker, it's test-time, unfortunately."

Sean turned around and smiled at the doctor, his eyes brimming, "By all means Doctor, run your blood tests." The man walked over and Bryce grinned at him, sitting up.

Dr. Martin raised both eyebrows, "Well, we need to run some tests before we determine whether or not we need to take him down for a second operation."

"Okay," Bryce shrugged.

Sean and Dr. Martin helped Bryce into the waiting wheelchair. The whole way down to the next level, both father and son couldn't help but grin. Dr. Martin shook his head incredulously.

~

The duty doctor looked from the report in his hands to the jubilant teenager sitting upright on the hospital bed with his legs crossed. "Where's Dr. Martin?" Sean asked from his seat by the window.

The duty doctor scratched his chin, distractedly, "Uh Doc Martin will be with you in a few moments."

Going over to Bryce, he took the boy's temperature and drew another vial of blood. Bryce rolled his eyes when he saw the needle, "I loathe those things." He grimaced.

Sean's eyebrows bobbed up and down, a slightly amused smile playing across his mouth. The duty doctor muttered to himself quietly about blood sugar and glucose levels as he walked out the room.

Bryce tucked his arms behind his head as he lay back down. Sean laughed, "You done then?"

"Yeah," Bryce drawled, "all in a day's work." He yawned, "Ya know, I'm really hungry."

Sean nodded and went over, sitting on the edge of his bed, "I know, we'll get you something to eat after Dr. Martin has been." The door opened and the doctor walked in. He stood next to Bryce's bed, shifting his feet.

"Uh, Mr Walker, the tests we did last night and the young man sitting on the bed grinning at me like that creepy pink cat from the Alice in Wonderland movie don't match."

Bryce raised an eyebrow, "I ain't no cheshire cat," he muttered.

"What are you saying?" Sean asked, leaning forward.

The doctor drew a deep breath, "What I'm saying is that the blood tests we took last night and the blood tests we took this morning tell a completely different story." He held up a chart, "Last night this young man was very, very ill. Near death." He flipped the paper over on the chart. "The young man before me right now is well."

Bryce blinked as the doctor walked out, shaking his head.

"Awesome." He said.

Sean removed his cap, messed up his hair and shoved his cap back down. He grinned, then let out a whoop and threw his fist in the air. Bryce laughed and pulled another face at the nurses' camera. The door opened and Sean sat down instantly, his face pinching into a concentrated look. Another duty doctor came in, a different one from last.

"Uh Mr Walker, you can take you son home. There is no point in him staying here anymore. He's better. None of us understand this, but this was not a natural recovery." She cleared her throat, pulled at her uniform, turned on her heel and opened the door, she spoke over her shoulder.

"He's discharged."

~Chapter Thirty-Five~
"You're a good, good father."

"Yippeeee!" Ivar ran out towards the barn tearing across the grass; his mom not far behind him, both of them hollering and yelling. Jason and Caleb who were working in the barns looked up.

Jason stopped milking Daisy. Wiping his hands on a towel, he walked outside and called to Caleb who was hauling bags of seed.

"What's going on?" Caleb came out, brushing his jeans down. Jason tipped his straw hat back and stared down the track at his daughter and grandson who were running towards them.

"We're about to find out."

Aubrey threw herself at her dad once they had reached the two men. She was crying so hard her words wouldn't come out. Ivar practically jumped on his uncle's back yelling like a mad cowboy. "He's coming home!" Ivar shouted.

His voice brought Cameron and Madison around the corner. "Jason what's-" she didn't get to finish her sentence as her husband bounded towards her and spun her around laughing. Aubrey and Caleb were hugging and crying, while Ivar wrestled Cameron to the ground.

"Whoa," Cameron gasped as he hit the ground at such a velocity that the wind was knocked out of him. He tried to get his brother off him, but Ivar was a strong lad.

Cameron got his breath back and turned Ivar onto his back. Pinning him down, he asked laughing, "What's going on, man?"

Ivar grinned up at him, a light sparkle in his eyes for the first time in two and a half weeks.

"God healed Bryce overnight. He's coming home! The doctors don't know what's happened and they don't know what to do so they've discharged him!"

Cameron stared at him, stunned for a moment. Then, like the dawn breaking through the middle of a night-sky, a grin spread across his face.

"Whoohoo!" He jumped up and tore around the yard, before running in the house only to come back out with Reese on his shoulders and Jade clinging to his arm, laughing with joy. Hunter and Emma were the next to join the fiasco.

Jason picked his daughter up and twirled Aubrey around. Ivar threw Hunter in the air. Caleb laughed and hugged his mom and wife. It was Aubrey's idea to thank God.

The family gathered in a semi-circle outside the barn, smiling at each other with tears in their eyes.

Pushing back his hair, Ivar watched as one by one, each family member gave thanks. Daisy's mooing joined in as he prayed. "God, thank you." He choked, "You're a good, good father."

Ivar blinked and looked away to hide his tears.

Aubrey walked over and pulled him into a tight hug. "It's okay to cry," she whispered through her own tears. Ivar buried his face in her neck.

Madison stared at Jade and Reese, "You girls want to help me cook up a feast for dinner?"

Aubrey joined the girls and Emma as they headed back to the kitchen with Madison. As they walked down the track she could feel the morning sun warm the back of her head. She smiled properly for the first time in weeks.

~

Ivar swiped across his phone and hunkered down behind a stack of hay bales wiping tears of joy from his eyes. He scrolled down his contacts list, hit one and waited as it dialled. "Hello, you have reached Savannah Van Dyke. Please leave a message after the tone and I will try and get back to you. Thanks!" The voicemail ended.

"Hey Sav, it's Ivar." Ivar paused and gathered his thoughts. He grinned at himself. "Uh, I have great news for you. Well, actually great news for everyone." He laughed slightly. "Uh, we got our miracle. Bryce was discharged this morning, he's gonna be home within the hour. I-I can't wait to see him again. He's not using a wheelchair, but still needs to use one crutch a little, but." Ivar choked up, "but he's coming home." The voicemail box beeped and Ivar's message finished. Staring down at his phone, Ivar grinned. "Thank you God."

He heard the sound of car tires on the drive.

His heart rate sped up and Ivar felt his stomach twist with anticipation. He crouched back down behind the hay for a brief moment as he heard the ecstatic voices of his family. Then he heard it.

His voice.

His laughter.

"Bryce." Ivar whispered his brothers name.

His eyes burned with tears again.

Slowly he stood up from behind the bale and started to walk towards the barn doors.

Someone came running up the track. Hunter burst into the barn, his hair messy. He went straight up to Ivar, gripped his hand and pulled him out of the barn and down the track towards the farm house.

Ivar saw the familiar Stars and Stripes blowing in the wind from the flag pole first.

Then he saw his dad's truck, then his dad. Sean grinned, wandered over and ruffled Ivar's hair. "He's inside."

Ivar ran up the porch steps, into the hallway and froze outside the sitting room door.

His hand hovered over the handle.

Taking a deep breath he swung open the door.

Bryce's smile was the first thing he saw before his eyes filled with tears.

~Chapter Thirty-Six~
"But you didn't let that fear get the best of you,"

Thursday morning brought bright sunshine, bird song and the end of the summer warmth. Aubrey pushed the general store's door open and the little brass bell rang out joyfully.

She had just enough time to fulfil her promise before she had to meet up with Emma in town.

Aubrey grinned. "Sarah? Miss Foster?" She called while looking around the store.

"Aubrey!"

Before she could look in the right direction, Aubrey was swept up in a larger than life hug. Sarah's beaming face filled her vision. "Now what do I owe the pleasure of seeing your lovely face again in my store?" Sarah pushed her dark curly hair back over her shoulder and continued with the task she had been doing; stacking the back shelf with cans of fruits. Her Colorado accent was as thick and broad as ever.

Aubrey loved it.

"Well, I needed to get a few things and I while I was at it, I thought I would fulfil a promise I made ya."

Sarah put down the can of pineapple chunks she was holding and picked up a tin of green string beans.

She stood on her tiptoes and placed it on the top shelf. "Now, Aubrey, what promise would that be?" Her eyebrows drew together in confusion. She picked up another tin and slid it into place.

Her entire body went rigid when she heard a voice.

"Howdy Miss Sarah."

She turned and saw Bryce leaning on one single crutch. He wore a pair of stone-wash jeans that covered the white bandage on his leg and a shirt with a denim jacket thrown over it. Aubrey laughed.

Bryce's face was a picture as Sarah rushed at him, hugging the breath out of him.

"Oh you darling! Praise God!" Sarah pinched his cheeks before holding him at arm's length and looking him over. "This is Bryce?"

She lifted her chocolate-coloured eyes towards his mom. Aubrey nodded.

Sarah turned back to Bryce, looking him over once more, "How old are you, dear?"

"Sixteen." Bryce smiled back.

"Well, young man, you're looking a little skinny!"

Bryce laughed. "Yeah, I guess so. I lost a lot of weight in hospital."

Sarah nodded, "I bet Madison and your mom are trying to fatten you right up."

Bryce tilted his head and let out a nervous laugh. "Well they're tryin' but Grandpa and Dad say nothing but good old farm work will get me back into shape."

Sarah patted the side of his cheek. "You sweet thing."

Bryce smiled awkwardly as Aubrey laughed.

~

That evening, Bryce picked up his fiddle and set the bow to the strings. He sat on the sofa, filling the sitting room with music. Ivar played alongside him on the guitar as Aubrey and Sean watched with Madison.

Cameron danced with Jade and Reese around the room. When the doorbell rang, Ivar set aside his instrument and got up, "I'll get it," he said, going to the front door and swinging it open.

His jaw dropped when he saw Savannah standing on the doorstep. "Sav?" He said, surprised, then recovered and grinned.

"I got your message." Savannah smiled at him. "I thought I'd come say hey."

Ivar blushed and stepped aside so she could come in.

Half an hour later, Ivar and Savannah left the farm heading out towards the back fields, talking as they walked.

"You're a strong person, Ivar." Savannah observed. "Emotionally, I mean." She smiled up at him.

Ivar laughed slightly. "Mostly, but the past two weeks have left me utterly afraid."

Savannah shook her head, "But you didn't let that fear get the best of you."

Ivar rubbed the back of his head with one hand and with the other he reached up and plucked a leaf off an overhead tree. He rubbed the small stalk between his thumb and forefinger.

"I had a strong family around me." He smiled shyly at her, letting the leaf go and taking her hand in his own. "And strong friends."

Savannah blushed and smiled gently.

Ivar drew her under his arm, holding her in a side hug. "So what would you say if I asked you to start going out with me?" He said lightly.

Savannah turned her brown eyes toward him. "I'd say yes." Ivar grinned boyishly and planted a soft kiss on top of her head, laughing as her cheeks heated.

~Chapter Thirty-Seven~

"He's a miracle-working God, who loves us desperately despite our flaws and mishaps. The miracles never stop...they just go on and on. Just like a never-ending harvest."

Two weeks later, the leaves on the trees had taken on a golden-brown tint. The tips of the leaves turned an almost-blood red that indicated the start of Autumn. Picking up one of the juicy red apples that filled the barrel to the overflow point, Bryce tossed it into the air and caught it again.

He rubbed it against his shirt and took a bite, relishing the sweet tangy taste in his mouth.

The watery juice from the apple made his tongue tingle. A loud protesting snort came from behind him.

Bryce swivelled, the apple still in his mouth. He raised his eyebrows at the horse as if to ask, 'What do you want?' Bryce's eyes fell towards the apple in his mouth.

He bit off a chunk and chewed slowly. He smirked slightly, "You want one?"

He asked, holding the apple in front of Charis's eyes. Bryce tossed the apple up, he went to catch it but Charis caught it first between her teeth. She munched on her prize happily, her dark eyes seeming to mock him.

Bryce laughed and leaned over the stall. He rubbed her velvety nose gently, "That taste good girl?"

The horse let out a snort and stamped her foot against the ground. Bryce rubbed her side gently, "What? You want a ride as well as an apple?" He moved his hand up and over her nose and down her neck, he gently brushed back her long mane. Leaning back he looked out of the barn doors. "Well,

Cam doesn't seem to be around, and Ivar isn't around either. I guess they wouldn't mind if I stopped working for a bit so you can stretch your legs."

Bryce grinned as he swung open the stall door, he walked in and put a bridle and saddle on Charis, then taking the reins, he gently led her out of her stall.

He nudged the barn door open a little wider and led Charis out into the afternoon sun. Putting his left foot in the saddles stirrup and swinging his right leg over the other side, Bryce sat up on Charis and led her around the back of the barn towards the open fields that weren't used for growth and harvest.

The movement of the horse caused him to bounce slightly as Charis walked briskly up the back path to the further pastures.

Above him, birds swooped on air currents in the cloudless blue sky. Birdsong filled the air.

A light breeze blew through the grass, the trees swaying ever so slightly as if the very nature around him moved together in their own kind of dance.

Bryce followed a well-trodden path along the edge of a cliff side that ran along the back of his grandfather's property. The path was a steep incline angling towards the left.

Bringing Charis to a gentle trot, Bryce glanced down at his right leg. He was wearing shorts and he could see the thin caterpillar-like scar running from his knee a little way up his thigh. He let go of the reins with his right hand - keeping Charis steady with his left - and reached down to trace the scar with his index finger. Lifting his hand back up, he rubbed it over his face. "Mmm,"

Pressing the flat of his palms over his eyes Bryce released Charis's bridle for a moment. "You know what, girl?" he murmured, leaning forward so he spoke close to her ear. "Spring and harvest; they are the best times of year. You wanna know why?" Charis stopped walking for a moment and turned her head to stare at him as if he were a two-headed cow. Bryce laughed. "Ride on." He said after a moment's hysterics and clicked his tongue. Bryce grinned as the path evened out a little.

At the top, the pasture's fence line came into view. "I'm gonna tell you anyway. They are both the seasons of miracles. I mean think about it," he patted the side of her neck. Wondering for a moment why he was talking to a horse as if it were a human, he blinked, smiled crookedly and went on. "Take spring for instance. I mean, birds come back from migration, new animals are born, flowers bloom and the weather starts to warm up. I mean what can be more miraculous than a baby's birth!" He tilted his head back and felt the brush of warmth against his face as they rode under a tree bursting with colour and life.

"And the autumn, I mean, c'mon. If you want to see colour, come riding along Pike's Peak or in the upper pasture at the start of fall. It's like God himself has chosen this season as a canvas and is gently painting each and every piece of it as Autumn takes over." He reached down and traced the scar again. "Just two weeks ago I was dying," he said gently and tossed back his blond hair. "But now?" He shook his head and laughed. "Hey did you hear? They started calling me the miracle child back at the hospital."

Bryce rubbed his forehead, "Miracle child."

Grinning, Bryce stroked Charis gently, "He's a miracle-working God, who loves us desperately, despite our flaws and mishaps."

Bryce pushed Charis to a canter as they entered the large open space. A wooden fence lined the pasture's perimeter. Towards the far western corner a small corps of colourful trees swayed gently in time with nature's song. "The miracles never stop, Charis, they just go on and on. Like a never ending harvest."

The Rosetta Stone
Part Two

For a child is born to us, a son is given, the government will rest on his shoulders. And he will be called: Wonderful counsellor, Mighty God, Everlasting Father, Prince of Peace.
Isaiah 9:6

But to all who believed him and accepted him, he gave the right to become children of God.
John 1:12

~Chapter One~
"Never take on a firefighter."

"And who is this?" Bryce laughed between intervals of the wet dog tongue slapping across his face. Jason came down the stairs and leaned on the banister, watching the large brown and black collie dog's tail whack back and forth.

"You better step back, Ivar. That tail is gonna leave some bruises on your legs."

"And slobber on my face." Bryce grinned, trying to push the large dog off of his chest.

"Awwww, who's a cute doggie!" Ivar was on his knees, stroking the collie's soft fur. "Why the dog, Grandpa?" He said, not looking up from the new member of the Davis's farm.

"This is Kit." Jason said, he walked down the stairs and joined his two grandsons on the floor with the dog.

"Well, hello Kit!" Bryce laughed again and half sat up, Kit's large black face inches from his own.

Hot dog breath rolled off of Bryce's cheeks and he winced, half squinting and trying to push the dog's face away.

"He's great, Grandpa! Always wanted a dog around this place, but why now?" Ivar asked.

Jason's eyebrows bobbed up and down as he rolled back onto his ankles, "Maddie thought he'd be good."

"Grandma thought he'd be good." Bryce repeated, squirming out from underneath the dog and rolling onto his knees.

Ivar took the dog's large face in his hands, "He's so cute!" He looked up and saw both his brother and grandpa looking at him amused.

"What?" Ivar smiled, "Kit's awesome!"

"Ivar…it's a dog…slobbering…wet…" Jade came into the hall behind her cousin, she grimaced.

"Jaaade!" Bryce reclined back on the floor, his tone languid, "It's a dog! Tell me that's not like totally amazing."

"That's not totally amazing." Jade said.

Both Walker boys' faces went blank.

Cameron chuckled as he walked in from the yard with Reese and Hunter hanging on his arm, "You were asking for it Bryce-boy." He snickered and swung his arm as Hunter let out a squeal and jumped down, throwing his arms around Kit's neck.

"Dogwwwyyy!" He screamed, delighted.

"Yes doggy." Reese said smiling, she picked Hunter up, "Now say goodbye to the doggy, Mommy and Daddy are waiting in the truck."

"Bye bye doggy." Hunter waved as Cameron walked the three Davis kids out of the hall and towards the front door.

"Ya goin' already Reese?" Bryce ran after them, leaving Ivar to smoother the dog in the hallway.

Reese grinned and tucked a strand of her blond hair behind her ear, "Yeah, Dad wants to catch the break in the rain."

Bryce stopped on the porch steps, "What rain?" He asked, sticking his head out from under the porch's shelter.

A bucket full of water hit him full in the face and Bryce gasped for air.

"That rain!" Bryce's dad—Sean—called from the top window. Rolling his eyes, Bryce shook the water from his head, strands of his blond hair sticking to his face and neck.

Caleb sounded the horn in the car as Jade, Reese and Hunter all bundled in after their mom.

"Later Bryce! We'll see you later this week for the harvest camp out." Caleb called, waving as they pulled out. "See ya Uncle Caleb!" Bryce shouted back, then ran and pinned his unsuspecting older brother to the ground.

Cameron rolled over as the lanky seventeen year old jumped on him. Grinning, he flipped over, pinning Bryce underneath him. "I'm the fireman, remember Bryce?" Cameron gloated, flexing his muscles, "Never take on a firefighter."

~Chapter Two~

"Your mom has never liked sleeping bags."

"I'm pretty sure that you're going to need more than one shirt." Ivar commented from the doorway.

Bryce looked up from where he was standing by his bed, trying to pack his rucksack for the harvest camp out later that week. "Yeah I know." He frowned and picked up another shirt, jamming it down the side of his rucksack.

Ivar laughed and shook his head, "Bryce, that's not going to work."

Bryce mumbled something about needing a bigger rucksack and went to find his dad.

Sean was in the kitchen, hunched over a large pile of stuff that his mom had created. "Aubrey," Bryce heard his dad say as he straightened. "There is no way we can take all of this."

Aubrey sighed and rubbed a strand of her hair between her fingers, "You sure, Sean?"

Chuckling, Cameron who was with them, reached down and plucked a hairdryer from the pile, "We don't need this Mom." He grinned.

Aubrey blushed and Sean, seeing her embarrassment, got up and kissed her gently, "Hun, I'm sure we can cut this pile in half yeah? It's just one week of camping. You did go camping as a girl."

Aubrey smiled at him weakly, "Yeah. But that was a long time ago…"

Cameron, who was still going through the pile, held up three sweaters, "Three! No wait, four!"

Bryce hid a laugh behind his hand watching from the doorway. Aubrey saw him and pulled a face, "Oh that's it Bryce, laugh it up."

He thought she was mad, but then saw her sparkling eyes.

Sean shook his head, "Sweaters, now they are good. We only need one each though, the nights are gonna get colder now that the summer is over and we are heading into autumn."

"Okay," Aubrey murmured, "But I do need the quilt."

Cameron sat back on his haunches, "Mom, this is camping. You do know that right?"

His mom nodded.

"Then use a sleeping bag?"

Sean reeled back, gasping in mock horror, Bryce and Cameron looked at him. Ivar, hearing the large, over-exaggerated gasp came skidding into the room, "Where's the fire?" He asked.

Sean was thumping his chest with a fist, Aubrey folded her arms across her front and glared at him.

"Your mom? Sleep in a sleeping bag?" Sean pretended to cough, he looked up at Bryce and said, "That's like getting Bryce to cut his hair short."

Bryce dragged his fingers through his shoulder length blond hair. "Hey, what's wrong with my hair?"

"Nothin'" Ivar smirked, reaching over and messing his brother's hair up. "Dad's just drawing a comparison."

Bryce blinked, "No way, it's not like I know that." He winked.

"Heavy on the sarcasm here you two." Cameron laughed absently as he watched his mom thumping his dad on the back as he had actually started to choke on his own breath. *How's that possible?* Cameron thought to himself.

After Sean pulled himself together he smiled wryly at his sons, "Your mom has never liked sleeping bags."

Bryce looked at his mom, dumbfounded.

Aubrey shrugged, blushing helplessly, "Even as a kid."

Bryce shook his head and reached into the pile, pulling out a large rucksack, "Can I use this?"

Sean cast his wife a sly look, "Unless your mom wants it as her third backpack."

"Ohhh." Aubrey's eyes flashed and she brushed a strand of her strawberry blond hair back behind her ear before lunging at her husband.

Sean grinned, sidestepping out of her reach and then chasing her around the kitchen diner.

Getting up off the floor, Cameron put an arm around both of his brothers, "We might as well go finish our packing. They could be at this for a while." He laughed and started walking towards his room at the other end of the bungalow.

"When do you need to get back to the station, by the way, Cam?" Ivar asked as he walked with him, trying to ignore the faces Bryce was pulling.

"Ah, well, since I didn't take any vacation time this summer, I have from now until after Christmas."

Bryce let out a whoop and then dived into his own room to finish packing before Cameron could think of pinning him down like he had done the day before at the farm.

~Chapter Three~
"I'm just feeling grateful for my son."

"Oh Bryce." Aubrey stopped at her son's bedroom, she stuck her head around the door.

"Yeah?" Bryce looked up from playing his fiddle, sitting cross legged on his bed.

"I'm gonna drop you off at Grandpa's early on Friday, okay? You can help Grandpa get a jump at clearing the space for camp and collecting wood yeah?"

Bryce smiled, "Cool."

"Oh! And before I forget," Aubrey had taken a few steps, but backtracked, "Ivar wants you. He's in the yard."

"Righto." Bryce got up as his mom left and put his fiddle back in its case. Not bothering with his shoes, he padded into the kitchen barefoot and out into the back yard. The late September air held traces of the heat from summer but carried a chilling breeze that brought the promise of winter.

He spotted Ivar laying on his back in the grass, staring up at the sky as clouds passed overhead.

Bryce walked over and stood over him. Ivar, feeling a shadow block the sun from his face, squinted open his eyes, "Bryce?"

"Mom said you wanted me?" Bryce smiled and then flopped down on the grass next to his brother.

"Oh yeah," Ivar rolled over and passed him a piece of paper, "I'm thinking of giving this to Sav. What do you think?"

Bryce gave his brother a sly look and then unfolded the paper, "Before I read this, is it going to be all mushy?"

Ivar rolled his eyes and flung his arms back over his eyes. "Just read it, would ya."

Smirking, Bryce read the note quickly, snickering slightly.

"What's so funny?" Ivar's voice was sleepy.

"Nothin' nothin'" Bryce smiled, "just you. So you finally got around to askin' Sav to marry you, did ya?"

Ivar cracked open one eye to glare at his brother, "You know sometimes if I wasn't so happy that you lived through last summer, I swear I'd give you some bruises."

Bryce handed the paper back and sprawled out his long limbs in the cool grass, "Nah, you wouldn't."

They were quiet for a moment and then Ivar asked, "So, is it okay?"

Bryce looked across at him, surprised at the small shy tone his brother spoke in. Suddenly Bryce saw how much it meant to Ivar for Bryce to agree to this.

Smiling softly, his green eyes luminous in the evening light he assured him, "I think it's perfect, big brother."

Ivar visibly relaxed, a tired smile turning up the corners of his mouth. "Thanks."

~

Friday morning was chilly and Bryce hoped it would get even a little bit warmer as the day wore on. He rode with his dad through their hometown of woodland Colorado to the countryside on the outskirts of town, towards the farm.

"What music do you want?" Sean asked, fiddling with the dials while keeping his eyes on the road.

Bryce slapped his dad's hand, "Both hands on the wheel." He laughed. Sean grinned and clipped his son playfully around the head, Bryce shook it off, smiling and turned to the music, fiddling until he found the country stations.

Once the music was playing, the fast paced, swift beat of the fiddle and guitar filling the cab, he turned to look out the window at the passing fields.

They were like oceans of golden corn and then oceans of trees turning from green to vivid reds and oranges. Bryce sighed contentedly and rested his head against the window, he glanced across at his dad to find Sean watching him thoughtfully.

"What?" Bryce asked, his nose crinkling up.

Reaching over, Sean put a hand on the side of Bryce's face, gently running the crook of his finger across his cheek.

"I was just feeling grateful for my son."

"Aw Dad."

Sean shook his head and took Bryce's hand, feeling it in his own, "I can't believe that it was a year ago that I held this hand, pale, thin and feverish while you lay at death's door."

There were tears in both of their eyes now and as they pulled up to the farm, Sean wiped at his eyes with the back of his hand. He jumped out of the truck and hauled Bryce's rucksack out of the back of the truck.

He was surprised as he found Bryce's arms around him in a hug. Holding his youngest son close against himself Sean murmured, "I love you Brycy-boy."

~

Bryce wandered aimlessly through the barns, stopped outside of Daisy's stall and leaned over to stroke the cows leathered hide, "Good girl." Looking up he blew out his breath and adjusted the backpack straps, "Grandpa!" He called, "You around here?"

The barn was quiet save Daisy's excessive mooing.

"Grandpaaa." Bryce sung out as he walked the entire length of the barn, "you here?"

He bent down to stoke Kit, who was lounging in the sun by the doors. "Grandpa?"

Bryce froze as an apple smashed into the wall inches from his head. He swallowed and looked at where the fruit had smeared on the wall, *that was almost my head, how did they miss that-* he paused and looked up. He only knew one person that could throw that well and deliberately miss.

"Grandpa?"

Then he heard it. Laughter. Jason's deep rich infectious laughter. Following the sound, Bryce dropped his rucksack on the barn floor and started to climb the large stack of hay bales that were piled against the wall for the horses, once at the top of the pile he leaned over the top and glared down at his grandpa who was curled up on top of a bale laughing.

"Oh, I suppose you think that's so funny." Bryce murmured dryly, resting his chin in his hand.

Jason sat up and nodded, letting out a long breath and running both hands through his greying hair.

"That's the best thing I've seen all day."

A grin split Bryce's face, "Grandpa, you gotta teach me to throw like that."

~

Jason scrubbed a hand through his hair, knocking his straw hat backwards, "So I was thinking about this field for camp? What do you think Brycy-boy?"

Bryce surveyed the large open green field with folded arms, "Looks good." He glanced to his right and laughed.

"What?" Jason asked.

Bryce shook his head, "Nothin'" he said still laughing, "I was just wondering, the lakes right close, if we swam down to the bottom, would we find the old wagon we used last summer to bomb down the hill?"

Jason shrugged and shook his head, "Dunno, but you boys can hold your breath for quite a while, I'm sure we could have a swim down and see at some point."

~Chapter Four~

"It was that or Atlantic, can you imagine me naming my horse after the second-largest ocean in the world?"

"Cam, slow down and back up."

Bryce balanced his phone between his shoulder and ear as he pulled a bag of potato chips out of the pantry and then reached for the sour cream and chives dip.

Cameron's voice was muffled across the line as he was walking through fields, the wind buffeting against him.

"I saaaid," Cameron drew out the words, "does Grandpa have room for another horse?"

"Dunno, why?" Bryce bit down on his lip as he tried to open the dip pot with only one hand.

"Coz I've got a beautiful horse here just waiting for a smashin' home."

"Nice! I'll go ask Grandma, hang tight." Bryce cradled the phone and shouted down the hallway, "Grandma! Do we have enough room in the barn for another horse! Cam's found one that he says could use a real good home."

Madison stuck her head out of the front room, "Bryce," she laughed, "I'm not deaf. Now what's this about Cam and a horse?"

Bryce held out the phone, Madison took it, taking the jar of dip from him at the same time and unscrewing the lid.

"Thanks!" Bryce grinned, wandering back into the kitchen where he sat down, straddled a seat, dipping the potato chips into the salsa.

Kit padded into the kitchen a few seconds later, he stood by the back door and shook, his long brown and white fur splaying out and then fuzzing as he stilled and trotted across to Bryce. Sticking his nose between the young man's knees he sniffed, trying to get a lick at the chips.

"Hey boy," Bryce fondled the dog's silky ears before dunking a chip into the dip and then dropping it for the dog.

Kit's dark eyes grew large and he gave a small jump, grabbing his snack in midair.

"Cooool," Bryce said, shovelling another sour cream and chive covered potato chip into his mouth.

He had almost finished both chips and dip when Madison walked back into the kitchen and passed him back his cell phone.

"You better get out front Bryce Walker, we have a new horse here."

"Already?" Bryce's mouth was filled with food and his cheeks puckered as he tried to drink a mouthful of water at the same time.

Laughing, Madison cleaned away the potato chip bag and dip jar, "Cam, as it turned out, was talking about the horse that Mr Shaw owned. The Shaw's are getting along in life and can't care for the old boy as much as they used to. So they called Cam to see if we wanted him."

"Does he have a name?" Bryce asked, getting up and pulling his denim jacket over his checkered shirt. "I'll put him in the stable next to Reese's horse Apple yeah?"

"Alright, oh and don't stay long out in the barn. Your mom texted me, the rest of the gang will be here soon to set up camp."

"Yes ma'am." Bryce shoved his grandpa's Stetson that he had pinched from the hook by the back door down on his head and ran out of the farm house barefooted.

~

"Woohhweee." Bryce let out a long slow whistle.

Cameron raised both reddish brown eyebrows, "He's a beaut ain't he?" He reached inside the horse trailer and stroked the horse's soft black coat.

Bryce nodded, he opened the front of the horse trailer and reached for the reins, gently walking the horse down the ramp and onto the gravel driveway. "Stunning, looks a lot like pepper don't you think?"

Cameron tilted his head to the side, bird-like. "Pepper is a solid black. This boy is more bluish black. Like a Raven."

Bryce grinned, "Raven's kinda a cool name don't you think?"

Cameron laughed and shoved his ball cap back, "Out of all of us, you and Ivar have the best horse know-how. Name him what you will."

"Oh yeah that reminds me." Bryce said, "I keep meaning to ask you. Why did you name your horse Trojan?"

"Trojan?" Cameron repeated, he grinned and ran his hands through his messy hair, "It was that or Atlantic, but can you imagine me naming my horse after the second largest ocean in the world?"

He laughed and shook his head, "I'd never hear the end of it from the guys at the fire station."

Cameron clapped his hands together, "So Trojan it was! Ya know, a big strong name for a big strong firefighter."

Bryce smirked, "Just reminds me of Mr Jenkins' history lesson where he droned on and on about the Trojan horse." He reached up and scratched behind the new horse's ear.

Cameron laughed and glanced down at his watch, "You alright to handle the horse Bryce? I have to go and collect a bunch of gear and stuff for Uncle Caleb and Aunt Emma for the camp out."

Bryce nodded, "Sure," he stroked the horse's soft mane, "You'll be back to help set up camp though yeah? The rest are already heading over!"

Cameron shut the trailer and jumped in the front of his truck, "Absolutely! See you later Brycy-boy."

Bryce waved, preoccupied with the new horse.

He gently led the nervous animal up and into the barn, walking him into the stable and into the stall between Charis and Apple.

"There we go boy," Bryce closed the stall behind him as he stepped out and grabbed an apple from the barrel, holding it out to the horse with one hand, he stroked the horse's nose with his other hand.

"Now…what to name you."

Bryce looked towards the front of the stables as he heard his grandpa's truck pull up.

"Bryce, you around here?" Jason's voice bellowed.

"Comin'!" Bryce yelled back, he gave the horse one last stroke and then jogged out and down the drive.

He paused by the porch steps, his eyebrows raising as he saw the large rucksack on Reese's back as she jumped out of the back of their truck.

"Uh Reese." He covered a smiled and trotted over towards her, "You know it's only a week right? We're just camping in the field, if you need anything you can go to the house." He reached tp help her with it.

Reese sighed and nodded, "I know, but I couldn't figure out what I would need and Jade wasn't much help."

Jade grinned from her seat and got out, giving her cousin a hug, "Is that dog still around by the way?"

Bryce smirked and whistled, Kit flew out of the front door and down the steps, jumping up and planting both of his paws on the front of Jade's top.

Bryce cracked up and doubled over laughing as he saw Jade's face crumple and her head squeaking while asking their grandpa if she could use the shower.

~Chapter Five~

*They are grieving...
Grieving for what though?*

"So this is camp." Reese smiled around at the large open field.

Caleb who was nodding and looking around came back towards where everyone was standing, "It's perfect!"

He turned to Jade and Reese, "Okay, where do you girls wanna pitch your tent?"

Jade opened her mouth to state her preference but Reese had already dumped her stuff in the shade of a tall tree, "Here will do." She announced flopping down in the tall grass.

Bryce raised his eyebrows at Jade, "Well, looks like you're all sorted."

Jade rolled her eyes at her cousin and then dodged as Kit tried to jump up at her again, "Bryce, can you keep that wild thing away from me? Please?"

"Awwww, Jaaade." Bryce squatted down and stroked Kit's soft fur, "He's so cute."

Emma walked over, she crouched down to stroke Kit, "You know Jade, I grew up with a dog."

"Really?"

"Yep,"

Caleb who had been eavesdropping shamelessly sauntered over and draped an arm around his wife, "Yeah, I forget about old Chester. He was a good boy wasn't he?"

He noticed tears prick Emma's eyes and gave her a strong hug.

"You okay, Mom?" Jade asked, frowning. Emma nodded and shared a look with Aubrey and Sean who had arrived and were walking towards them, "Yes." She said after a while, "I just remembered someone else who loved dogs."

Bryce saw his mom's face crumple, he had only ever seen her that shaken once before. That day they had all thought he was going to die in hospital.

"Mom?"

Aubrey glanced at him and then looked away, her eyes tearing up, Sean quietly put his arms around her, holding her close and rocking her back and forth.

Caleb, seeing his nephew's forehead pinch together in confusion, said, "We all knew a young man once, Bryce. It just brings back memories, that's all."

"Right," Bryce tugged on Jade and Reese's hands, "C'mon." He said, pulling both of them under an arm each as they walked away from the campsite.

"We need to give them some time." He looked back over his shoulder as they walked towards the barn where the horses were kept.

They are grieving...Grieving for what though?

~

"Where're Ivar and Cam?" Reese asked as she dragged her fingers through her horse, Apple's, mane.

Jade stood by the water trough, staring at her reflection in the clear water, "Yeah Bryce? I wanna swim in the lake with Cameron. He promised to teach me how to dive this time."

"They'll be here soon." Bryce said, stroking the new horse, "Cam went to grab some gear for you dad and Ivar was dropping something around at Sav's before coming here." He smiled over his shoulder and then stood back.

"Well girls," he folded his arms, "This boy needs a name. Any suggestions?"

Reese inclined her head, studying the beautiful creature before her. "What about Vista?"

"Vista?" Bryce rolled the name around in his mind, "could work."

Jade pulled her hoodie off and tied it around her waist. Walking over, she folded the horse's ears back, stroking him. "What about Panorama? It's like Vista, but can be shortened to Pano."

Bryce and Reese looked thoughtful for a long time before Bryce patted the horse and said, "How about it, old thing?" He turned to the rest of the horses stabled in the barn.

"Well you all? How does Pano sound?"

Sean's horse Chilli let out a snort and turned his back, causing Reese to laugh.

Grinning at his cousin lopsidedly, Bryce shook his head and chuckled, Charis and Apple stopped on the floor, seeming to enjoy the new member to their herd.

Carson, Pepper and Trojan lifted their heads and kept eating.

"Well." Bryce smirked, "that went well."

A truck horn blared outside and the three bolted out of the barn and down to the drive where Sean and Caleb stood with Jason, helping Cameron to unload the back.

As soon as Jade saw Cameron she grabbed his elbow, "You promised to teach me to dive."

"Whoa! Hold your horses Jade," he put a large rolled up tent on the ground, he smiled at her and tugged playfully on her ponytail. "This evening okay?"

Bryce picked up a large cooler, helping Ivar, who had tagged along in the back of the truck with his rucksack, carry it down to the field.

"What do you think of the campsite?' He asked.

Ivar looked up and glanced at it, then nodded his approval. "Perfect."

Once they had put the cooler down, Bryce nudged his brother, "So."

Ivar shot him a withering look, "So what?"

Bryce's face fell, "Really? So what?"

Ivar shoved him in the shoulder, stooping to take his trainer off, "If you're referring to whether I dropped the letter off or not, I did."

"Aaannd." Bryce sat on the cooler, tugging his own shoes off as the adults carried the last of the gets down.

"And nothing,"

"Seriously."

Ivar straightened, his eyes laughing at his brother. "I put it in her letter box. She'll get it tomorrow."

"And he prolongs the agony!" Bryce announced tossing his shoes into the open tent he and Jason had set up earlier. He swivelled expectantly as Madison announced that it was time for hotdogs.

~Chapter Six~

"For the word of God is alive and powerful. It is sharper than the sharpest two-edged sword, cutting between soul and spirit, between joint and marrow. It exposes our innermost thoughts and desires. Nothing in all creation is hidden from God. Everything is naked and exposed before his eyes, and he is the one to whom we are accountable." Hebrews 4:12-13

The lake looked cool, tempting and the perfect escape to the last of the heat that was tailing on to the end of the summer weather before autumn and winter took over completely.

"Okeeey!" Cameron stretched out by the lake's edge, "You ready for this Jade?"

Jade sat up from where she had also been stretching, "Yup." Her dark blue and pink swimsuit shimmered slightly in the light.

Cameron nodded, "Great, okay. So, stand by the edge of the lake." He stood by the edge and got ready himself, "So keep your feet together and extend your-" he broke off as a wild yell filled the air, both Jade and Cameron turned, getting out of the way just in time as Reese and Ivar, led by Bryce came sprinting down the hill and cannon-balled into the lake.

Stepping back from the spray that they caused when they all landed in the water, Cameron grinned wickedly, "Or you can just do that." He ran at Jade and caught her up, throwing her over his shoulder and pelting up the hill, before turning back on himself and running full pelt down the hill with Jade thumping him on the back as he neared the lake, he jumped and curled his legs underneath himself, propelling both him and Jade through the air and into the centre of the lake. They surfaced, laughing and choking on water.

Bryce swam towards them, grinning, "Ivar and I are gonna go under to see if we can find the wagon we used last summer, wanna come?"

Cameron laid back in the water, back stroking, "Na, I'm just gonna float." He drawled lazily.

"I'll join you, Bryce." Jason called from the edge of the lake as he and Sean waded in.

"Awsome." Bryce grinned and turned to his dad, "Dad?" Sean nodded in response and jammed his cap down further onto his head.

"Honey," Aubrey called from the shore where she was reclining with Emma and Madison who were watching Caleb stalking a small grass snake with Hunter. "I don't think wearing that is a great idea."

Sean smiled at her brightly and dove beneath the surface, he came back up and shook like a dog. Aubrey's eyebrows rose to her hairline. "All good babe!" Sean hollered back, his cap sliding over his eyes.

Bryce laughed as his mom rolled her eyes and went back to talking to her sister in law and mom.

"Okay, you ready boys?" Jason asked as he and Sean joined Ivar and Bryce in the centre of the lake, Cameron was busy swimming lengths of the lake with Reese and Jade.

"How far are we going down?" Ivar asked while looking down into the water, squinting to see the bottom.

"As far as our lungs will let us!" Bryce quipped.

Ivar shot him a look, "Didn't you get close enough to death last year?"

Bryce's face puckered and Jason shook his head, "We are only going down as far as we are able to try and find this wagon." He assured.

~

When Ivar placed his hand flat against his throat and moved it back and forth in the underwater signal for he was out of breath, Sean motioned for them all to surface.

When Bryce broke through the water, he glanced across at Ivar, "You okay?"

Ivar nodded, holding a hand up to say he couldn't talk at that moment. Sean helped his son stay afloat while he caught his breath, "I'm okay." Ivar said hoarsely.

"You sure?" Jason asked, concerned.

Ivar nodded and flicked his dark hair out of the way, "yYah. I'm fine grandpa." He smiled at his dad when Sean gave his shoulder a squeeze, "Really, I'm fine Dad. Just stayed under a little too long. We goin' down again?"

Bryce was frowning, "Ivar maybe-"

Ivar shook his head, "I'm fine, let's do one more dive down to see if we can spot the old thing yeah?" He swam towards his brother and nudged him in the shoulder, "Bet I can get further than you."

Bryce grinned, took the largest breath he could and disappeared under the waters.

Ivar gave his dad a reassuring look before plunging under the waters himself.

Jason was the first to notice the peculiar look that was playing across Sean's face. "You okay, Sean?"

Sean blinked as if he was coming from a deep sleep, "Huh? Did you say something Jason?"

Jason clapped him on the shoulder, "I understand if this is too much for you."

Sean swallowed and nodded, "It never normally bothers me. But Ivar just now having to come up for air…it…it shook me."

Jason's smile was sad, "it's ok, Cameron and I will help Ivar and Bryce, you go back to shore."

Sean nodded and swam his way to the shallows, once his feet found solid ground he waded to where the women where reclining in the grass against fallen trees.

"Sean, honey?" Aubrey got up and went towards him as soon as he got onto the grassy bank, "Sean."

Sean pulled his shirt on and then stared at her, for the first time in years, Aubrey saw her husband speechless. He gasped for words but couldn't find them.

Sean ran a hand across his eyes, "Aubrey."

Smiling weakly, Aubrey pulled him into a hug, "Faith is the substance of things hoped for Sean, of things not, Sean."

She put a hand on the side of his face, wiping away a lone tear with her thumb. "Last year," she said softly, tilting her head to the side, "Someone told me that the doctors' report wasn't the last. When our boy was dying he said that what the doctors said wasn't the final word ."

Aubrey gripped his hand, "We can trust him Sean. We can trust God with anything."

"We haven't heard anything in so long, Aubrey."

"And *their* words ain't the last. Just like for Bryce, the same for him."

Sean nodded slowly, he breathed deep and then let out his breath, ransacking his hair with his fingers. He closed his eyes and when he opened them again he smiled at his wife, pulling her into a hug and kissing her gently.

~Chapter Seven~

I think I prefer the way my great grandpa used to know it was harvest. That big old lovely harvest moon.

Bryce's wild gesturing caught Jason and Ivar's attention. He motioned towards a shadowed part of the lake's bottom.

Jason shook his head and pointed back towards the surface. He made a hand motion saying it was time to go back up for more air.

Once they broke through the surface again, Ivar said, "I think I'm done, if I hold my breath any longer I'll burst."

Jason laughed and splashed the water with his fist, "Too right. It's getting a bit chilly now as well."

The dark horse that had been used to help bring down gear for the camp out lifted his head from eating grass.

Ivar grinned at the horse, "Not you Chilli. It's a metaphor."

"Yeah, I don't think a horse will understand that." Jade said as she swam towards them.

Reese was right behind her, disappearing half towards them as she plunged under the water.

Everyone glanced down into the water, watching as Reese's slender figure gracefully sliced through the water.

"We do this differently." Jade commented, "Reese swims gracefully whereas I swim with power."

"And that's why you win contests and I don't." Reese breathed as she surfaced right by Ivar's elbow, shocking him out of his treading water routine.

She ran a hand down the front of her bright green swimsuit before turning in a circle and saying, "Are we going back under?"

"Best not." Jason said, "we should get back to the shore."

"Just one last go, Grandpa. Cam and I can dive." Bryce asked, the water was getting cool, but he wanted to see if he could find the wagon so badly that he was willing to put up with the cold water.

"I don't know," Jason said.

"Don't worry, Grandpa." Cameron stopped backstroking and came to join them in the centre of the lake. "We'll be fine."

"Ok." Jason said, "You have ten minutes."

~

Bryce loved the feeling of cool water as it flowed past his body. Pushing forward in the water he swam further down than Cameron.

Next to him, his brother had stopped swimming and was squinting in the direction Bryce was pointing. He shook his head and wildly gestured towards another part of the lake.

A few more moments of pushing against the water with his arms and his lungs started to burn for air.

Reaching out to touch Cameron's arm, Bryce made the 'all out of air' signal and angled his body back up towards the surface.

Cameron nodded and then both started swimming towards the surface.

Once they had both broken through the water it hit them as to exactly how cold it was getting.

They made their way to the shore and got out, taking the warm towels that their mom had been warming by the campfire for them.

"Find it?" Ivar asked hopefully from where he was smearing ketchup on his hotdog.

Cameron shook his head and smiled at the familiar autumnal cinnamon smell that clung to the towel. "No," he said, "the lake's deeper in some parts. It's probably pretty far down. No hope in getting it just by diving down like we were."

"Aw, that's a shame." Caleb smiled, "Though we can all breathe now and be assured that Bryce won't be riding a wagon down the hill with the others anytime soon." He said reclining back in his camping chair.

"Oh ha ha, uncle Caleb." Bryce dried himself down and reached for his shirt.

His uncle grinned at him and winked while passing him a large roasting stick with marshmallows all the way up it.

~

Jason breathed in the night air deeply, "We start harvesting the wheat and corn tomorrow."

Madison, laying next to him in the tent, burrowed deeper under her blanket, "It's gonna be a good one." She murmured sleepily.

Jason glanced across at her "Mmm," he laughed quietly and pulled the blanket back so he could smile down at her, "I still can't believe I got you to agree to stay in a tent."

Madison's pale-coloured eyes blinked back at him happily, "I cant believe that Sean got Aubrey to stay in a tent."

Jason agreed with her and put his arm around his wife's shoulders, the trees outside caused patterns to dance across the tents fabric. "I still don't understand why you never liked sleeping bags."

Madison smoothed a hand over the quilt that Jason had carried down from the house for her. "I don't know, Bryce and Aubrey are the same, we don't like small spaces, I happen to include sleeping bags on that list."

Jason's nose crinkled as he swatted a fly away, "Bryce doesn't like sleeping bags?"

"Not really, he unzips it and then uses it as a blanket."

"Ahhh." Jason idly would a piece of Madison's hair around his finger as they laid together listening to the sounds of the night. After a while he glanced down to find Madison asleep on his chest, he smiled fondly and kissed her on the forehead, "Goodnight, love."

Resting back against his pillow, Jason started up through a small mesh-covered gap in the tent roof at the stars, he smiled slightly as he saw the large moon; he knew that it would be a full harvest moon soon.

Rolling onto his side and wrapping Madison in a hug, Jason suppressed a yawn. "You know what God, when lookin' at the sky, I think I prefer the way my great grandpa used to know it was harvest. That big old lovely harvest moon."

He sighed and curled under the blanket, "It's amazing isn't it." He paused and a ironic smiled pushed up his mouth, "but then you know that don't you." His eyes crinkled at the edges, "I really got to stop doing that haven't I."

Pushing a hand through his hair he sighed and rested his cheek on the top of Madison's head, "I need to know what to do Lord. After what happened today with Sean at the lake, it reminded me that Bryce never knew. Is it time he knew? Cam and Ivar know. Are we not being fair by keeping it from him?" Jason paused for a breath, he could hear the young voices of his grandkids in the large group tent as they played with their torches making shadows.

"Should he know, Lord?" Jason had never felt so confused. "If you want Bryce to know, show us Lord. Show us."

~Chapter Eight~
"None of y'all are gonna let that go, are ya."

Bryce was up with the sun the next day. Sneaking out of the tent before anyone else was awake, he grabbed his fiddle and his trainers, carrying them while walking barefoot across the fields towards the barn.

When he reached the hay barn, where the bales were stacked precariously high, he dumped his trainers and fiddle case at the bottom of the ladder and holding his fiddle and bow in one hand climbed up onto the rafters.

Bryce settled himself among the rafters like a barn pigeon. He balanced on the beams, swinging his feet as he tuned up his fiddle. He traced the thin hairline crack on the back of the fiddle's neck, remembering how his uncle had fixed it for him last summer.

Smiling, he lifted the fiddle, placing it on his shoulder and tucking it under his chin, where the red mark on his skin showed how often it had come to rest there. He blew a little sand off of the bow and then set it to the strings.

Bryce felt himself relaxing as music started to spill and leap from his well-loved fiddle.

He had only been playing for a few moments when he let out a deep breath, allowing the music to warm him against the slight autumn chill. For as long as he could remember he had played music. It was a part of him. His life blood and the pounding of his heart.

With fingers dancing across the strings, Bryce's smile grew until it reached his eyes. He stopped playing as he heard the horses in the barn across the yard start to wake up.

He flipped his fiddle over, rubbing a dirt smudge off of the back of its smooth wooden body.

Pulling the sleeve of his shirt down over his hand, he rubbed vigorously at the mark.

Then stopped.

Bryce stared at the mark. He had never seen it before, but it wasn't a mark; it was a small engraving.

Out of habit, Bryce's hand slipped beneath the top of his shirt and his fingers grasped the wooden cross that hung from the leather cord that his dad had given him.

You'll know when it's time to pass it on. Sean had said. Bryce hadn't felt or thought it was time for that quite yet. He knew that he would pass it on one day, when the time was right and when God told him too. But until then it hung around his neck and was there to stay until that time.

Bryce felt tears fill his eyes as he stared down at the small engraving on the back of his fiddle, it was tiny. Small intricate words in the most detailed manner etched into the base of the fiddle on the back in the far right corner.

The engraving was old, but Bryce was able to make out the words by squirting hard at it.

David Bryce Walker.

"David Bryce walker?" Bryce repeated. His voice echoed in the barn sounding hollow.

Who the heck is he? He turned the fiddle in his hands, looking it over as if with new eyes. He'd never thought about who the fiddle might have belonged to before it found its way into his capable hands. He had been given it when he was twelve, he had supposed it used to be one of theirs, or even grandpas. Ivar had been the one who told him it had been in the family for a long time.

It had been Ivar's for as long as Bryce could remember until he stopped playing to learn guitar. Ivar had then passed the fiddle onto Bryce. He had often wondered how many years back into the family generation it went.

Whenever someone saw it, they always mentioned and pointed out how it was such a beautiful piece of work.

For a brief moment, Bryce wondered if he had been named after this David Bryce Walker, if he was some sort of great grandfather no one liked to talk about.

No one had ever mentioned him and he had never seen the engraving so he supposed that like him, everyone just hadn't thought about it.

Bryce ran his fingers across the engravings, he smiled. For some reason just knowing it was there, made him feel closer to the music, made his smile that bit brighter and his dedication to the music that much stronger.

~

"Three! Two! One!"

At the count, all the men from the Davis and Walker household pulled on the large canopy that covered Jason's combine harvester. As the cover fell away, folding in on itself on the ground, Cameron beamed, "Well ain't she a beauty."

Caleb slapped him on the back, "And since you missed Harvest last year, you get to be the one to drive it."

"Seriously?" The firefighter-turned-country boy's eyes grew as large as saucers as he stared up at the large machine.

"Aw c'mon Cam." Ivar teased, "You're twenty four, surely you can take on this." He raised his eyebrows at the large machine that even he hadn't ridden yet, "I mean, it can't be any harder than running into a burning building? Can it?"

Cameron snorted and grabbed the handle, opening the door and pulling himself up, "We run on pure adrenaline when going into those fires."

Sean folded his arms, watching amused as Cameron fumbled around in the driver's seat, trying to figure out how to drive it. "Come on Cam!" He hollered, "can't be too different from a fire truck can it?"

Cameron's gaze flew to his dad, "I don't drive the truck!"

Bryce and Ivar laughed as Caleb slapped his hand against his forehead.

"Is this safe?" Bryce asked.

Sean's eyes widened and he shrugged, "No idea." He walked over to the combine harvester and patted its exterior, "Just know son." He looked up at Cameron, "if we lose the entire harvest-"

"And in turn, all of my orders!" Jason put in as he tried to prise a large piece of scrap metal out of the barn door.

Sean grinned, "And all your grandpa's orders, then it's all your fault."

Cameron's expression was blank. He leaned out the door as his mom walked into the barn, Hunter on her back, holding on like a monkey, "Mom, did you know how encouraging my brothers and dad are?"

Aubrey winked and blew him a kiss, and Hunter, upon seeing his dad, clapped his hands and called, "Daddy! Mommy said you would do mwe awroplane!"

Caleb held out his arms, and Aubrey passed her nephew across, "Sure thing buddy!" The proud father announced, swinging the little guy around in circles, everyone enjoying the sound of his laughter.

"Hey Uncle Caleb." Cameron called, "Can Hunter ride on my lap?"

Caleb toyed with the idea, while trying to stop Hunter from attacking one of his mom's chickens that had found its way into the barn.

"Sure, it can't be any more dangerous than Bryce and his wagon last year."

At the mention of the wagon that he had never even found at the bottom of the lake, Bryce rolled his eyes and stuck a long piece of grass between his teeth, chewing on it as he grabbed Jason's Stetson on the hook on the wall and dropped it onto his own head, "None of y'all are gonna let that go, are ya."

"Nope!" Ivar sung out while trying to defend himself from a surprise attack from Jade and Reese, "Be back in a second." He waved before ducking out of the barn chasing after his cousins.

~Chapter Nine~

You haven't done this before. Ask, using my name, and you will receive, and you will have abundant joy.
John 16:24

"Ivar, where are you going?" Aubrey put down the bowel she was using in the farmhouse kitchen as her son made a wild dash past the window towards the truck.

"Ivar?" She went to the door and swung it open, hugging herself as she regretted not grabbing a jacket.

Kit followed her out of the house, sitting back on his haunches on the porch as Aubrey walked down the steps and onto the drive.

Gravel kicked up as Ivar dug his trainers in, stopping. "Mom? Did you say something?"

"Yeah, where you going, whirlwind? Shouldn't you be down helping bring in the harvest?"

Ivar nodded and leaned through the open window of the truck, fishing around for something, "Yeah, Dad said I could make a quick run into town."

Not finding what he wanted in his car he shrugged and ran up the steps to where his mom stood, "Sav got my letter."

Aubrey laughed and kissed her grown up son on the forehead, she remembered what it had been like for Sean and her during their younger years. "And what did she say?"

"She wants to meet me in town at the milkshake shop."

"Well, go then!" Aubrey urged, pushing him towards the car, she reached back into the door and grabbed his coat, "While you're in town, grab us two pumpkins would you?"

"Pumpkins?"

"Mmm," Aubrey nodded and pushed a strand of her hair back behind her ear, "Madison and I wanna make some pumpkin pies for the end of bringing in the harvest." She handed him his coat.

"Right okay." Ivar smiled at his mom and stuck the car into reverse, almost backing out into Cameron who came sprinting up the drive, "Ivar!"

"Cam!" Ivar slammed his brakes on, almost smashing his forehead into the windscreen of his truck, "Bro! Seriously!"

Aubrey frowned, "Cam?"

"Sorry." Cameron said sheepishly, he jogged up to Ivar's window and knocked on it, "can I catch a ride into town? Dad asked me to grab some gear we forgot."

Aubrey's forehead creased and she shivered slightly in the evening breeze, "Cam, you sure that's necessary? The crops are almost in and we pack up camp tomorrow."

Cameron turned to grin at his mom, "Yeah, it's necessary. Dad, Caleb and Grandpa are planning something and I am sworn to secrecy."

Aubrey shook her head, "Alright, just don't let them go crazy okay?"

Cameron slid into the passenger side seat, "Can't make any promises Mom!" He waved as Ivar backed the car out of the drive.

Aubrey sighed and turned to look at her mom who stood in the doorway, "They are gonna take it overboard ain't they mom?"

Madison nodded, "Definitely." She held out an arm and Aubrey walked up the steps and into her hug, "Come on, let's do some autumnal themed decorticating. I got your dad to agree to a small campfire type party on Sunday evening to celebrate the end of bringing in the harvest. I think that's what your husband and brother are going overboard on. Don't tell them I told you though."

"Ooh," Aubrey's eyes lit up, "Where're the girls? They can help us."

Madison picked up an armful of dried leaves that she had swept from the steps earlier that day, "I sent them to grab the fairy lights from the attic."

"Great, oh wow," she shivered again, "it's colder than it was last year."

Madison walked into the warm kitchen and dumped the leaves on the table, "I know what you mean. Last year about this time, it was still warm enough for them to all walk in shorts and T's. Now both Bryce and Sean have swathed up in long sleeves and jeans."

"Mmm," Aubrey warmed her hands over the steaming cup of coffee that was sitting on the table, "So what are we doing with those leaves?"

"This!" Madison said grinning as Jade and Reese came in with an armload of fairy lights. She picked up a string of it and tied a red leaf between two lights, going along the string of lights until between every fairy light was a colourful autumn leaf.

"Oh Madison." Her daughter in law breathed, "That's beautiful."

Madison smiled softly as she worked, "Jason and I have been making leaf and light wreaths for harvest every year since we were married."

"I love them," Aubrey said, picking up the finished trail of lights to show Jade and Reese.

~

Aubrey looked up as Ivar dumped a large pumpkin on the table in front of her. His face glowing as bright as the lights strung around the entire farm house.

"What's that look for?" She asked, folding her arms as she looked Ivar over.

"Oh Mom, I think I'm in heaven." Ivar's eyes had never been so bright.

"Sav said yes didn't she?"

When Ivar nodded, Aubrey squeezed him in a hug, "Ohhhh!!! I always wanted a daughter!"

Ivar's grin spread across his entire face, "I asked her to come to the harvest campfire on Sunday, Mom, that okay?"

"Of course," Aubrey bit her lip, flicking through cake recipes in her mind, "I need to get Madison to help me make an engagement cake."

Ivar's laughter rumbled in his chest as he hugged his mom, "Nothin' too big or fancy ok? Sav and I wanna keep it low key. Stay true to our roots."

"Absolutely," his Mom beamed, "just let us do a cake."

Ivar hesitated but then relented, "ok." He grinned again, "I'm gonna tell the others."

Aubrey caught his hand on the way out, "Where's Cam?"

"He's using his truck, he left it at the house." He threw over his shoulder as he sprinted from the kitchen, giddy and in love.

Laughing, Aubrey turned back to the pumpkin, she washed it before putting it up on the counter and starting to cut it open, removing the insides of the pumpkin and putting it in a separate bowl. *My son...engaged.*

She smiled at the thought.

She was so engrossed in the idea of Ivar and Savannah's wedding day, that she didn't notice Sean until he had walked in, dropped a soft kiss on her lips and nudged her out of the way so he could wash in hands, "Gee, babe, what's got you so dazed?"

He grabbed the bowl of orange stuff from inside the pumpkin and tipped it into the blender with milk, sugar, cornflour and honey.

"Ivar hasn't told you?"

"Haven't seen him, what's he need to tell me?" Sean put the blender on and leaned against the counter top lazily.

"He and Sav are engaged." Aubrey said casually as if it was no big matter. She sliced a piece of pumpkin off only to drop it as Sean grabbed her around the waist and whirled her around the kitchen.

The screen door banged open and Ivar appeared with Bryce on his back and Jade and Reese hanging from his arms while Hunter clung to his leg like a limpet.

Sean laughed and pulled Ivar into a hug, Bryce, Jade, Reese, Hunter and all.

Kit, who had been asleep by the door, started to bark and jump up, wanting in on all the excitement.

~Chapter Ten~

What you plant today, you will harvest tomorrow.

Cameron lifted the garage door, leaned inside and grabbed the extra length of rope that his dad had asked him to pick up. Halfway back to his truck he gained a thirst for coke so turned around and went inside the sunlit spacious bungalow, making a beeline for the refrigerator.

Finding what he was looking for, Cameron popped the can open and took a sip, flipping idly through the mail on the countertop. His phone buzzed and he picked it up.

Hurry uppppppp XD

Cameron laughed at his uncle's message and turned his phone off, as he did, he smiled at his screen saver, Ivar had made it when taking a digital design course in his last term at collage. The photo was of a field in full bloom, an eagle swooping down across the top of the page and written across the centre of the image where the words, *what you plant today, you will harvest tomorrow.*

"A word in season." Cameron murmured rolling the stiffness out of his neck and drained his can, then tossed it in the trash can by the back door. As he walked towards the door he bumped into the table where the mail was and knocked it onto the laminate.

Groaning, Cameron bent down to pick it up.

His heart stopped.

A crisp white envelope addressed to his parents was supporting the US airforce insignia.

Instantly Cameron was thrown back to the day an envelope just the same but edged in black had arrived at their door when he was fourteen.

He forced himself to swallow and picked it up, stuffing it into his back pocket before dumping the rest of the mail onto the table and staggering out of the house.

It wasn't until he was in the car that he noticed that his hands were trembling.

~

Bryce was the only one who wasn't present in the kitchen. Jason swallowed and looked at the open letter lying on the table, the reason for Bryce running from the room pale-faced and shaking.

The look of disbelief on Aubrey and Sean's faces echoed on the faces of everyone seated around the table.

"H-he's alive?" Came Ivar's muted question.

Sean blinked, "Yeah…after all this time, I-I don't know what to say…"

Aubrey was busy pressing her hands against her face, trying to figure it all out. "He's alive." She kept muttering. Even Emma and Caleb were numb.

"I thought the Air Force said his plane had gone missing over the Pacific years ago." Madison said.

"They did." Sean replied, "New evidence must have surfaced." He folded the corners of the letter back and forth, a slow, tired smile creeping across his face and then he started to laugh until tears were rolling down his face and his back ached.

Cameron flickered a smile and then grinned, "We all look like we've been told he just died. I don't think a funeral could look more down in the dumps,"

Ivar recovered next but his mom remained dumbfounded. "He's alive." She muttered away, tears pooling in her eyes.

The sound of fast-paced fiddle music quickly knocked her out of her dazed stupor though and she got up from the table, "I need to talk to Bryce," she said quietly.

Sean stood also and took her hand, "We both do."

As soon as they had left the kitchen, Ivar bolted out the back door and started to turn cartwheels in the backyard.

Emma squinted out of the window above the sink, "I didn't even know he could do those."

~Chapter Eleven~

Faith is simply seeing things from God's perspective.

"Bryce, honey?"

Bryce looked up as his parents crossed the front yard towards the tree he was up.

"I'm sorry," he said, putting his fiddle down, "I know I reacted like a kid. Not an almost adult."

"Hey," Sean pulled himself up into the tree and then bent to help Aubrey up. "You did nothin wrong, in fact it's your mom and I that need to be sayin we're sorry."

Bryce was quiet for a long moment, then, "I've known of David Bryce Walker for a few days now."

His mom's forehead crinkled, "Huh?"

"All I knew was a name," Bryce said, he flipped the fiddle over and traced the engraving so his parents could see the name, "didn't know who he was though…"

Sean took the instrument and stared down at the name, "I'd forgotten this was here."

'Why didn't you tell me?" Bryce asked suddenly, his green eyes misty as he looked at his parents, "Why didn't you tell me that I had another brother? That he was older than Cam?" He shook his head angrily, "I don't even know who he is and he's turning up here this week?"

Sean opened his mouth but Aubrey shook her head, she reached across and wrapped her arms around Bryce, "He's tall." She started, "About your dad's height, you were named after him, you are also the spitting image of David. People used to say that you were baby David all over again when you were little. Both of you have the same eye colour, the same windswept blond hair, love for the country and music."

Aubrey ran her fingers through his shoulder length hair, "He was a fighter pilot. Not home much. Flying for the US Air Force. It was just a routine flight. We received word a few days before your seventh birthday that his plane had gone missing. You didn't remember David very well so we decided not to tell you. Cam and Ivar remembered him so they knew, we didn't want you to grow up knowing you'd lost someone."

Sean squeezed his arm, "We know we were wrong not to tell you Bryce. We should have, he's your brother and you deserved to know who he was."

"How old is he now?" Bryce's voice was small.

"He should be about thirty-one now."

Taking a deep breath, Bryce tipped his head back to look up at the sky, he watched as a leaf fell from a tree and floated down to the ground, "Is that why you freaked out at the lake, Dad? Coz he went down over the ocean?"

Sean's expression was pained.

"Bryce sweetie, we're so sorry." Aubrey blinked back tears and rubbed his shoulder, "Your dad and I don't know what else to say."

"I have another brother, Mom…" Bryce's lips trembled, "and I never knew?" His voice rose an octave and his accent which was normally quite lax became stronger as he spoke, "Mom, how in tarnation am I meant to face him next week not knowin' nothin' about him?"

Bryce scrunched his eyes up and balled his fists, pushing them into his eyes so he wouldn't cry, "Is he the one that Kit reminds y'all of?"

Aubrey nodded.

Sean watched him for a long moment before reaching for him and hugging him. "I'm so sorry son." He whispered, rocking Bryce slightly. "Please, please forgive us."

When his dad said this, Bryce leaned back and rubbed at his tears. Pulling himself up to his full height, he told himself sternly to act like the young man he was.

"It's okay." He managed finally. "I understand you were trying to protect me," he rubbed at a stray tear on his cheek and then took a shaky breath, "this is gonna take some processing."

"We understand that." Aubrey said.

"I think I need to walk," Bryce said, "I'm gonna go for a walk." He jumped down from the tree, waiting until his parents got down also, he picked up his fiddle, smiled and gave them both a hug.

"Sure you're okay?" Sean asked, worried.

Bryce nodded "Yeah, just—just need to think this all over."

~

Faith is simply seeing things from God's perspective. When someone does something to you, instead of just reacting in the natural physical realm, based on your emotions, faith considers, "What does God's word say?"

A sigh escaped Bryce's locked chest. Rubbing his forehead he looked up at the golden leaves on the tree as he watched the tree branches above him move.

The words from the book his grandpa had lent him buzzed around his head like an annoying fly.

Grabbing a handful of the grass he was laying it, Bryce threw it in the air and watched it disperse.

He groaned and rolled onto his stomach, pulling his fiddle towards himself he ran a finger over the engraving.

"God I don't understand. I feel so...so confused." He bashed his fist into the ground, wincing as it caused his hand to ache, "Stupid idea Bryce." He muttered.

Bryce got up and picked up his fiddle, walking towards the fence line that looked down over his grandpa's entire farm land he started to play. Slowly and deliberately, allowing the music to wash over him in an unspoken prayer.

His heart raced in a turmoil of emotions, thumping wildly like a horse at full gallop.

He felt angry.

Angry at his family for not telling him. Angry at his brother from going missing. Angry at himself for feeling angry. He let out a tightly-held breath, trying not to let it tie him in knots on the inside.

Now, what's the right thing to do Bryce? He asked himself while playing. Bryce watched the sky, the vast blue was slowly turning a deep orange and red, pink and purple swirled together to make a scattered pattern with the clouds.

Taking a deep breath, Bryce closed his eyes, feeling like he had aged all of sudden. He wondered if this was how Ivar had felt last summer, Ivar had told him after he had come out of hospital that it had been like he'd grown up suddenly during Bryce's stay in hospital.

Now with high, quick-paced music spilling from the fiddle, Bryce sighed, his forehead creasing, he felt like that. Like the knowledge of his new—not so new—brother had caused him to age, grow up and think.

Stopping his playing, Bryce reached for the cross he always wore. *Okay.* He prayed inwardly. *I'm hurting. But Lord, I forgive them for not telling me. I'm older now Jesus and although I'll always be the playmate and the jovial one, I need to realise the enormity of what this is I've been told. Show me, I need to know what it is you would have me do with my life.*

He let the cross pendant fall back against his chest, then shivered slightly in the breeze.

The sun was starting to set, casting a beautiful orange glow across the fields. Like they were on fire.

Fireflies had also started to come up, dancing among the tall grass. He was reminded of his mom's favourite song from the year before.

Looking back on all you've done, the miracles, how far we have come.

The story of your faithfulness, I won't forget.

When all around was shifting sand, you raised me up and made me stand.

I'm anchored in your perfect love. I will not fear.

Yet I'll say, arise, arise my soul and sing.

Remember all the greater things that he has done.

What's yet to come.

Oh, my soul, arise!

The song made him smile. It reminded him of the strength his mom had had while he was in hospital.

Then it struck him.

Even while his mom had been dealing with him in hospital. His mom had been fighting the fear of losing another child.

That small nagging fear that had been growing in the corner of his mind—that he was just another David—died and he knew his parents loved him for *him*. For being Bryce. Not a replacement of David.

He was loved. He had his brothers. His family. His friends. But David had missed out on all of that for so long.

It wouldn't be easy. He knew that for certain.

It would be hard.

"But a harvest takes some work." He reminded himself. "If I want to be able to let David into the family and love him like I love Ivar and Cameron. As a brother…" he trailed off and his heart finished his sentence for him.

Then I need to love him as a brother in my heart, before I can to his face.

He dropped back onto his back in the grass and let out a long breath before smiling sleepily.

"God. This is gonna be *haaaard.*"

But worth it. The spirit of the Lord replied, speaking to his own spirit.

~Chapter Twelve~

The sweet voice was familiar and they all knew who it was because Ivar actually fell off of the ladder this time.

The harvest was almost in. Jason and Cameron were in, bringing in the last of it with the combine harvester, while the others either finished baling up the wheat, helped finish decorating the barn for the harvest campfire or joined Bryce in teasing Ivar mercilessly about Savannah.

Reese looked down from the hay bales she was standing on and tossed her long blond ponytail out of her way, "Get used to it Ivar," she laughed, "When Savannah gets here, all Bryce will do is make faces at you the entire night."

Ivar rolled his eyes and smirked. He climbed up the ladder and reached down for the string of fairy lights his aunt held up for him.

"No, Ivar, a little to the left." Emma pursed her lips, she waved a hand, "Up a bit. No, too high. Down a bit, to the right."

Caleb came into the barn and Ivar gave him a long look as Emma said the lights were too high again.

Caleb grinned, winked at his nephew and went to help Sean with the wheat. Ivar huffed and once more lifted the lights to where his aunt wanted them.

Jade came in with Madison and Aubrey, arms ladened down with bowls of food and Madison's famous chicken casserole and Aubrey's famous pumpkin pies.

"Smells good!" Ivar shouted from his perch, "Need someone to taste them?"

Jade shook her head and swatted Bryce away as he pecked at the pies and cinnamon and oatmeal biscuits. "No need, Bryce has already taken the job." She frowned and smacked his hand once more as he went in for his second biscuit. "Bryce!"

"What?" Bryce tried to look innocent though his cheeks puckered with the food he had in his mouth. Aubrey laughed and handed him a pitcher to go and fill up in the kitchen, "The punch is on the table," she instructed as his blond head disappeared out of the barn and into the farmhouse.

Hands on hips, Aubrey surveyed the barn, nodding with approval as she smiled up at Ivar's laughing face, "When's your girl getting here?"

At the mention of Savannah, a deep red blush crept into Ivar's face, he smiled crookedly, "Any moment."

Reese jumped down from the hay bales and picked up one of the pumpkins she and Hunter had carved and put battery candles in, "I can't wait for Sav to get here. I want to see how Bryce will embarrass Ivar."

"Reese!" Emma bit down on her lip, trying to be on her nephew's side but also looking forward to Bryce's escapades.

Aubrey waved it off, "Oh don't worry Emma, Bryce has been embarrassing Ivar in front of Savannah since the first day Ivar blushed at her name."

"I do not blush!" Ivar protested loudly, almost falling from the ladder.

"Oh yes you do." Sean grinned, pushing a hay bale into place to act as a seat, "Whenever someone mentions her name."

Jade looked sly, "Savannah."

Ivar glared at her and almost fell off the ladder again. Bryce hooted with laughter as he came back in with the pitcher of punch, "He's blushing!"

"Oh shut up," Ivar frowned, he hammered the last hook into the barn wall and then smacked his hand with it. "Uhhhhhh!" He shot his brother a look as if to say, 'This is all your fault."

Bryce grinned up at him and then grabbed his dark blue checkered shirt off of the nearest hay bale and pulled it in over the solid T-shirt he was wearing.

"Very handsome, country-like and very you." Aubrey smiled, brushing a piece of straw off of his shoulder.

"Hello?"

The sweet voice was familiar and they all knew who it was because Ivar actually fell off of the ladder this time.

"Does anyone know why Cameron and Jason were laughing like a pair of jackals when I walked up here?" Savannah asked as she walked into the barn, a denim jacket slung over her arm. Her long maroon skirt swished as she skirted around hay bales to give her friends hugs.

Bryce grinned, "Yeah, probably coz they knew Ivar would react like this." He stepped aside and Savannah hid a smile as she went over to help Ivar up off the floor.

"What, are you falling for me now, Ivar?" She laughed slightly and held out a hand.

Ivar took it and stood, pulling her into a hug and kissing the top of her head, "Absolutely."

Bryce bent over and made retching sounds. Hunter laughed and clapped his hands, mimicking Bryce.

~

Sean looked down at Aubrey as she sighed and rested her head on his shoulder, "You cold?" He asked, reaching for one of the blankets that Madison had brought into the barn.

"No," Aubrey smiled up at him, "I was just thinking about Ivar and Sav." She nodded in the direction of where Bryce and Ivar were making music, everyone who had come to the harvest campfire stood by, listening or dancing.

Every now and then, Ivar looked up from his guitar and smiled across the barn at Savannah.

Sean shook his head, "Never thought I'd see the day when Ivar was so head over heels for someone."

"He's in love, Sean."

"I know what that's like," Sean grinned, "First time I saw you, I was smitten."

Aubrey sat a little straighter and looked at him intently, "And when was that?" She raised an eyebrow coyly.

Sean thought for a moment and then took her hand in his, "I'd just joined your family's church. You were helping your brother carry something into the building, you were all rushing around and your strawberry-blonde hair was a mess." He reached out to brush a strand of her hair back.

"Despite being busy though, you stopped to help me find where I saw going," Sean laughed, "You told me that I looked as lost as a kangaroo in the arctic."

Aubrey squeezed her eyes shut, smiling brightly, "In my defence, you did look as lost as a kangaroo in the arctic."

Sean grinned again, he sighed and leaned back on his hands, enjoying the sound of Bryce's fiddle mixed with the gentle tunes of Ivar's guitar.

"Did Jason get all of the crops in?" He asked after a moment. Aubrey nodded and yawned, curling up next to him on the hay bale. "Yup, Dad says it was one of the best harvests on record."

Sean smiled and tucked his arms around his wife, enjoying the fading sunlight and the warmth from the campfire, his stomach filled to satisfaction with Madison's chicken casserole and Aubrey's pie.

~

"Well Cam, what do you think?" Caleb asked as he and Jason joined the firefighter by the snack table.

Neighbours and towns folk crowded around, swinging and dancing in time to the music that two of the Walker boys were playing with Madison.

"I think," Cameron said over the noise, "That grandma's sweet peppermint coffee is the best!"

"Better than your grandma's Tuesday vanilla coffee?" Jason said as he helped himself to a drink from the urn.

Cameron swished the dark creamy liquid around in his mug. "Tied. Depends what mood I'm in I guess."

Caleb took a sip from his forest fruit punch, "I think she should mix them." At the idea he turned towards the table and with his dad and nephew peering over his shoulder he grabbed a mug full of the sweet peppermint from one urn and a mug full of vanilla coffee from the other.

"Prepare to have your minds blown." He said while emptying one mug into the other.

Jason passed him a spoon and Caleb swirled the two together in his mug.

"Well?" Cameron asked as he watched his uncle take a drink from his concoction.

A slow but luminous grin broke across his uncle's face, "Man, I think I just beat mom's coffee."

Jason raised both eyebrows, "Now that is not possible. Maddie makes the best coffee ever."

"Here let me try that." Cameron said taking the mug from his uncle, he took a sip and his eyes grew as big as the saucers that the pumpkin pie was being served on.

"Ohhhh maaan, this is goood." He drained the end of the mug and smacked his lip, "I gotta get more of that."

Jason laughed and reached for his own mug, "I'm sure it's good. But I'm partial to Maddie's coffee blends."

"Just like you're partial to mom's aromatherapy blends. Ain't ya, Dad?" Caleb teased.

Jason jabbed his son in the side, "Oi. The farmhouse smells like lemongrass, cinnamon and lavender most days instead of mud, dirt, horses and multiple grandkids. Who am I to complain?"

The three men laughed quietly to themselves in the corner while they watched the people at the harvest bonfire from over the top of their steaming mugs.

After a few sips of Caleb's coffee blend, Jason groaned softly and said, "Don't tell Maddie I mixed these."

Cameron burst out laughing and gained several looks from his brothers and the friends.

Caleb grinned and nudged his dad back in the side, "Don't worry, Dad," he drawled, "Your secret is safe."

Jason nodded and took another sip of his hot drink. He groaned again and rolled his eyes heavenwards. "So good."

~Chapter Thirteen~
"You're David?"

The music stopped, Bryce half-dropping his bow as it screeched across the strings.

Cameron followed his brother's gaze to the barn door and saw the tall blond man standing there, leaning against the side of the band wearing a clean Air Force uniform.

His jaw dropped, he turned sharply as he heard Bryce drop his fiddle. A quick glance around told him that everyone from his family was staring at the man in the barn door.

Cameron moved towards him but his parents were on their feet and at his side quicker than he could have ever imagined they would be.

~

For former fighter pilot David Bryce Walker, it was the first time in eleven years that he had seen his family.

Strange, that was how it struck him. That even after all the time apart, he recognised his family, they hadn't changed. He had heard the bow on the fiddle go wonky and looked over to see a tall teenager who looked almost exactly like he had at that age, staring at him with wide green eyes.

He then saw Cameron, his younger, but now adult brother staring also, and then he was moving towards him.

Before Cameron could reach David though, David saw both of his parents getting up off of the hay bale they were sitting on and running across the barn towards him. His mom's arms were around his neck, almost knocking him over before he had time to breathe.

"Oh! David." Aubrey's voice was emotion-choked and close to his ear as her hot tears rolled down her face. Sean wrapped the both of them in a hug, holding him close as if at any moment he would be taken from them again.

Moving back, so Sean could have a good look, Aubrey put her arm around Cameron who had come to stand next to her, Sean cupped David's face in his hands and studied his weary face. "You haven't changed." Sean whispered.

David smiled weakly at him, he grasped his dad's hand and was then pulled into a tight embrace.

"Can we go inside the house?" David croaked, his voice was hoarse and had a distinct Carolina twang to it.

Sean nodded, he looked across the barn to where Jason was standing with half a burger falling out of his open mouth, "Jason, can you and Madison take care of this campfire?" He looked back at David, "We have something more important to deal with."

Jason closed his mouth, swallowed his food and nodded. He hadn't expected Aubrey's oldest son to turn up at the campfire.

Only a few days after the letter had arrived.

David saw his grandma push his younger brother Ivar forward, watching, fascinated as he stopped next to a young woman with reddish brown hair wearing a denim shirt and maroon skirt, to kiss her gently on the forehead and whisper something in her ear before coming to join the parents and Cameron.

His eyes were then drawn to the young blond fiddler, the young lady who Ivar had kissed on the forehead went over towards him and gave him a playful shove in the shoulder, "Go on Bryce." She said, loud enough for him to hear.

The boy didn't put his fiddle down. He walked across the barn, making a straight bee line for the group by the barn doors.

As he got closer, David saw the strong likeness between him and his dad.

"You're David?" The boy asked once he was standing in front of him.

David swallowed and nodded, the last time he had seen the boy, he had only been six, almost seven.

"And you're Bryce." David reached out a hand, his youngest brother's youth making him feel old.

Bryce nodded slowly.

"You don't recognise me do you?"

Bryce's eyes flickered across to where his parents stood, he then looked back at David and shook his head.

Sean put a hand on each of their shoulders, "Let's go into the house."

~Chapter Fourteen~

Bryce's smile gave him a release to fall back into his old farm boy life and place.

David spread his fingers out across the coffee table. He felt shy around his own family, *I hardly know them anymore.* As soon as the thought occurred to him he laughed inwardly, *they are your family, David. You spent the first seventeen years of your life with them. You face-timed and called them every day until your plane went down.*

David looked up to see Ivar's face inches from his own, "Yahoo, earth to David."

David blinked at him, "Huh?"

"You zoned out." Aubrey said from the other sofa, Sean who was sitting next to her raised his eyebrows, smiled slightly at him. "So." Sean said, stretching his arms along the top of the sofa, "What happened?"

David appreciated them all giving him space to sit on the sofa alone. He felt nervous, jittery and out of place in his uniform surrounded by checkered shirts, work boots and floral dresses. He could see his dad's hand on his mom's shoulder, a signal for her to stay next to him and not crowd David.

He swallowed and tried to ignore Bryce's penetrating gaze from across the room.

Finally David looked up, the room smelt of cinnamon and soft pine chips, it was familiar and comforting. The sound of an owl outside in the barn calmed David's ragged nerves.

A dog he had never seen before padded into the room, his large dark eyes looked around everywhere, before going across to David and putting his chin on the man's knee.

Dogs had always made David feel comforted and safe. After all, they were called man's best friend for a reason.

David absently stroked the dog's silky ears.

"Kit, you traitor." Ivar hissed to the dog from the other side of the room.

Cameron smiled, "That's Kit."

David nodded, "Like a kit kat?"

"Yeah, he's a bit attached to Bryce and Ivar. Ivar's gone a bit green-eyed now he's giving you attention."

David smiled down at the collie, it felt good to have a dog by his side again. He looked up to see Ivar smiling also.

Why am I so nervous? He tried to figure out an answer to his own question, *it's because I've been away so long,* he glanced sideways at Bryce who was leaning against the fireplace, the glowing embers in the grate reflected off of the boy's face, causing him to look young and vulnerable.

Bryce looked up in that moment and caught his brother's gaze. David swallowed and then knew why he was feeling so out of it. *Does Bryce accept me?*

Across the room, Bryce held his gaze for as long as possible, unblinking.

God! You gotta help me. He prayed. The lord the words from the book Jason had lent him back to mind for the second time that week. Instead *of just reacting in the natural physical realm, based on your emotions, faith considers, "What does God's word say?"*

Bryce stopped himself from grinding his teeth, he took a deep breath and whispered to himself in his spirit.

"I love your David. You're my brother and I choose to love you as a part of my family."

When he looked up David was still watching him.

Cameron saw the exchange, he knew Bryce didn't know a thing about David. He also knew what David must be feeling like.

Finally, David pulled his gaze away, only to see Bryce grin quickly like a young schoolboy who had just caught sight of his oldest and best friend across the classroom.

David felt a twinge inside of him and he wondered what he had missed out on all those years.

Bryce's smile gave him a release to fall back into his old farm boy life and place.

"So?" Ivar prodded, "What happened?"

David leaned back into the sofa, grabbing one of the winter themed throw cushions that Madison had put out, and hugged it to himself. "What do you know first of all? I'll fill in the blanks."

"We were only told that your plane went missing over the Pacific. They assumed that you had crashed and drowned." Aubrey said weakly, all the emotions from that day rose up in her throat.

Sean gave her a gentle squeeze, kissing the side of her forehead, "Shh, it's okay."

Aubrey nodded and took up the knitting Madison had left half-done on the side board. The needles flew back and forth as Aubrey kept her eyes on the wool, trying not to cry.

Someone squeezed her hand, stopping the panicked knitting. She looked up to see that David had leaned forward, reaching across the space between them to touch her, he smiled faintly and Aubrey touched a hand to his face, she swallowed and closed her eyes, "I missed you so much."

"I missed you too." David's voice broke and he blinked rapidly, sitting back he ran a hand through his wavy hair, he waited a moment before continuing.

"My plane went down but it didn't crash. I noticed there was an engine fault, and that if I didn't land I'd crash, so I belly-landed the plane onto the water. It was stormy and a wave threw her back up in the air causing me to smash my head against the top of the cockpit, it knocked me out and the plane was left to float and slowly sink, when I woke up I was surrounded in water up to my chest. I got out and onto the wing, staying there until the plane sunk and then I was left to tread water until a small boat found me."

David tilted his head listening as it started to rain outside, *perfect,* he thought, and then smiled.

His mind still worked according to the farm, they would have just brought the harvest in and the rains would do the dry ground good.

Turning back to his family he said, "It turns out my plane had gone down somewhere in the Pacific near the California coastline. A small boat that had gone too far out that day found me just before I gave up all hope."

Bryce noticed that his accent became slightly more pronounced as he talked.

"My knock on the head during the landing had caused me to lose my memory." David said slowly.

Bryce thought his mom's eyes were about to fall out, they were so wide.

David shook his head, "For the next eleven years I stayed in California, memories slowly came back but I couldn't remember where I was from and who I was."

"Sorta the two most important things to know." Ivar commented from his perch on the coffee table.

David rolled his eyes, smirking slightly, "I know that."

Ivar wiggled his eyebrows at him.

Swallowing, David continued, "it wasn't until last year that the couple I was staying with took me to one of those large open air rallys. There I learnt that faith is basically seeing things from God's perspective. That if I planted words of healing and good memory, I would reap a good harvest."

He looked up as Bryce practically bolted up from his seat at his words, Cameron grabbed him by the back of his trousers, yanking him back down. "Hold your horses cowboy."

Bryce sat back down and pulled the ends of his shirt sleeves over his hands, tucking him under his chin.

"Anyway," David said, "last month I got my miracle. I went straight back to the Air Force base and they contacted you. I am now out of the Air Force and plan on staying exactly where I am the rest of my life."

Sean let out a long whistle from between his teeth, "Looks like this family is just full of miracles."

David squinted, "What do you mean?"

Sean smiled slowly, "Cameron, how's about you tell your story first."

"Right." Cameron got up, slapping his knees as he did so, "David, let's go riding."

"Riding, you mean you still have Trojan?"

"Yup, hey Bryce is that new horse ready to ride?"

Bryce nodded, "Panorama, Pano for short."

"Nice name," Cameron winked and clapped Bryce on the shoulder as he walked past him with David on his way out.

Bending down so that Bryce could hear him, Cameron whispered, "Remember, It's going to be okay. And, what you plant today, you will harvest tomorrow."

Bryce nodded slowly, smiling at him, "Thanks Cam."

David watched from the door, feeling a twinge of jealousy at the relationship his brothers had with each other.

He'd missed out on it all. It wasn't his fault, it wasn't anyone's fault. But he had a lifetime to make up for it.

~Chapter Fifteen~

I will say of the Lord, he is my refuge and my fortress, my God in whom I trust.
Psalm 91:2

"Hey, you okay?"

Bryce looked over his shoulder at Reese as she came out the back door and stood on the porch, watching him as he gathered the chopped logs and piled them into the wood store. "Yeah, I'm okay. Why?"

Reese shrugged and zipped up her hoodie as she walked towards him and started to help pick up the wood, "I dunno, you just seem…confused? Conflicted?"

Bryce dumped an armload of wood, "Conflicted is a good word for it." He glanced skywards, "It's going to rain again. You should get inside, Reese."

Instead of doing as he said, Reese sat down on a large tree stump and watched her cousin as he finished splitting logs, "It's funny. You boys are so alike and you don't even recognise it."

"Huh?" Bryce looked at her quizzically, his blond hair hanging down over his eyes as he bent to pick up the ax again. "What do you mean?"

"Well, last summer when you were in hospital," Reese had to stop, talking about the year before always choked her up.

She'd never tell anyone, but Bryce was her favourite cousin, she was closest to him. Maybe it was because they were closer in age, only three years apart, but it was something else. Bryce wasn't just Reese's cousin, he was like a brother to her.

"Last summer when you were ill, when you had that second wave and went so downhill we all thought we'd lose you. Cameron came out here and started splitting logs to let out some of his pent up energy and fears."

She rubbed the back of her neck, "I had a bit of a go at him." Reese bit the inside of her cheek, dragging the heel of her ankle boot through the dirt, "What's there to feel conflicted about Bryce?"

The ax stopped mid-swing, going limp in Bryce's hand. He straightened and stared at her, squinting so he could look at her face in the fading light. "I dunno. I just feel all mixed up about David. I know what I'm meant to do. I've chosen to love him as he's my brother. I've talked this through with God. It's just not easy. But it helps to know that he's my shelter and that he's helping me through it."

He shrugged and took another swing at a stubborn log. Lighting cracked, zigzagging across the sky in a flash of light. Thunder rolled and the heavens opened, Reese jumped up, screeching and making a dash past Bryce for the house.

Laughing, Bryce caught her hand and pulled her into the woodshed, putting his arm around her shoulders as they took cover from the freezing rain.

"I don't know," he said, speaking as if they had been deep in conversation about the subject for hours and not just mere minutes. "I guess I feel conflicted because I've never met him, didn't even know he existed and he's here now and I don't know what to do? But also, on the other hand I can see that David needs help, help to settle back in, help to feel like he belongs with us again."

Bryce sighed, peering out of the woodshed and into the rain, "I want to help him. But I'm confused as to how to be.

It's like having a stranger walk into my life, but yet, he's my brother…am I making sense?" He glanced down at Reese.

Reese stopped picking at the loose thread of a hessian bag she had found under a stack of wood, "Yeah it makes sense. You two seem to have a lot in common though."

"Oh?" Bryce joined her floor, dragging his fingers through the piles of wood chips that covered the floor.

"You both love the fiddle, animals, the farm and you both have had a miraculous healing."

"Yeah that's another thing, how do I tell him about everything that happened last year? He'll want to know all about me Reese." Bryce closed his eyes, taking a deep breath,

"I just…" he shook his head and let go of a handful of wood chips, watching as they hit the floor, dust and sand swirling in a small tornado before settling back down again.

"So tell him." Reese said.

Bryce pursed his lips, he created a small hammock with the end of his red shirt, pouring the wood chips into it.

"Bryce, Aunt Aubrey ain't gonna be best pleased with ya pouring wood shavings all over your shirt."

Bryce grinned at her, "Aw Reese, don't ruin my fun." He created a small hollow part in the pile of shavings and picked up an acorn from the floor from where it had fallen from the trees outside the woodshed, "Ta da!"

He brushed off his hands by clapping them together.

His cousin stared at him blankly.

"What?" He asked.

Reese pointed at what he made, "What the heck is it?"

"A wood and sand tower, topped with an acorn."

"You're such a child," she laughed, reaching over and pushing the pile off of him.

Bryce pouted playfully. "Reeeesey…" he frowned down at the mess and then smiled up at her, a glance out the door told him the rain wasn't going to let up, getting up he brushed the dirt off of himself and held out a hand, "C'mon, we might as well run for it. Besides, I think it's dinner,"

Taking Bryce's hand, Reese got up and followed him as they ran across the yard and into the kitchen.

~

Sean looked up from his dinner, "So Jason, how did the rest of the campfire go? Sorry we missed the end of it."

Jason shook his head and put his fork down, swallowing the food in his mouth before speaking, "Nah, it's fine, we all pretty much made a run for it when the rain came." He laughed and turned his eyes onto Madison, her hair had just started to dry, causing it to curl slightly around her face. "Maddie and I had a bit of a mishap when running back down to the house."

"Oh? What was that?" Cameron asked before popping a baby potato into his mouth.

Caleb sniggered and then choked on his water, Emma patted him on the back as Jade said, "Dad, you really have got to stop doing that."

Caleb looked at her helplessly before trying to clear his throat.

He motioned for Emma to speak, Emma smiled at her husband, rubbing his back as he tried to get his breath back, "Jason and Madison slipped on the path and both went sliding in the mud all the way down to the gate."

There was silence at the table.

Then Bryce broke it by saying, "Aww, grandma, ya should have used a wagon."

Aubrey sent her youngest a look across the table.

Jason grinned, "Don't worry Aubrey-girl, Bryce is right, it would have been better to use that than sliding down on our backsides."

Madison snorted and reached for the gravy, "You're tellin' me. Say David, has anyone told you about Bryce and his wagon yet?"

David raised an eyebrow, "No?" He cocked his head to the side, a smile playing across his tired face, "What happened?"

"Who's gonna tell him?" Caleb asked, taking a second attempt at drinking his water.

Emma's hand hovered behind his back, just in case.

Bryce caught Reese's eye across the room and waved his fork in the air, spraying gravy everywhere, "I will,"

"Bryce, put your fork down. I swear you act like a five year old sometimes." Aubrey said firmly, though her eyes twinkled as she mopped up splotches of gravy off the cabinet behind him.

Bryce grinned sheepishly at his mom before turning to face his brother who could have easily been his twin if it wasn't for the difference in age. "Last summer it was stinking hot, so Uncle Caleb inspired me with this amazin' idea."

Caleb waved his hands as if in a time out, "Hold it. I ain't got nothin to do with nothin." He choked on the peas he was eating and Emma ended up slapping him on the back again, trying not to cry with laughter.

Savannah who was seated next to Ivar nudged him slightly, he glanced down at her, "What?"

Savannah smiled, "I see where you get your clumsy side from now."

Ivar almost spat out his chicken, "I'm not clumsy."

"The ladder."

Ivar's cheeks reddened and he tried to focus his attention back on Bryce's story, but Savannah was hiding a laugh next to him and he ended up in the same situation as his uncle.

Bryce raised an eyebrow at his brother before finishing his story, "We got the wagon from the barn and all of us piled in, we coasted down the hill and right into the lake." He slammed his fist into the table as if it were the lake.

"I wode the wagon too!" Hunter exploded from the other side of the table, flinging his arms out and sending food everywhere.

Bryce watched David's face from across the room as he ducked Hunter's peas. His older brother seemed almost lost. Like he wasn't sure how to react.

A glance around the dining room showed him how blessed he was. And David had missed out on it for ten years.

All of a sudden he felt an overwhelming sense of importance hit him. Like the Lord was showing him what he needed him to do.

It's a field, Bryce. The spirit whispered. *It's a field that needs cultivating and harvesting. I want you to plant seeds.*

It seemed like a mammoth job to Bryce. That was until he saw his mom laughing with his dad and saw Savannah trying to help Emma stop both Caleb and Ivar from choking. Then he knew. It wasn't going to be hard.

In fact, he knew with God it would be easy.

All David needed to know was that he was loved.

By all of them. Even him.

~Chapter Sixteen~

David looked confused and Bryce looked sad, like he was remembering something.

Later when Ivar was saying goodnight and goodbye to Savannah on the porch, Cameron caught Bryce peeping through a gap in the door. "What, you spying now?"

Bryce grinned and shook his head, putting a finger to his lips, indicating for him to be quiet. "I've never seen Ivar be so mushy before."

"Say who is she?" David had come up behind them, and was leaning over both of their shoulders, spying on Ivar along with them.

Cameron shook his head and rolled his eyes, "Ivar is gonna whoop us you know that right?"

"Eh," Bryce shrugged it off and brushed his hair back out of the way, "He's our brother, gives us licence to spy on him." He grinned, "That's Savannah." He said, answering David's former question, "She's his fiancée."

David blinked, then his nose wrinkled up, "Ivar's engaged?"

"No, he's a widower." Bryce said dryly.

David elbowed him and the two laughed, Cameron clapped a hand over both of their mouths as they grew too loud. "Shut up." He hissed, "you want Ivar to catch us?"

"Catch you, huh?"

The three young men who had been kneeling on the floor, peeking through the key hole, looked up to see Ivar standing in the now open doorway.

Savannah was gone and their brother wasn't looking too impressed.

"Really Bryce, you stooped to spying." Ivar planted his hands firmly on his hips, frowning.

Bryce got up slowly, it was clear that his brother was actually ticked. "Sorry Ivar, I didn't know you'd take it this way," he blushed, embarrassed and half hung his head as he stuffed his hands into his jean pockets and scuffed the side of his riding boots along the floor.

Ivar let out a long breath. Eyeing up his younger brother for a moment, "Was this Bryce's idea?" He asked, directing his question at his two older brothers.

David shook his head and Cameron nodded, Ivar cracked a smile and patted David on the shoulder, "One thing you need to know about Bryce, he's always getting into trouble. If it was his idea, just say so." He laughed, "Trust me. It's easier."

David bit his lip and looked at Bryce, the boy was grinning wickedly at him. "I don't like the looks of that." David started, motioning to Bryce.

Cameron glanced at him and laughed, "Uh oh. Ivar, better run."

"Run?" David repeated as both Cameron and Ivar took off down the hallway towards the back porch.

David turned slowly back towards Bryce, only to see the blond boy spring at him suddenly, laughing as he pinned him down.

David, a strongly built former pilot, quickly overturned Bryce, pinning his arms behind him. He put his knee on Bryce's back, smiling in triumph as Bryce squirmed, turning to get free.

Reese came in just as David moved backwards, sitting on Bryce's legs so he'd stop flailing about.

Reese saw Bryce wince every so slightly and even though he was laughing and trying to get a shot at his brother, she saw the way his leg was bent while he tried to land a good punch. She knew it wasn't hurting him, but just seeing Bryce helpless—even if it was in a friendly wrestling match—and his leg bent at the knee troubled her.

She turned to David, her eyes flashing. "You get off of him right now!"

Her screaming brought the rest of the family running into the front room, Caleb was the first in, he saw his two nephews paused mid wrestle. David looked confused and Bryce looked sad, like he was remembering something.

Then he saw Reese, her face screwed up as she tried to stop herself from crying, her fists clenching and unclenching.

"Oh baby girl." Caleb pulled his daughter towards him, hugging her, "Shh, it's okay. No one or anything is gonna hurt Bryce. He's okay Reese, it's not hurting him. They're just wrestling."

David got off of Bryce and they both stood up, Jason and Aubrey barrelled into the room followed by Jade and Madison, "What's going on?" Aubrey asked, she looked at Caleb, her eyes asking questions.

Caleb nodded towards Bryce, his eyes flickering down to his leg, then back at Reese. "They were wrestling." Caleb said quietly.

"Ah," Aubrey nodded, understanding at once.

Going over she hugged Bryce with one arm, rubbing his shoulder, "Reese, it's okay love. Bryce is fine."

Bryce nodded in agreement and put a hand on the back of Reese's top, "I'm fine Reesey."

Reese peeked at her cousin, her eyes wet. Bryce grinned and opened his arms, she walked into them. Hugging him tightly.

David, who was already looking baffled beyond belief, was even more confused when Reese sniffed and said to him, "Sorry for shouting at you David. I…I just remembered last year. I freaked out, I'm sorry."

David nodded and said it was fine, but once Caleb and Bryce had taken Reese out of the room and to the barns for a ride on Charis, Apple and Pepper, he turned to Jason.

"I have no idea what just happened."

Jason looked at his daughter, his eyebrows pinched together, "Aubrey girl? You haven't told him yet?"

Aubrey tugged on her strawberry blonde hair that she had wound into a tight braid. "Not yet. Sean and I were waiting for Bryce to tell him…but maybe Bryce isn't ready yet." She smiled sadly at David, "Bryce didn't remember you very well once you went missing. We never…never told him about you. Thought you wouldn't want him to know at such a young age. Years went by and we never told him, and didn't want to hurt him."

She rubbed at the tears on her own face and then smoothed her hands down the front of her ankle-length red dress. "We know that was wrong now. But you can see why Bryce is so cautious around you."

Aubrey swallowed, "You're like a stranger to him, that's why he hasn't told you about last year."

David chewed the inside of his cheek, he hooked his thumbs into the front pockets of his jacket, "I see." He frowned and squinted at the floor, "I think I understand. Can't miss what you don't know you have, right?"

Aubrey shook her head distressed, "David, please don't think we didn't tell him because we didn't want him to know who you were. We were so proud of you. Loved you so much."

Madison walked across to her daughter, Jade had slipped out the room ages ago, giving them some space.

She hugged Aubrey to herself and spoke over her head to David, "Your parents were devastated when we heard the news, David. It ripped your mom's heart out. It was too hard for her to talk about."

David understood, reaching out he squeezed his mom's shoulder, "Mom?"

Aubrey turned and threw her arms around his neck. "I'm so sorry," she wept. David rubbed her back, after a moment he pulled back and said weakly, "It's okay. What happened last year?"

"Uh Aubrey, I'll tell him." Jason offered, he picked up his Stetson from the top of the piano and motioned David out of the room.

~Chapter Seventeen~
'And by his stripes, we are healed.' 1 Peter 2:24

"You rode Pano with Cam the other day, didn't you David?" Jason reached over the stall to stroke behind Pano's ears.

David nodded and grabbed the saddle, thankful he had pulled on his US Air Force jacket as he had left the house.

The camouflaged fabric brought comfort to David as he swung up onto the horse's back. He'd never fly with the airforce again. But he would always love aviation.

David heard laughter as they exited the barns on horseback, he looked over his shoulder and smiled crookedly as he saw Jade and Hunter watching him from the barn.

"What's so funny?" He asked.

Hunter squealed with laughter and buried his flushed face in Jade's skirt.

Jade laughed and brushed her dark hair back over her shoulder, "You look odd. A bit outaplace in your uniform jacket in cowboy boots on horseback."

David looked down at his outfit, he wanted to frown, he liked his jacket. But Jade was right, he did look odd. A bit out of place. Looking up at his young cousins he shrugged, "Don't have another jacket."

Hunter's face pinched together, then his eyes flew open and his mouth half dropped as he whispered loudly, "I get wyou new jackewet."

He then disappeared into the house.

David looked at his grandpa, Jason shrugged and smiled lazily. "Cute isn't he."

David nodded, tears in his eyes, "Didn't even know I had another cousin."

Jason smiled and reached down to stroke Maple's soft mane. "Mmm, Hunter's six soon."

As if on cue, Hunter came trotting out of the house, a jacket ten sizes too large for him flapping on his arms, "Here wyou gwo Dawid." He flapped his arms, looking like an overactive bird as the jacket sleeves billowed.

Laughing, David bent down and grabbed the jacket, "Thanks bud." He messed up Hunter's hair, laughing.

Jason waved as Jade took Hunter's hand and headed towards the chicken coop, "I thought we'd ride into town."

David nodded and pulled on the new coat, it was denim with a fleece inlining. "Ok."

~

"Any new places you don't recognise?" Jason asked as they rode Maple and Pano through the Main Street. Someone reclining on a chair on an old porch waved and called out a greeting to Jason.

"Who's that?" David asked.

Jason tipped his hat at the man as they rode past, "That's Bob Holler, he and his wife Maisy run the local hardware store."

Recognition dawned across his grandson's face, "Yeah, yeah! I remember now." He looked across the street towards the grocery store, "Do the Matthews still run the Peak grocery store?"

Jason grinned, "Only the finest fresh fruit and veg this side of Pike's Peak." He quipped, quoting the slogan that was written in fancy cursive across the top sign.

The next store that David saw was whitewashed and wooden with a curved blue sign above it that said, '*Van Dykes milkshakes and ice.*'

"That's new." He said flippantly, wondering if the Scandinavian styled building fitted in with the rustic cowboy styled town. The door to the café opened and David saw Ivar's fiancée walk out, her floral skirt swinging as she tugged on her coat and walked down the street.

"Hey Grandpa, ain't that Ivar's girl?"

Jason nodded and adjusted the collar of his coat as a cold breeze started up. "Savannah Van Dyke, her father Peter owns the café." He smiled and nodded towards the fork in the road where an old blue pick up had stopped and a young man jumped out.

Ivar waved at his grandpa and brother before sprinting down the road to catch his fiancée before she disappeared into the general store.

David's laughter thundered in his chest, "I still don't understand why we have Peak's grocery store and the general store. Say, who owns it now?"

"Uh," Jason scratched the back of his neck and eyed the general stores wooden exterior. "Miss Sarah Foster. A friend of your mom's actually. Miss Foster helped Aubrey a great deal during Bryce's hospital stay."

The words had slipped out and David pounced at his chance, "Bryce's hospital stay? Is that what happened last year?"

A sigh escaped Jason and he swept his blue eyes across what he could see of pikes peek. "There's a trail a little ways down here. Come on." He clicked his tongue and squeezed Maples's sides with his knees, "Onwards girl."

David followed his grandpa until they reached a small river trail that his grandpa said ran up and through his property. Large trees with red and golden leaves formed an arch overhead as they rode their horses across the leaf strewn path.

"So," David prodded, "what happened last year?"

Instead of answering, Jason reached into his back pocket and pulled out a folded piece of paper, "Bryce gave this to me last Christmas. Read it."

"Would he be okay with this?"

Jason thought for a moment before nodding, "Yeah. Yeah I think he would."

Carefully, David unfolded the paper and then read what was written on it in Bryce's small neat handwriting,

I was just sixteen. Yet that's never too young. I was dying, but a word from you made the sickness run. You're the God of my days. The God of all power. The strength in my weakness. The breath in my lungs. The reason I'm here, just seventeen years of age. When they said my life was over, you turned another page. Kept writing my story. Day after day. In the rain. In the storm. You were there, walking on the sea. Through the dark. Across the swells. Just to get to me.

"I don't understand." David said quietly, folding the paper back up.

Jason tilted his head, his greying hair falling across his forehead, similar to the way Cameron's reddish brown fringe fell across his when he inclined his head to the side.

"Last summer." He started slowly, as if groping for the right words to say. "Last summer, Bryce was rushed to hospital with high fevers and in agony. He had an operation that same day. For two and a half weeks the doctors fought for his life the only way they knew how. And we fought for his life in prayer. Halfway through the third week, Bryce went downhill. He wasn't with it, they had to sedate him and it was one of the bleakest times of our lives. His life was in the balance and it seemed we would lose him."

Jason pulled his jacket closer, turning up the collar as if he could still feel the chill that the sterile hospital walls sent down his spine every time he had walked down the hallway to Bryce's room.

"The doctors wanted to take Bryce in for a second operation. Sean asked for time to talk to your mom about it and we all got prayin'. While we were praying, God gave your mom a promise, David. No more surgery. Three simple words, but a promise nether the less. A promise we stood on and refused surgery."

David could only imagine what the doctors' reaction would have been to his family saying no to a life -aving operation for his younger brother.

"He was discharged the next day." Jason's voice rose an octave and he bounced slightly in the saddle as the energy and adrenaline of the moment surged through his veins once more.

David blinked. "Pardon?"

"He was discharged."

David blinked again, at a loss for words. "What?"

Jason shot him a look, "Boy. Don't you listen? I said, your brother was discharged the next morning." He grinned, revealing a set of perfectly white straight teeth. "God healed Bryce overnight David. The doctors were baffled. Confused. Challenged. They didn't know what had happened and they wanted him out. Bryce was laying on that hospital bed, his body racked with fever and pain, dying. Fighting for his life, struggling to stay awake and to keep on fighting. Then, during the night it switched, God held true to his promise David."

He took a breath and then kept going.

"Bryce was sent home to us the next day. Alive and well. Oh and get this, there had been another boy on the ward at the same time with the same illness, when Bryce went back a week or so after to get checked up, he practically waltzed into that room. Head held high, eyes all shining and bright. And the other kid was still using his crutches. It just shows you David, when our God heals, it ain't partial."

"No sir," David murmured quietly, without even noticing the fact that they were coming close to the farm now.

"He ain't into the partial business. It's whole. Complete and finished."

~Chapter Eighteen~
'The Lord is my shepherd. I shall not want.' Psalm 23:1

Bryce was looking over Reese's shoulder, watching the paint pool under her brush onto the canvas when the door opened and a pale-faced, shaken, David walked in.

Jason had his hand on David's shoulder, he smiled at Bryce, winked, and walked into the kitchen where Bryce heard his voice soften as he spoke to Madison.

Reese looked up from painting a blue border around a starlit mountain range. "Should I give you two some space?"

Bryce swallowed. His mouth felt dry and cottony.

One part of him wanted Reese to stay, he didn't know David. But then, on the other hand, something inside of him tugged, like there was an alliance that had been there from the day he was born because of one thing.

David was his brother.

It was the strangest feeling Bryce had ever had, he stared at David, half listening as Reese gathered up her paints and papers, almost spilling the blue paint down the front of her white shirt.

She grinned at Bryce as she passed, bumped into the dresser and almost spilled the bright red paint all over Bryce's khaki shirt.

He rubbed the back of his neck, a thousand thoughts running through his head and the musical part of him jumped towards the song that his aunt had been playing earlier that day when she had been changing the sheets in the bedrooms.

The words started to leap around his head as the catchy tune tried to get past his mouth.

Bryce pressed his lips into a tight line though and stepped forward, pushing the music and art he had just been watching from his mind.

Whatever was up with David was more important than watching sky blue and lavender purple ooze together in an ombré effect under Reese's brush as she swirled it across the page. It was the same fierce fire that had flared up inside of him the day he heard Cam had gone missing during a fire.

The same pulsing loyalty that had swept over him when he had led his brother Ivar and his cousins all on a wild goose chase to the river and gotten them lost in a massive rain storm.

Drawing a long breath and pulling on every ounce of selflessness and courage he had. He stepped off the edge and took the plunge into uncertainty.

Bryce saw the paper in his brother's hand and knew what his grandpa had spoken to him about on the ride.

Without a word passing between the two of them, Bryce held out his hand and David grasped it in a tight, firm hold.

A moment's indecision and then he pulled on his brother's hand, yanking him into a hug.

~

Bryce's hug surprised David so much that he was stunned into silence and numbness. He hadn't seen Bryce since he was so young. He closed his eyes and held Bryce close, like a father holds his son. His entire time in Carolina, he had been haunted by the memory of three boys he had left when he joined service.

The sensible red head of a brother that was closest to him in age. The sober brunette with smiling eyes and the bouncing blond baby that had hung onto his mom's shirt wherever she went, laughing and chuckling his way through life.

Tears burned behind his eyes and his heart settled inside of his chest. He finally felt like he had come home.

He knew his other brothers and his family accepted him. But he had been waiting; waiting and painfully wondering if Bryce would accept him.

"Thank you." He whispered.

Somehow he knew Bryce knew what he was feeling.

Bryce tossed his blond hair out of the way, his emerald green eyes shining. "You're my brother, it's what I'm here for."

"What was it like?" David asked.

"I don't remember the pain I was in while in hospital. I remember the confusion and the fear. But I also remember the sense of not being alone. That God had something special for me to do and he wasn't finished with me yet. No memory of the pain in the hospital. Just the sense that I wasn't alone."

~Chapter Nineteen~
"Don't say it!"

"Okay well it's finally time to actually get you behind the wheel." Sean stood by the truck, rubbing the back of his neck as he debated within himself whether or not it was a good idea to let his son drive.

Cameron laughed and leaned against the hood of the truck, "Come on, Dad. It will be fine, you taught all of us to drive. And now, it's Bryce's turn."

"'sides," Bryce added from where he was standing looking at the truck steering wheel as if it were about to jump out and bite him, "how hard can it be?"

David walked up pulling a coat on, it had been a week since he and Bryce had had their nonverbal conversation after his ride with their grandpa.

He smiled warmly at his brother before sliding into the passenger seat, "Ready Bryce?"

Bryce swallowed and nodded, getting in behind the wheel, leaning out the window he looked at the large whitewashed farmhouse with bright blue shutters, "Ivar." He said mournfully, looking across at his brother who stood on the porch steps, next to the pumpkin lanterns with his arm around Savannah. "If I don't make it out of this driving lesson alive. Tell everyone I love them."

Ivar rolled his eyes and smiled wryly, "sure."

Still not fully convinced, Sean shoved his cap back and messed up his hair, "If Aubrey knew you were usin' the truck." He muttered.

David smiled, "Dad. Chill, it's fine. I'm a great driver."

By the hood, Cameron choked.

David glared at him, "what's that meant to mean?"

"Nothin'." Cameron grinned and then retreated a safe distance from the car.

Inside the truck, Bryce turned the aircon on as his nerves got the better of him and he felt a sweat break out across his forehead.

"Maybe I *should* try another day." He pushed open the door and was halfway out of it when David grabbed him by the belt loop of his trousers and pulled him back into the truck. "Nu-uh, you're learning to drive. We booked your test already for after Christmas."

Bryce muttered something under his breath that David couldn't hear, but he adjusted the mirrors and buckled himself in. Staring at the wheel, his fingers tightening and then relaxing again.

David looked at him, amused, "Ready when you are. We have all day."

Bryce nodded, *ease off the clutch and slowly push the accelerator. What's the worst that can happen, right? I'm on a level surface and everything. Oh yeah, handbrake. Release the handbrake. Check. So now just slowly-*

His thought track ended quickly when David put an arm on the back of his seat and glanced out the blue truck's back window, "You'd better start soon. Ain't that Mom's SUV coming up the drive?"

"What?" Bryce, who had just started to shift the truck into first gear, spun around in his seat to see, all at the same moment he slammed both feet against all the pedals at the same time in his panic.

~

It was only once the smoke had cleared from the front windscreen that Bryce could see his entire family-including his mom-standing in front of the truck, watching the black smoke curling up from the hood.

He opened his mouth to say something and then closed it again. *Did I just…wow yep,* Bryce thought to himself privately, *I blew up the car. Personally, I'm surprised I didn't get knocked out with how loud that bang was. I hope it's not too bad cuz that'd be awkward…and it's dad's car and all.* He looked sideways at David.

His brother was staring straight ahead, his hand as white as death gripping the handle.

Slowly he turned to look at his brother, "Did you just?"

"Don't say it." Bryce said.

David looked back towards the bonnet where smoke was pouring out of and Ivar was hollering at Cameron to use his firefighter skills. Their dad was just standing there, his mouth hanging open and his cap half-falling off of his head.

Their mom had a look of pure disbelief on her face as she put her bag and car keys down on the porch steps.

The smoke was clearing a bit now and Bryce's pale face could be seen through the blacked out windscreen.

"Don't say it!" Bryce said again as David opened his mouth. They both swallowed and sat there for a few more moments, their mouths opening and closing, guppy fish style.

"I get the feeling dad's truck isn't blue anymore." David finally managed.

Bryce looked at him. "Really?"

"Well, you did just—"

"Don't say it."

Bryce took several long breaths, "I think I'll stay in here a few more minutes. Give them all a moment to cool off." He tried to still his shaking hands, "While I calm down from my near death driving lesson."

A look at David told him that he blamed him, "Not that I had a great driving instructor or anything."

David's mouth fell open for the sixteenth time since the loud bang when Bryce had jammed all the gears and floored all the pedals at the same time.

"You're blaming me for this?"

"Partially."

Instead of protesting, David nodded subliminally, his mind still reeling from what just happened.

There was a tap on Bryce's window and he opened the door, "Did you just—" Ivar began.

"Don't—" Bryce tried to interrupt.

"—just blow up the truck?" Ivar finished quickly.

"—say it…" Bryce trailed off miserably as David poked him in the back of the ribs, "He said it."

~Chapter Twenty~

Aubrey saw him coming though before he was even halfway through his dive and side-stepped, causing him to trip over his younger brother who had dropped down onto the floor and land face first in the tinsel box.

Two days before Thanksgiving on November 26th, Savannah turned up at the Walker bungalow, her arms ladened with a large box.

Ivar opened the door and his three brothers crowded in the corner laughing and mimicking his brothers blushing.

Ivar ignored them and invited his fiancée into the front room where Aubrey had been busy turning all the males in her house into her Thanksgiving elves—soon to be Christmas elves.

Looking up from the list in her hand, Aubrey smiled at Savannah and then swept a hand to the only empty seat on the decoration-piled sofa across the room from where she and Sean perched on the edge of the coffee table. "Oh Sav! Thank goodness you're here."

Her cheeks were flushed as she appraised her list again before skeptically eyeing the box of Christmas bulbs. "You don't know how much I long for female company some days. Would you sort my son out? He's not convinced that it's time to put up Christmas decorations yet."

"Ivar thinks we should wait *until after* Thanksgiving," Bryce chirped, pushing himself up onto the counter top, "He's being the grinch."

Hands firmly on her hips, Savannah turned to look at Ivar who had started sorting through the box of garlands she had brought.

He looked up to see her staring at him. "What?"

"It's never too early for Christmas decorations, Ivar! It's almost the first of December and they ain't up yet?" She shook her head and tucked a rebellious strand of hair back behind her ear.

Ivar looked at her dolefully for a moment before he held up a candy cane coloured hair ribbon, "Is this yours?" He asked, his eyes twinkling like the fairy lights Aubrey had ordered Cameron and David to string about the kitchen diner.

Turning red, Savannah took the ribbon from him, no one had ever seen her with the ribbon in her hair, Ivar grinned and followed her into the kitchen part of the open-plan front room. He cornered her against the worktop playfully, teasing her and coaxing her into putting the ribbon in her hair.

Bryce made a retching noise by shoving his finger down his throat.

Sean elbowed him, "Stop it,"

Bryce grinned, he rustled around inside of a large box and produced a turkey hat, "Hey David! It's definitely your turn to wear this." He hopped over a tangled pile of lights and slammed the hat down on David's head.

"Oh yeah." Cameron nodded in approval, his forehead creased in deep concentration, "Suits you very well."

Their mom waved a holly covered book, "Don't talk so fast Cam. I have a photo of each of you wearing one."

The mention of the photo album caused Ivar to spin on his heels, the candy cane ribbon quickly forgotten as he lunged across the room for it.

Aubrey saw him coming though before he was even half way through his dive and side stepped, causing him to trip over his younger brother who had dropped down onto the floor and land face first in the tinsel box.

Ivar emerged, spitting out pieces of the silvery plastic, he glowered at his mom who was producing baby photos of him with the turkey hat on his head with a flourish to his future wife.

Catching the look on his face, Sean smiled and shook his head, "Don't worry about it Ivar. She'll bring out the others when it's their turn to get married."

"I'm burning them." Bryce concluded, "before Mom has any ideas for my wedding day." He played with a lighter, causing it to flicker in and off.

Cameron confiscated it from Bryce, putting it away while Bryce trailed after him saying how becoming a firefighter had made him a spoil sport.

Sean snorted as he heard Bryce get called childish, he peered over a stack of Christmas books to see David enjoying the site of his family getting ready for the holidays.

"You okay, David?"

"Yeah," he held up a stuffed reindeer, "I remember this little guy. I used to put him on the window every year so we could see him from outside."

"Really?" Bryce asked as he came back their way, pulling a large fluffy Christmas jumper that he had found over his head. The robin on the front of the jumper had fair lights for eyes that flashed on and off.

David nodded, handing it to him.

Bryce looked the reindeer over, grinning, "Let's do it."

Standing up, David followed Bryce to the window. "Cam's right. You really don't act your age do you?"

Bryce shook his head, "Nah. I'm getting older, no use in acting older too."

The entire room paused at his comment.

Savannah looked at him especially confused as if she was trying to work out what he had just said in her head, a second past and she let out a small gasp that made Ivar look at her.

"You okay?"

"Yeah, yeah," she waved him away, "it's just what Bryce said."

"I know right." Cameron smirked, "he actually said something intelligent for once."

~

Aubrey sipped her cup of hot chocolate at the base of the Scandinavian-style decorated tree.

Savannah did decorating and interior design for work and Aubrey and Sean had asked her to help decorate their tree that year as she and Ivar were getting married on New Year's Eve.

She looked up from her frothy drink to see Ivar hovering by the back door. She could see Savannah's silhouette form outside as she paced the patio on the phone.

"Ivar love, come sit down." Aubrey held out a hand and he smiled, walked over and sat next to her.

Bryce had taken Reese, Hunter and Jade out for hot apple juice and cinnamon in the park while Caleb and Emma had a night to themselves up at the farm.

"Where's Cam?" Ivar asked, noticing David and Sean in the hallway debating whether or not the white garland should go above or below the small banister that led to the mezzanine level, the only part of the bungalow that wasn't on the same floor as everything else.

"He was dropping Bryce and your cousins off at the park but knowing him he's probably tagged along. A big kid. Both of your brothers."

"What about David?" Ivar asked, interested to know what his mom thought of his oldest brother.

Aubrey glanced over her shoulder, "He's more stoic and undemonstrative than I remember. When it's not to do with his family he's quite stoic," she laughed and shook her head, her strawberry blonde hair swinging across her back as she did. "I love him though, he's grown up plenty." She reached out and put a hand on the side of his face, "Like all of you. You did a lot of growing last year didn't you?"

A faint smile danced across Ivar's tired face, he yawned and slid down the sofa, enjoying the feeling of the cool leather sofa behind his back as he sat on the floor, stretching out so his feet hit the grey and white fur rug on the floor. "I've learnt another thing."

"Oh? What's that?" Aubrey squinted, running her fingers through his dark hair.

Ivar grinned up at her wickedly as his fiancée walked back into the kitchen diner, putting her phone away. "That being your Christmas or Thanksgiving elves ain't as easy as I remember."

Aubrey swatted his hand and smiled at Savannah as she got up to put her mug in the sink. "I hope you know what you're getting yourself into dear." She winked as they passed, Savannah blushed and pulled at the edge of her knee length woollen dress top she wore over jeans.

Ivar beckoned her over and she sat next to him on the floor, looking up at the tree with him.

"Ya know." He said after a moment of gentle silence, "I really like what you did with that old tree."

Savannah's laughter was like music, "Thanks Ivar."

"No, I mean it." His face was completely serious, "It's really great!"

He looked up at the tree that was decorated in pine cones, silver fairy lights, snowflakes and wooden decorations. All neatly arranged across the surface of the evergreen.

"In fact. I love it." As he said so, he looped his arm around her shoulders, holding her close. "Just like I love you."

The lights from the tree caused Savannah's hazel eyes to appear more green than brown as she blushed.

Sniggering came from behind them and Ivar glanced over his shoulder in time to see his dad drag David back out of the living room and into the hallway.

Savannah looked over his shoulder and laughed with him.

~Chapter Twenty-One~

"I was complaining coz Bryce is embarrassing."

It was cold and wet since it had started to rain. Hunter toddled across the park towards the bench where Cameron was sitting, huddled inside of his coat miserably, his hair hanging down over his forehead in wet strands.

"I blame Bryce for this." He said gruffly as he lifted Hunter onto his lap.

The little guy wiggled slightly, trying to get comfortable on his seat of wet denim and leather.

"Camwon angwy?" He asked, his eyes as blue as cornflowers. Cameron tried to look angry but his phone flashed up with a notification and he saw his screensaver—*what you plant today, you will harvest tomorrow.*

Rolling his head back he looked skywards, "Sometimes I wish you weren't so *to* the point."

Hunter's cheeks bulged as he took a deep breath and held it, trying to looking up into the rain to see who Cameron was talking to. When his small face started to go red from holding his breath too long, Cameron glanced at him, alarmed he squeezed Hungers cheeks with his fingers causing him to let out his breath and breathe again.

"Bud! What you doin'?"

Hunter panted, "twying to concentwate, who you tawking to, Camwon?"

"God."

"God?" Hunter echoed, crawling closer against Cameron's chest, he curled up inside of his cousin's thick fur-lined denim winter coat.

Inside of it, padded with the fur and the warmth of his cousin, Hunter felt sleepy.

"Yeah, God. I was complaining about Bryce." Cameron smiled crookedly and pulled his coat tighter around his little charge, tilting his head back to watch a robin stalk a worm across the park and catch the scent of the hot apple juice and cinnamon stand in the centre of the park where a group of carollers were making their presence known.

Jade was being obstinate, refusing to get involved with their songs, while Bryce and Reese had jumped right into it, swaying and singing away like two cheery larks.

"You complaining at God, cause Bwyce sing?"

"No," Cameron shifted so he was more comfortable on the hard bench and wished it would stop raining.

The path was wet, the trees were wet, even the air was wet, and to make it worse, he was wet.

"I was complaining coz Bryce is embarrassing." He laughed and shook his head.

Hearing Cameron's laughter, Hunter realised his cousin was only joking. He sighed and stuck his thumb into his mouth, a habit his mom was slowly trying to wean him off. When Cameron next looked down he saw the cute golden curly head asleep against his chest wrapped in his coat.

He sighed and smiled tiredly.

Bryce and Reese bounced over towards him while Jade trailed behind, kicking at the wet leaves that scattered the path. Bryce called to her and she pulled a face, but then laughed and ran to catch up.

"Hey Cam," Bryce grinned as he snapped his feet together in front of his brother, "Reese and I have had a great idea!"

"Yeah? Whassat?" He nodded at Jade as she sat next to him on the bench, "Figured out a way to get her to join the singers?" He earned a punch in the arm from Jade for that.

"We wanna do a Thanksgiving hike-"

Reese jumped in, "We wanna start off really early, like say nine in the morning, and we hike up Pike's Peak and then get back in time for dinner at seven!"

Cameron scratched a hand through his hair, "And who's going with you?"

"It'll be me, Reese," Bryce counted it off on his fingers, "Jade doesn't want to come. So Ivar, Sav, David, you."

"Sorry Brycy-boy. I promised Grandpa I'd help him all day that day until dinner, David too."

Bryce frowned but shook it off, "Right, okay. Just me, Reese, Sav and Ivar then."

~

Ivar winced and waved his phone, "Sorry Bryce, Grandpa just enlisted my help also."

Bryce pouted, he hoisted himself up onto the countertop and rested his chin in his hands, "Ok, so just Reese and I then for the hike yeah?"

Savannah, who had been listening while pulling her coat on before Ivar dropped her home, spoke up, "I'll join you Bryce." She smiled and pulled the baseball cap that Ivar had given her down over her forehead, buttoning up her jacket.

"Really?" Bryce looked hopeful.

Ivar's voice had traces of doubt, "Sav, you sure?"

"Sure I'm sure. Besides, it will be fun to hike with your brother and cousin. Also, it gives me a break from the café, preparing for thanksgiving and Christmas, and preparing for a wedding."

"Oh!" Reese who had been sorting through a bowl of the small peanut butter Reese chocolates, looked up, "Have you got a dress yet, Sav?"

Savannah put a finger to her lips to shush Reese and then motioned her across to see a photo on her phone.

Bryce smirked as he heard Reese's oohing and ahhing and saw Ivar blush.

"Seriously." He snickered, elbowing him in the side.

Ivar shoved him back, "You take care of both the girls up on that mountain."

"Me?" Bryce looked as innocent as an angel, "I'm great at leading expeditions."

"Ha!" Reese exploded, "Keep telling yourself that." Bryce emptied the bowl of Reese chocolates over her head.
Reaching over, Savannah ruffled up his long blond hair, "See you on Thursday."

She smiled, hugged Reese and then followed Ivar out of the door to get into the car.

~Chapter Twenty-Two~
"Love, God's kind of love, is a lot of things isn't it?"

Thanksgiving was to be a day Bryce would remember forever as the day he decided Savannah was good for Ivar.

While Aubrey, Madison and Emma rustled up food in the kitchen, Ivar hovered nervously around Bryce and Reese on the front porch as they pulled on their coats and laced up their hiking boots.

"Now, you're sure this is a good idea?" He asked.

Bryce laughed, he ran a hand through his hair and turned his eyes into his brother, "Ivar relax! Sav's about to become my sister-in-law. I'll look after her as if she were my own." His words seemed to calm Ivar a little, it wasn't until he saw Savannah's car pull up outside of the farmhouse and saw her jump out and come towards them, her face spilt in a big grin as she hugged him, that he felt a bit safer with letting Bryce look after her.

"You're worrying." She mused, shaking her head she gave his hand a squeeze, "I'll be fine. Reese and Bryce are the best I know, it will be a laugh."

Ivar nodded, "Yeah, wish I could come."

Jason, who was leaning on the porch railing watching them all get ready winked, "Instead you're hauling feed and stacking pumpkins and bringing that large evergreen in from the back yard."

"Whoopee…" Ivar drawled, he flashed his grandpa a genuine smile. Turning to Savannah he said, "Did I hear your car having trouble as it came up the drive?"

"A little," Savannah admitted, squinting in the cold sunlight towards the Ford park by the gate. "It stalled halfway, then sorta spit back into life."

Ivar was nodding, rubbing dirt off of his hands and onto his jeans he said, "I can look at it if you like?"

Savannah tilted her head to the side, "Thank you, that would be awesome."

"Come on Sav!"

She turned as Bryce called, he and Reese were already half way to the field gate.

Smiling at Ivar she swung her rucksack onto her back and jogged after Bryce and Reese, falling in step with the two as they passed through the gate and into the fields.

Ivar shaded his eyes as he watched them going, he knew he shouldn't have felt so nervous.

But he did. O,h he trusted Bryce with his life, but the weather had been foul and he didn't want anything happening.

"I think that was good for young Bryce to see."

"Huh?" He looked towards his grandpa as they walked back into the farm house, Jason stopped in the hallway and put his hat on the rack, "I think what he just witnessed was good for him."

"I don't think I understand." Ivar folded his arm and leaned against the wall, smiling as the smell of spice and turkey floated out of the kitchen.

"Well, Bryce has been getting at you and teasing you for being in love. He's thought it to be all mushy and icky, as he so tentatively put it." Jason said, chucking slightly. "I think that exchange between you and Sav just now showed him that love isn't just that. It's also selflessness and practical love."

"Yeah," Ivar rubbed the back of his neck, "Love, God's kind of love is a lot of things isn't it."

"It's tough work, that's for sure."

"Mmm," Jason's grandson squeezed his eyes shut, "It's gonna be hard ain't it Grandpa?"

Jason nodded, "Yup," he clapped a hand on Ivar's shoulder, "But you have the best helper to be there with you."

"You're not moving in with us grandpa."

Jason laughed, his eyes filling with tears as the thought of moving in with his first married grandchild tickled him silly, "Don't worry, I'm not."

Ivar smiled, "I know Who you mean." He nodded and let out his breath, stuffing his hands into his back pockets he scuffed the side of his boot along the wooden flooring.

"Tell you what. Cam, David and I will haul the feed. I want you to do something for me."

"Whassat?"

Jason ripped a piece of paper off of the legal pad by the telephone and passed it to him with a pen, "Go read 1 Corinthians thirteen verses four to seven. Also Philippians four verses six to seven. Then I want you to write them out in your own words. Remember, you're gonna need a large, constant harvest of selfless love once you're married."

He patted him on the shoulder, "Better start planting some of those seeds."

Taking the paper held out to him, Ivar nodded, "Alright," he bit down on his lip and tilted his head, listening to the noisy house, "Anywhere quiet I can go?"

Jason pursed his lips, "The attic?"

Grinning, Ivar nodded and headed for the attic, grabbing his dad's bible off of the hall table as he passed.

~

"Hike two three four. Hike two three four. Hike two three four. Hike-"

"If you say that one more time I will dunk you head first into the stream."

"Hike two three four—no! No! Bryce! Stop—" the words were cut short as Bryce hurled Reese over his shoulder and ran back down the hill towards the river they had just passed.

Reese's screeching could have been heard halfway across the farm, Savannah was sure.

It was at her word that Bryce put his cousin down and the two of them made their way back up the path towards her.

"Aw Sav. You ruined my fun." Bryce whined, winking at her.

Savannah grinned at him before shoving him in the shoulder, "And I saved your aunt a load of laundry. 'Sides, if you had dunked Reese, we wouldn't have been able to keep going." She smiled, knowing she had one over Bryce on that.

Twisting his lips to the side, Bryce thought about it before shrugging in acceptance.

"Where are we, by the way Bryce?" Reese tucked loose strands of her wild blond ponytail back up under her hat.

"Halfway up Pike's Peak." Bryce said slowly as he turned to glance back down the path, leaning over the edge he could see the farm land and the town sprawled out beneath them.

"Another half hour then we need to turn back." He added looking at his watch then at the sun that had started to set. He knew he was responsible for both his cousin and his brother's fiancée. He didn't want anything to go wrong.

~Chapter Twenty-Three~

"Love is patient. Love is kind. It does not envy, it does not boast. It is not proud. It does not dishonour others. It is so self-seeking, it is not easily angered, it keeps no record of wrongs. Love does not delight in evil but rejoices with the truth. It always protects. Always trusts, always hopes, always perseveres." 1 Corinthians 13:4-7

"Should we stop here for a moment before turning back to go home for Thanksgiving dinner?" Savannah suggested as they reached the peak of their accent, "We've been hiking for quite a while."

Bryce squinted down at his watch, it wasn't working. Water had gotten into the watch face from where he had dropped Reese's boot into the river and he had to dunk his arm in to grab it.

"Well, that will be a story to tell." He muttered, the watch face was stuck at five thirty pm. Who knew what time it was now. Neither of the girls had a watch and all of their phones were either dead or had been left behind.

"Peachy." He said dryly, "Just peachy."

"And that's our cue for going back." Savannah chimed, seeing Bryce's dilemma and not wanting to worry Reese. "The suns almost set anyway and Bryce's stomach is growling which means it's time for dinner."

"What about stopping for a break?" Reese asked as she undid the laces on her one dry boot and tipped leaves and acorns out of it, Savannah shook her head, "Think it's best we go back. There's a freak snowstorm coming tonight. I heard about it on the news,"

Bryce grinned, "And you didn't tell my brother cuz you knew he'd freak."

Savannah laughed, "He's not that bad Bryce."

Both Reese and Bryce's faces were blank, "Yes, he is." They chorused.

Laughing again, Savannah shook the hair out of her eyes and shifted her rucksack, "Well then, we don't want to add his worry onto your mother's do we?"

Bryce grinned, he liked Savannah. In fact, despite being nervous about having his brother married, he was looking forward to having her as a sister. Even if it was a sister-in-law.

Reese ran ahead as they started walking back so she could get a good photo of the view before they had to move on. Falling in step with Savannah, Bryce tried to think of something intelligent to say. Instead though all he could come up with was how proud he was of Savannah and Ivar.

Nope. Not sayin' that. As soon as he rebuked himself for thinking about it, he chided himself for not being brave enough to tell his future sister-in-law what he thought about her and his brother being together.

"What is it?"

Bryce blinked and looked at Savannah, her reddish brown fishtail braid was swept back under a blue scarf with small pink flowers dotted over it.

"Pardon?" He asked.

Savannah smiled at him, "I said, what is it? You and Ivar both share the same thinking face."

Bryce laughed dryly, "Gee, thanks."

"What's wrong Bryce, you can tell me." She nudged him and he shoved her back playfully.

Keeping her footing Savannah asked once more.

When she did, Bryce shook his head and smiled, "I was just thinking about how good you and Ivar are for each other."

~

"What ya doin?"

Ivar looked over his shoulder as David stuck his head through the attic hatch, his blond hair sticking up everywhere with cobwebs he had collected from climbing up the ladder.

"The one place I thought I'd be alone." Ivar kidded.

"Oh, should I go?" David started to clamber back down the ladder but Ivar called after him, "No, it's okay. Come up, actually, it would be good to show someone."

He waited until David had climbed back into the attic and was sitting next to him on the old trunk.

"What you writing?" David asked, pushing his hair out of the way with a sweep of his hand.

Ivar passed him the paper he had been writing on, "Grandpa said it would be a good idea for me to read one Corinthians and Philippians four and then write them in my own words,"

"The love chapter and the peace chapter." David affirmed, he glanced at the bible passage for Philippians four before turning to the paper Ivar had written on.

Peace, God's peace is so powerful, so whole and fully complete that it goes beyond what we understand and clarify as peace. Like an ocean, it is so tangible that it affects everything, washing away all of our fears and anxiety. It comes in so quickly and wonderfully when we pray and give all of our worries to God. It's so whole that we can't understand just how amazing it is. Complete peace that stands at our hearts and minds like a watchman, ready to ward off attacks.

David was quiet for a moment before saying, "That's good. That's really good,"

Ivar smiled and pointed to the next part of the page, "That's One Corinthians."

David smiled and shook his head, "In a moment. First off, why is the word *worries* underlined?"

Ivar looked uncomfortable, "Well…I worry a lot. So, I'm learning to not worry and let God handle the stuff I worry about."

"Uh huh, you're worrying now ain't ya?"

Ivar looked at his brother out of the corner of his eye, "Maybe." He shook his head, he hadn't seen David for years and his brother still had the knack of reading Ivar's emotions like a whiteboard.

David grinned a bit crookedly, "About Sav, Reese and Bryce?"

Ivar nodded and glanced out of the attic window. "Yup." He shook his head again, "I dunno. Last year I learnt to not give into fear over Bryce, now I just keep worrying though." He picked at a piece of peeling paint.

"Ivar, you know perfect love casts out fear." David said softly from behind him.

Ivar sighed, his shoulders heaving, "I know."

Turning to the paper in his hand, David read aloud what Ivar had written about God's kind of love.

"Love doesn't get impatient and fretful. Love doesn't keep to itself. Love is always thoughtful, it doesn't push itself to the front, only thinking of itself. Love is not easily agitated. It doesn't store up the wrongs of others to use against them later on in life. Love isn't vindictive. It doesn't take revenge because it wants to. Love cries with those who cry, laughs with those who laugh and rejoices with those who rejoice. Love is for the truth. It fights for those who can't fight for themselves. Love keeps going no matter what."

He folded the corner of the page back and forth, musing to himself, "Huh, funny. That doesn't say a thing about worry."

Ivar opened his mouth to speak but David stopped him, "No, listen, it's good to be concerned, if you weren't I'd say you didn't love them. But concern and worry are different Ivar. We are to put all our cares and worries at the feet of Jesus. Don't worry about tomorrow," he tilted his head and smiled, "sound familiar?"

Ivar looked at his brother through half-closed eyes. Reaching forward, he shoved David off of the trunk playfully, causing his older brother to land backside first in a cardboard box of feather hats from the days western gun fights and long silk dresses. "Yeah, I get it." He said smiling.

David lifted one of the hats and plunked it down on top of his head, a large indigo plume pointed out the side of the berry red bowler hat.

"Suits you." Ivar said.

Rolling his eyes, David twisted so he could see himself in the old half shattered mirror that Jason had put up in the attic last spring. "Beautiful," he admired, "I think I should wear this more often."

Ivar's mouth twitched.

"Maybe even to your wedding."

All the blood in Ivar's face drained leaving him as white as chalk, "If you even," he breathed, David hooted with laughter, almost falling out of the box and crushing his beloved hat.

The colour returned to Ivar's face and he sat down on the floor, glaring at his brother in mock anger.

"*That!*" David cried, pointing to him while removing the offending article off of his head, "was beautiful."

Ivar picked up one of the larger, more sturdy hats and threw it at his brother, "Oh shut up." He laughed. "You're way too much like Bryce."

David grinned, his eyes sparkling over the rim of the hat he held against his face.

~Chapter Twenty-Four~
"Where's Reesey?"

"Oh? Is that right," Savannah teased.

Bryce cackled and shook his head, "Yeah, you're good for my brother."

The smile Savannah gave Bryce was warm and sweet, "Thank you Bryce, that means a lot."

Bryce nodded and kept on, "You're not like the other girls in our schools and colleges, your sensible, you love God, your humble, you know how to be responsible—"

He stopped as Savannah shook her head, "Bryce, I have plenty of faults, just like everyone else—"

She stopped as they both heard a cry cut short suddenly. Turning in a slow circle Savannah looked back up the path, it had started to rain and a part of the path had crumbled.

Bryce touched her shoulder, "Where's Reesey?"

As the dread of what had happened settled in Savannah's stomach she shook her rucksack off and ran back up the path, her boots slipping in the mud that was quickly forming with the rain.

Bryce had also dumped his rucksack and was making his way along the cliff edge, holding onto tree roots and branches to keep himself from falling.

"Reese!" He shouted, cupping one hand around his mouth as he did so.

There was silence and he looked across the path at Savannah alarmed.

"It will be okay." She said calmly, getting onto her knees she laid down flat on her stomach, inching her way forwards, towards where the path had fallen away, *Jesus, help me reach Reese. Keep her safe. Give me wisdom Jesus.*

For a fleeting moment she was reminded of a verse she had read the day before in psalms.

Like a drowning man who has just been thrown a life ring, she clung to every ounce of strength that the verse gave her as she repeated it to herself and over Reese while crawling closer to the edge, "Keep me safe, my God, for in you I take refuge."

The words of Psalm sixteen brought her comfort. Savannah was now at the edge, she pushed herself forward one more time and her upper body was over the edge.

"Reese?" She squinted down into the rain.

Reese's voice came back up in a reply and Savannah heard Bryce breath out in relief.

Waving a hand in his direction, Savannah called, "Bryce pass me your jacket," she started to shrug off her own and when Bryce gave her his she knotted them together.

Behind her, Bryce prayed while crawling towards the edge himself, "Keep us safe, oh God, for in you we take refuge." He positioned himself where Savannah had been once she moved away, she crouched on the edge, letting Bryce take the jacket line they had made.

Looking down the landslide, Bryce saw Reese balancing on a large piece of earth that had gotten stuck, it held her weight, but didn't look like it could for much longer.

A glance over his shoulder gave Bryce a view of a large blue spruce through the rain, curling his legs around its base, he inched his way over the edge until he was hanging down, "Reesey, you hear me girl?" He called.

"Bryce?" Reese's voice was watery.

Bryce squinted through the rain, Reese balanced precariously on the clump of earth, it shifted and crumbled away as a tree limb was swept down the mountain side, almost taking Bryce and Savannah with it.

"Reese!" Savannah shouted, "Hold on!"

She held onto Bryce with one hand while holding onto the roots of a large bush as a Bryce lowered himself down over the edge. Arms extended to grab ahold of Reese, who was laying with her back to the wall, holding onto a weak branch.

"Reese." Bryce's voice was low, it was getting cold and he had started to tremble slightly, "Reese, look up."

Reese did and saw her cousin a foot above her, "Bryce…I can't hold on any longer." She was pale and the wind was getting stronger. Every few moments a strong gust would blow and she would be shifted a few inches before being slammed back against the wall.

"It's ok Reesey. It's ok, I'm gonna get you," Bryce twisted, "Sav, I need to get a little lower."

"Alright, get her to grab hold of the line Bryce."

Bryce nodded and then tossed his head trying to get the hair out of his eyes. "Reesey. I'm gonna hold this out okay, I need you to grab it and wrap it around your wrist…Reesey ya hear me?"

"I hear you Bryce. Please hurry."

Bryce dropped the line down, waiting for Reese to grab it, as he waited, watching as Reese held on with one hand while trying to loop the jacket sleeve around her wrist with the other, he felt the strongest wind he had yet. With it, the rain turned from water to sharp ice.

Above him there was a groan and a soft thud, looking back over his shoulder he saw Savannah struggling to get to her feet. The wind had knocked her over and she was having a hard time keeping hold of Bryce's ankles while keeping her balance in the soft ground.

Mud was oozing out from underneath her hiking boots as she dug her heels in. "Bryce, I can't hold in much longer!"

"Just a moment, Sav! Almost got her," Bryce's hopes rose as he saw Reese let go of the tree limb and then swing to grab his arm while he pulled on the clothes line he was holding down. "Come on Reesey, c'mon."

Jesus help us! Bryce screamed inside as another strong wind slammed his body against the wall the landslide had formed, he felt Reese's fingers brush his and he strained to grab hold of her hand.

Jesus.

The name became the centre of his thoughts as another wind slammed him.

Then. It died.

The wind stopped as suddenly as it had started, the rain slowed and the wind became still.

Bryce reached for Reese easily, the muscles in his arms screaming from tension as he pulled her up.

"Little higher, come on, come on," Bryce grabbed Reese's arms and pulled her up, while Savannah reached for the back of her shirt, helping to haul her to the ground.

Reese kicked until her knees touched the edge, panting, she grabbed a hold of Bryce's hand.

One more kick and a strong pull from her cousin and friend and she was on the ground.

Taking a large gulp of air, Bryce ran both hands through his wet hair before putting both arms around his cousin, resting his cheek on the top of her wet ponytail.

Reese's laugh was shaky as she patted his arm, "I'm okay Bryce. I'm okay."

Letting his breath out through his teeth, Bryce tightened his grip on his cousin, when trying to get her up he had been on autopilot, running on pure adrenaline.

Now he felt shaky and cold.

Reese hugged him harder and the two rocked back and forth in the mud for a moment before Bryce turned to Savannah.

"Thank you." He said, his voice husky.

Savannah smiled weakly, "I'm just glad Reese is okay." Savannah made sure to remain calm as Bryce and Reese got up and they started back down the trail.

~Chapter Twenty-Five~
Perfect love casts out fear.

Aubrey put the pumpkin pie in the centre of the table, everyone was seated except for Ivar who stood by the window, hands in his pockets watching the rain hitting the SUV in the drive. "Don't ya think they should be back by now?" He asked.

Sean leaned forward, he ignored the fact he was hungry and that food was on the table, "It's raining hard, Ivar, Bryce has probably stopped them."

Caleb put down the reindeer ornament he had been admiring, "Thing is Sean, it's gonna change to snow soon."

Picking up his phone, Sean rang his father in law who had run into town to grab some bits for Madison.

Jason's voice came across the phone, "Hey, what's up Sean?"

"Bryce and the girls ain't back yet Jason. We're getting a bit worried."

At the word, Ivar's head snapped up and he levelled his eyes on David who was leaning back in his chair, lazily inhaling the aroma of hot coffee.

Over the rim of his mug though, David caught Ivar look. He then glanced across at Cameron who was straddling a chair with Hunter on his back.

Cameron saw the look on both of his brothers' faces, getting up, he swung Hunter off of his back, "Dad, let's go a little way up the trail."

Sean covered his phone with one hand and looked from his wife to Caleb, "What do you think?"

Caleb nodded and reached for the door, "I'll go with—"

"No Uncle Caleb." Cameron stopped him with a hand, "Stay with Aunt Emma and the others." He swallowed and grabbed his winter coat from the hook on the back of the door, "Ivar, David and I will find them."

Caleb hesitated, he looked like he wanted to argue but then gave up and allowed Emma to take hold of his arm and lead him across the living room diner towards the coach.

Jade occupied Hunter with dancing carrots on the table. Ivar squeezed her shoulder as he whisked past, grabbing his phone as he went.

"You think they're okay?" David asked as he got into their grandpa's offroad truck next to Cameron.

"They're fine." Cameron's firm voice made Ivar relax, he sat in the open back part of the land rover, feeling the pelting rain on his face as they drove. It reminded him of Bryce's escape the year before and he smiled.

Perfect love casts out fear.

As the words crossed Ivar's mind, he felt a change in the weather, the wind died and the rain stopped.

Cameron pulled the truck over and stuck his head out of the window, "What just happened?"

David opened his door and peered into the light flurry of snow that had started to fall, "That was sudden…" he then grinned suddenly.

"What?" Ivar asked.

David stuck his tongue out to try and catch one of the falling snowflakes, "It was too sudden to be anything but a miracle."

Cameron turned the heating on the truck and glanced at Ivar, "You think they're okay?" He said, repeating his brother's question from before.

"They're fine." Ivar said.

"I'd say they are," David said, and pointed towards a part of the field further up, both Cameron and Ivar turned to look. Ivar was the first one to jump down out of the truck and run across the field towards Bryce and Savannah who were supporting Reese between them.

~

"What happened?" Ivar asked as he hugged the breath out of all three of them.

Savannah let her head drop down onto his shoulder, "We had fun." She said.

"Yeah?" Ivar looked over her head at Bryce, "Everything okay? Mom was gettin' worried."

Bryce nodded and adjusted Reese's arm around his shoulder, the snow was getting heavier and Ivar motioned them towards the truck where Cameron and David were waiting. "It was fine," he said finally, "we had a small mishap but it was good."

Cameron caught Bryce's last sentence and saw the amused look Reese and Savannah shared. He shook his head, laughing to himself, Bryce saw him and grinned knowingly.

David turned the heating in the truck up while Reese and Savannah bundled into the back seat of the truck and Bryce jumped into the flatbed with Ivar.

Halfway down the track Ivar shouted over the rush of the falling snow, "Déjà-vu or what, am I right?!"

Bryce nodded, he was soaked to the skin and was shivering now with cold.

Ivar pulled a handful of rugs out of the box his grandpa kept on the flatbed. He tossed one around Bryce's shoulders and his brother nodded his thanks.

"So what happened out there?" Ivar asked.

"Not much," Bryce said, shrugging under the blanket, "you underestimate me as a hike leader, brother."

Ivar grinned at him as his dark hair was whipped back and forth across his face, "Maybe."

"A lot." Bryce said, under the blanket he pressed a hand against his side, it was bruised slightly from being pummelled by the wind against a wall. "One thing I will say though," He shouted over the wind, "you made a good choice with Sav. She's level headed when she needs to be."

"What?" Ivar looked at him.

Bryce grinned and burrowed further down into the blanket. Using it as a hood to shield his face from the cold, "Nothin', didn't say nothin' at all."

Ivar looked at him again, then shook his head and tilted his head to look up into the swirling snow.

When he looked back at Bryce he could have sworn Bryce was six and not seventeen. The boy was sitting there, staring at him wide eyed and grinning stupidly.

Eh, never mind. Ivar thought, *it's almost Christmas, thanksgiving dinner is waiting back at the farm house. Bryce can be weird if he wants.*

As if on cue, perfectly timed to his brother's thoughts, Bryce cackled and threw one of the blankets at him.

Bemused, Ivar threw it back, laughing.

~Chapter Twenty-Six~
"You're missing a brother."

Bryce wasn't convinced.

But all the same, he found himself being pushed towards Ivar's car by David a week before Christmas.

"David! I'm not sure learning to drive is such a good idea in all this snow." Bryce said.

Dais squinted and opened the driver's side door, pushing his brother into the truck, "It's a great idea. 'Sides, if you get stuck in a snow drift or something," he grinned and gave the collar of Bryce's fur lined denim coat a tweak, "you have your warm coat on."

Bruce rolled his eyes but looked nervous all the same, "You sure? I don't want what happened to dad's car to happen to Ivar's car, especially with him getting married at the end of the month."

David smiled, "It won't."

"How are you so sure?"

"Because I'm gonna be teaching you. Your usin' my car, I'm the driving instructor." Ivar said as he stepped out of the bungalow, pulling his coat on as he shook the snow that had fallen off the roof and onto him, off.

"Oh. Yay." Bryce cheered sarcastically.

Ivar looked at him and slid into the passenger seat, "David, get in the back."

"What? Why me? Why not Cameron?"

"Because Cameron is going to get a Christmas tree with mom. And I don't want to push this car all the way to the garage on my own once Bryce blows it up."

David got in the back reluctantly as Bryce muttered, "Oh ye of little faith."

Ivar smiled at him, "Don't worry, out of all the Walker boys, I drive the best. If anyone can teach you to drive it's me."

"Don't we have a tree already?" David asked as Bryce put the car into gear.

Ivar nodded, "Yup." He said while twirling his index finger in the air, indicating for Bryce to turn the wheel.

"Then why is Cam gettin' another?"

Ivar stopped his finger turning and frowned into the rear view mirror, "That, my ever-so-slightly annoyingly smart brother is a good question."

He got out of the car and sprinted through the snow up to the house, returning a few moments later dragging a very begrudged looking firefighter behind him down the drive.

Bryce leaned back in the driver's seat as both got into the car, "Hey," he drawled, smiling lazily at Cameron, "How's that tree comin' along."

Cameron mimicked his smile before jamming his cap down over his hair.His reddish brown fringe fell out over his forehead though and he pulled the ends of his coat sleeves down over his hands.

"What, didn't you want to watch me learn to drive?" Bryce asked, still leaning on the seat.

Cameron pushed the cap up a little so he could glare playfully at the smiling boy.

"Na, I just thought it would be better to have a firefighter not in the crash. So he could rescue y'all."

Bryce whistled loudly, "Whoa! A hundred percent of the positive confessions here bro's."

Then, to get his point across, he stuck the car in reverse like Ivar had shown him and started to *very* slowly back out of the drive and onto the country rode lines with evergreens that led into town. All the while countering what his brothers had said.

"I will not crash this car. This drive will be smooth and carefree. We will not crash, we will not be rescued by any emergency services. We will live and not die. I will become a good driver. This car will not explode. Ivar's car will be fine and in good order."

Then just for the fun of it, he grinned as the back tires of the car hit the icy tarmac and said, "And thank you Lord that when they get married you give Savannah the patience to deal with my brother."

The car swerved as Ivar smacked his brother around the back of the head.

"And forgive him for being reckless and physical." Bryce added.

Ivar didn't look impressed but Cameron and David slid down their seats trying to not laugh.

~

The snow swirled around the car as Ivar got Bryce to slowly back it into the parking lot of the general store.

"Great, now everyone out." He ordered.

Bryce raised his eyebrows and put the car brakes on. "Why?" He asked as he pulled his coat on tighter as he stepped out into the chilling blizzard.

"We need some extra things for Christmas and I thought why not combine your driving lesson with a trip to the store."

Bryce grinned and watched as Cameron dragged himself into the store with a chirpy David humming Christmas carols behind.

The bell on the door rang as the four walked in, tracking snow behind them that started to melt as it hit the warmth of the general store.

The store was full of tinsel and smelled like oranges and candy canes. Ivar looked down at the list he had created on his phone and then back up when Cameron snickered.

"What?" He asked.

Cameron picked up a can of chicken soup and inspected it, "You're missing a brother." He said.

"Huh?" Ivar looked around the store, "Bryce?"

David grinned and shook his head turning he started towards the back of the store to hunt up eggnog.

~

Bryce grinned, she was there. At the back of the store, stacking the shelves with Christmas tins of biscuits.

Grabbing one of the floppy red Santa hats off of the shelf covered with trinkets and knick knacks for stockings, he tugged it down over his head and walked up behind Miss Foster.

Leaning around Bryce covered the grocery store clerk's eyes with his hands, "Guess who."

Straightening, Sarah Foster laughed, her voice sounding like silver bells. "Well if it isn't Bryce Walker himself!" she turned around and gave him a hug, squeezing the breath right out him.

"How's your momma?"

"Mom's good," Bryce said looking over a barrel of candy canes, "She wanted to know if you would like to have Christmas dinner with us up at the farm, Miss Foster."

Bryce selected a bright red candy cane and fiddled with the holly green bow. Sarah Forster had been a great help to his mom during his stay in hospital. She and Aubrey had become good friends over the last year and Bryce had even taken up a part time job at the store doing half days when he was studying.

Sarah's curly brown ponytail swung across the back of her maroon shirt.

She always wears maroon, Bryce noted. *Maybe it's coz it accentuates her dark skin colour.* He nodded to himself and peeled back the cellophane on the candy cane, *Mom's right, Miss Foster is beautiful.*

"Now Bryce Walker. You tell your Momma that I'd be sure right proud to join your family for Christmas dinner." Her broad accent was as strong and clear as ever.

Smiling, Bryce looked up, "Great!" He stuck the end of the candy cane in his mouth and sucked on it while tapping his foot to the catchy Christmas song playing over the speakers. Grabbing an armload of gravy granule pots he started to help her load up the shelf.

Hearing his name called, Bryce looked over his shoulder and gave Ivar a grin, the candy cane hanging out of his mouth as he did so. Walking down the aisle towards the pair, Ivar grimaced, "Take it out Bryce."

His brother obeyed, took another bite of it and smacked his lips, "These are the best candy canes in the county."

Sarah smiled and dimples indented her cheeks, "Why thank you Bryce. My own Momma makes those. She sent them across just for the season."

Bryce's eyes grew larger as he realised they were bespoke candy canes and not the usual he could get online at any time of year.

Sarah turned to Ivar, "And I hear congratulations are in order. Madison was in here just the other day gushing about an upcoming winter wedding?"

Ivar blushed, "New year's. But yes and thank you."

Bryce wiggled his eyebrows up and down and Sarah elbowed him in the side, "He finally got around to asking that Savannah Van Dyke to marry him did he?"

When Bryce nodded Sara laughed, "Ah, we all saw it coming." She said, patting Ivar's shoulder as he looked at them both mournfully.

"How come everyone saw it coming before I asked her?" He replied indignantly while scouring an array of mugs that were hanging from hooks in the wall.

"Face it. You were smitten the first day Savannah walked up to the counter in the café and said hello. You didn't even touch your milkshake that day, I had to drink both of them. Mine and yours." Bryce said. His brother waved him off and took a large coffee mug with a red robin on the front off of a hook.

"So is this a family outing?" Sarah asked, turning back to her work as it started to get dark outside and the store fairy lights came on.

"No," Ivar said, "Just all four Walker boys."

"They were teaching me to drive." Bryce put in, "Say, Miss Foster do ya have sliced apples or do I need to slice the actual fruit?"

Sarah raised an eyebrow and pointed the pen she was using towards the centre aisle. "You have to slice the actual fruit."

As he walked off to find the apples, Sarah turned to Ivar confused. "Four Walker boys? I thought it was only you, Bryce and Cameron." Ivar's eyes darted around the store, as if he was looking for someone. Before he spoke, his eyes settled on a tall blond that was bent over a shelf of beef jerky packets.

"My older brother came home."

Sara hid a gasp behind her mouth, "David?"

Ivar frowned, "How do you know about David?"

"Your grandma, Madison, she brought you and Bryce into the store when you were wee babies. David was with her, I helped behind the counter with my dad."

Ivar nodded, "Yeah, well. David's home now."

Sarah's smile was warm and loving, "I'm glad. I was so devastated when I heard about the accident. What happened?"

"He landed the plane and managed to tread water until he was found. He lost his memory for a long time, only remembering snatches. He got healed at a tent meeting last year and is now home." Ivar found that retelling the story that marked another miracle in his family brought tears to his eyes and he had to blink them away.

Sarah saw the tears in the young man's eyes and reached out to touch his arm, "Never be ashamed of tears Ivar. They show strength, not weakness."

Ivar laughed and shook the mug he was holding, "You guys are all the same!"

"Who?"

"People like you and my grandparents." Ivar said, smiling fondly, "You're like my grandpa, last year he told me never to be ashamed of my tears."

~Chapter Twenty-Seven~

"And Bryce, get your hand out of the candy cane barrel. Seriously man. Grow up a bit! I feel like a father already and I'm not even married yet!"

"Eh," Sarah Foster shrugged, her curly ponytail bouncing. "It's just us getting old." She smiled flippantly and stacked another can on the shelf.

"Who's getting old?" David asked, coming around the corner, he held a over large pumpkin, "Ivar, is this too big of a pumpkin for the pie?"

Sarah took one look at the large pumpkin and shook her head, "It's perfect if you're feeding the entire population of woodland park Colorado."

"Ha. Ha. Ha." David said.

Ivar grinned, "Miss Foster, the sarcastic man standing before you is my brother. David."

"Foster?" David repeated putting the pumpkin down on top of a barrel of chestnuts. "Not Sarah Foster? My grandpa mentioned you were working here but I didn't click it until I saw you. Didn't you work here when my grandma brought me and the others in?"

"Uhuh." Sarah said, she held out her hand and he shook it.

"Man, it's good to see familiar faces again." David said smiling.

"Ok, come on chatty boy." Ivar grabbed David by the back of his hoodie and pulled him down the aisle, "Let's go find a smaller pumpkin." He passed an aisle and called back over his shoulder, "And Bryce, get your hand out of the candy cane barrel. Seriously man. Grow up a bit! I feel like a father already and I'm not even married yet!"

~

"I have officially postponed your driving test!" Sean said walking into the lounge later that evening.

Bryce looked up from the game of monopoly he was playing with his brothers, Savannah and his mom.

"Really? Awesome. Thanks."

"Why postpone it?" David whined, "he would have aced it."

Cameron rolled the dice and moved his silver car token three spaces. "I'm sure he would have David, but with you teaching him he would have to retake it five times just so he could get to gears with what his examiner was saying.,

Taking his turn, Ivar snickered and moved his character across the board.

It landed on Savannah's property and she held out her hand for payment.

"Cam has a point, David. We ain't the best of teachers, I mean he blew up the car with you doing it." Ivar said passing the paper bank bills to Savannah.

"Yeah," Bryce added, "At least with Ivar I drove to the general store."

Aubrey almost chocked on her hot apple juice and cinnamon drink.

Sean patted her back, "You ok?" He asked leaning over her so that he was smiling at her upside down.

Aubrey nodded and paused to catch her breath, she waited a moment before trying to take a drink from her mug.

"You let Bryce drive your car?" She asked Ivar after a moment.

"Uhuh," Ivar said, half scowling as he picked up a chance card and got sent to jail.

David rolled and landed on Savannah's property, he eyed up the large pile of paper bank bills smacked neatly next to her. "I don't think you need this." He said.

Savannah grinned and took the money from him, "Thank you." She said sweetly folding the notes and adding them to her stack.

Aubrey shook her head, "Brave."

Ivar smiled up at his mom and then looked down as Savannah took his hand under the table. She gave it a squeeze and he grinned at her.

"Oh boy." Bryce said from across the coffee table.

Ivar shot him a look and then laughed, "One day Bryce." He said, "One day."

Bryce shook his head and dolled out another place in the game as Sean sat down to join in the fun.

Aubrey saw the look on Ivar's face as he glanced at Bryce. Moving closer to her son she whispered, "You okay?"

Ivar nodded, "Yah, I was just thinkin'"

"About?"

Ivar turned to face his mom, the lights from the tree accented his mom's reddish brown hair, making her seem younger than her age.

"I was just feeling grateful. About Bryce. He wouldn't be here today if it wasn't for Jesus. I mean, it wouldn't have been half as fun."

Aubrey put her arm around his shoulders and squeezed him in a hug.

"He'll grow up one day, Ivar. It will be him waiting at the altar, not you. He'll grow up and we can be grateful for each and every day we have with him, Hmm?"

"Amen Mom. Amen." He rested his head against her, laughing as David and Cameron engaged in a full war against Savannah with the bank bills and several cushions from the couch.

~Chapter Twenty-Eight~

'For a child is born to us, a son is given to us. The government will rest on his shoulders. And he will be called: wonderful counsellor, Mighty God, Everlasting Father, Prince of peace.' Isaiah 9:6

The multiple pages of the wedding planner splayed back and forth as Savannah sat next to Aubrey flicking through it.

Aubrey stabbed her pen down on a page, "Wedding dress. You got it?"

"Yeah,"

Another large flicked, another stab of the pen pinned a page down. "Cake?"

"Mmhmm."

Another page moved and Aubrey put her hand on the book instead of her pen, "Sav honey."

"Huh?" Savannah looked up at her future mother in law, her hazel eyes wide. "Pardon? I'm sorry I wasn't listening."

Aubrey laughed, "I can tell. What were you thinking about?"

"The Christmas Eve fair tonight in the park." Savannah said, brushing a strand of her hair back.

"Oh yeah, Ivar's taking you isn't he?"

Savannah nodded and reached for the blue glitter gel pen that was clipped in the centre of her wedding folder, she drew spirals up the side of the guestlist. "Yes he is," she said.

Laughing again, Aubrey got up and went over to the fridge, she opened it and reached for the bowl of watermelon slices, "Here." She said, setting the bowl down in front of the young woman. "Never too late in the year to eat watermelon in this house."

Savannah smiled and grabbed a piece, her eyes rolling heavenwards as she bit into the sweet fruit.

"Oh, that's good." She said around the watermelon in her mouth.

"What's good?" Sean asked as he stepped in from shoving the drive, he shook snow off of himself and smiled, feeling incredibly pleased with himself.

Aubrey put her hands on her hips, "Shovel in the garage Sean. Then coat off, wipe your boots and wash your hands. Then go dry off."

Sean put the shovel back outside and then crossed the open planned kitchen diner towards wife. He put his wet gloves on her shoulders and kissed her softly.

"Alright." He smiled into her face before sidestepping her playful slap and going to the sink to wash up.

Once he had left, Aubrey stared mournfully at the muddy snow tracks he had left across her clean floor.

"Tell me one thing." Savannah said, her eyes shining as she tried not to laugh.

"What?" Aubrey asked wearily.

"Is your son as messy as his dad?"

Aubrey paused her mopping, he glanced towards the meticulously decorated room and fireplace. Then thought about the inside of Ivar's car.

"No. He's not messy." She said finally, banishing another footprint with her mop.

Smiling in triumph at her once more clean wooden floor she placed the mop back into the cupboard and inclined her head as he heard laughter coming from the mezzanine level where Cameron, David and Ivar were wrestling Bryce, trying to get their younger brother to wear the famous Christmas Eve elf costume for the late night Christmas Eve bash up at the farm.

Hearing the sound also, Savannah smiled and grabbed her knee length coat from the back of the chair.

"I don't want to ruin their fun. Tell Ivar I said goodbye and I'll see him later. I've got some sketches for a floor plan back home that someone wanted finished tonight." She smiled at Aubrey's expression, "I don't work during the holidays I promise. It's my cousin's back home and I'm making an exception for her."

Aubrey nodded and buried her head back into the fridge trying to find the iced coffee she kept on the top shelf.

"Alright, see you later, Sav. Will your parents be coming to the Christmas Eve bash?"

Savannah stuffed her feet into her Norwegian fur lined boots.

Aubrey had always loved her clothing tastes.

"Yup." Savannah said cheerfully while reaching for her bag, "They will be there. Thank you again for inviting us, Mrs Walker."

Aubrey's head came back out of the fridge and she shook the bottle of iced Coffee she was holding, "Sav! I said to call me Aubrey sweetheart. Mrs Walker is too formal now you're gonna be my daughter in law."

Going over to hug the woman, Savannah smiled and said, "Alright. Thank you, Aubrey."

Then with a wave she was out the door, battling the snow to get to her car.

~Chapter Twenty-Nine~
"If you can catch me, you can have it."

"And you're sure you have everything we need?" Jason planted his hands on his hips and surveyed the large farm living room that had been decorated by his wife.

Sighing, Madison put down the large bowl of popcorn she was holding and took the stocking that was slung over her arm off and hung it on the peg by the fireplace.

Jason couldn't help but notice how young and pretty she looked in the holly green sweater and jeans she was wearing with her hair pulled back.

"Everything is ready," Madison said.

"You sure?" Jason teased, his eyes having caught sight of something she had missed.

Hearing the laughter in her husband's tone of voice, Madison turned and folded her arms, sweeping her gaze across the front room.

The blankets were out. Food was there. The Christmas tree was looking beautiful and the fairy lights twinkled in the dark. The garlands were out and there was a fire roaring in the fireplace.

Kit had taken residence on the large family sofa, sprawled out among the cushions and blankets, the tips of his furry ears could be seen peeking out from under a squirt shaped pillow.

"I don't think-" Madison stopped mid-sentence as Jason came behind her and covered her eyes.

She smiled and allowed him to move her so she was facing a certain point in the living room.

"Thou must openeth thine eyes." Jason said in a dramatic, knightly voice.

Once he had removed his hands, Madison blinked and squinted at the marble nativity set she had put out in the mantle piece. Joseph was missing.

"Jason!" She cried, "Give it back!"

Kit raised his head as he heard his owner squeaking, he yawned and then curled back up.

Grinning wickedly and feeling like a teenager again, Jason abided Madison's attempts at getting the nativity character back and ran from the room.

"If you can catch me, you can have it." He called as Madison ran after him, commencing a game of hide and seek that lasted until Caleb and Emma turned up with their kids and coaxed Madison and Jason out of hiding with hugs and Christmas greetings.

~Chapter Thirty~

"For God so loved that he gave..."

"Ready?"

Bryce hovered by his older brother's side as they both stood side by side looking in the floor length mirror.

Ivar swallowed and adjusted the collar to his suit jacket, "Nervous, yet excited." He glanced at his brother in the glasses reflection and smiled weakly.

Bryce didn't look away from the mirror but he kept his eyes on the flower bouquet that was reflected in the top corner of the glass.

"Chill. You'll be fine."

"Ya think so?"

Bryce grinned and lifted his chin, "If I say 'I know so' is that too cheesy?"

"Incredibly cheesy." Ivar laughed, it felt good to laugh. Especially now. In under two hours he would be a married man. Gone was his last Christmas of being single and living at home. The next year of his life would be spent with Savannah as together they searched out God's plan for their life. Together.

The idea of it all enthralled him but also made him nervous, what if he messed up? What if he wasn't a good husband or later, father? What if he couldn't do it right?

All the thoughts raced through his head as he studied one of the bunches of roses and ferns that had been placed everywhere in the building for the autumnal New Year's Eve themed wedding.

Bryce nudged him in the side and they both laughed.

Ivar pulled a folded piece of paper out of the front pocket of his jacket, "Here. Look at this, I wrote it on Thanksgiving."

Bryce unceremoniously unfolded the paper and spread it open on the dressing table.

"Love doesn't get impatient and fretful. Love doesn't keep to itself. Love is always thoughtful, it doesn't push itself to the front, only thinking of itself. Love is not easily agitated. It doesn't store up the wrongs of others to use against them later on in life. Love isn't vindictive. It doesn't take revenge because it wants to. Love cries with those who cry, laughs with those who laugh and rejoices with those who rejoice. Love is for the truth. It fights for those who can't fight for themselves. Love keeps going no matter what."

Bryce nodded slowly as he read the passage, "It's good."

"But?" Ivar squinted while fighting with his tie.

"But David already told me about it."

Frustrated with his tie, Ivar stopped trying to righten it and turned to Bryce, "Really? Is nothing private anymore?"

"Nope!" Bryce sang out while grabbing his own jacket and pulling it on over his dark blue shirt.

He modelled his clothing choice of denim jacket and dress shirt in front of the mirror. "What do you think the guests will think of having your best man dressed in a denim jacket and cowboy boots?"

The door to the room opened and their mom walked in, catching their conversation she said, "They'll think it's a very Walker wedding. With a very Bryce best man."

Aubrey smiled and straightened Ivar's tie, "You ready?" She asked.

"He's fine." Bryce said as he slipped from the room to find Reese.

Aubrey smiled at her son as he left before turning back to the one who was about to get married.

"Well?"

"I'm ready." Ivar said, "And excited. And nervous."

"That's normal." Aubrey patted Ivar's arm and brushed a piece of straw from his shoulder, "How in tarnation did you get straw on your suit?"

"Sav and I helped bring the hay bales in."

"Was she in her dress?" His mom asked.

"No," Ivar smiled crookedly, "Jeans and shirt." He looked his mom over, "You look beautiful, Mom." He said quietly, "The dark green really suits you."

Aubrey shook her head and looked down, "Your dad thought so too."

"He has good taste." Ivar smiled.

There was a knock on the door and they both looked up as Sean stuck his head around the door. "It's time kiddo."

~

"Dr. James Dobson once said, 'God is there with us even in the darkest hours, and we can never escape his encompassing love.' Ivar and Savannah Walker, your life together will have highs and lows. But remember, you're not doin' this alone."

The pastor turned towards Ivar and said, "Love your wife as Jesus loves the church."

He looked at Savannah, "Honour, respect and submit to your husband just like the women in the bible did to their husbands." He grinned suddenly and added, "I don't think you have to call Ivar, Master or Lord though."

Pastor Richards winked, "Don't want it going to Ivar's head." The room full of people laughed and Ivar rolled his eyes, smirking as Bryce made a face at him.

Pastor Richards looked down at his bible and read one final thing from the side notes he had written especially for Ivar and Savannah's wedding.

"For God so loved that he gave. He gave his only son. He gave of himself. And that's what you two here today are committing and promising to do. Give. Give of yourself selflessly, out each other before your own wants and needs. *Love* just like Jesus loved the church. Willingly laying down his life to save us."

On the front row, Cameron leaned over to whisper to Bryce who had sat down after Ivar and Savannah had exchanged vows. "Love. Giving of yourself. Loving with God's kind of love."

Bryce looked back at his brother as the pastor kept speaking, "Eh?"

Cameron jerked his head towards where David was sitting next to their grandpa and Sarah Foster. "You're loved Bryce. Not like this," he said, motioning with small gestures towards their brother who was staining at the altar.

"But you loved by allowing David into the family and accepting him even though you didn't have a single clue as to who he was."

Bryce smiled faintly, "He's our brother Cam."

Cameron grinned and shook his reddish brown fringe out the way, "Exactly." He gave Bryce's shoulder a squeeze, "I'm proud of you little brother."

Bryce grinned and turned to face the front as Pastor Richards finished speaking and Ivar leaned in to kiss his bride for the second time since they had been pronounced man and wife.

~*Epilogue*~

"Ha!" Bryce slammed his hands down on the steering wheel of *his* truck as he pulled up outside of the school building. "I finally got my licence!" He sung out while doing a sorta dance in his seat.

Laughter outside his window caused him to open the truck door and get out, "What's so funny, Randy?"

Bryce's friend from their first day of high school sniggered, "Didn't know you could dance." He finished drinking his can of coke and crushed it before tossing it in a trash can.

"Har. Har." Bryce drawled.

He grabbed his rucksack out of the back seat of his truck and swung it onto his shoulder as he walked with Randy into the school building. "So you ready for the first day of our last term?"

"Definitely." Randy stated as they walked through the large high shook double doors and into the hallway. "I can't wait to leave school."

"Your not goin' to college?" Bryce asked.

"Heck no! I'm gonna sit home and join dad's business all cozy-like. Don't need another three years of education, no thank you."

Bryce rolled his eyes and laughed, he jammed his key into the locker and opened it up, sliding his books in.

"Oh hey, isn't your cousin joining our high school?" Randy asked as he balanced a pile of textbooks while trying to close his locker with his foot. "A little help?"

Leaning against his own locker lazily, Bryce just watched as Randy got jolted around by the hundreds of kids that surged through the school corridors.

"Nah, I'm just enjoying the show."

"Oh you think you're so funny, Walker."

"Yeah, in fact I do." Bryce said, he bent to help pick up the textbooks all the same though, "And yeah, it's Reese's first day. She's coming with Jade though."

"Jade...Jade..."

"She's a sophomore. Reese is a freshman."

"Right," Randy nodded, "and we are finishing up as seniors!" He sighed dramatically and threw his arms up in the air, sending his books flying again.

Laughing and shaking his head, Bryce turned to his locker and grabbed his textbook, slammed the locker shut and locked it before stuffing his books into his rucksack.

"I'll see you in class." He said over his shoulder as he joined the current of young people moving down the hallway.

~

Bryce put his lunch tray down on the cafeteria table and then stood on the bench so he could see.

Ah. There she is.

Weaving in and out of all of the seniors who had congregated at a certain set of tables, he moved through the juniors and then the sophomores.

Finally he reached the freshmen and slammed his tray down on the table next to Reese.

"Hey freshman." He said smiling as he slid onto the bench next to his cousin. "Where's Jade?"

"She has a class during lunch." Reese said, she tucked a strand of her blond hair behind her ear and looked down at her lunch.

"Aw, shame. You'll just have to put up with your cousin then." Bryce said as he speared a grape on his tray with a fork.

"Ain't you a senior though?"

Bryce shrugged, "It don't matter."

"Won't it, I dunno, embarrass you to be with your little cousin?" Reese asked, she and Bryce had always been close. But along the way she had started to wonder if her cousin that had always been like a brother to her would be worried about his reputation.

Looking up into Bryce's smiling green eyes she realised how stupid it was to think that.

Bryce wasn't like that.

I mean, Reese thought as she pinched some of the chips off of his tray, *He's sitting with his cousin right now. How could he be worried about his rep here?* She laughed to herself and Bryce looked at her weirdly.

"What?" He asked, his mouth full of grapes.

"Nothin', I was just thinkin'."

As if he could read her thoughts Bryce nudged her in the shoulder, "I don't care about that." He said so only she could hear him. "If I did, do you really think I would have started a small prayer group by the flagpole every Thursday?"

"It could get you into trouble, Bryce. Not many people that are in charge of schools and stuff are too keen on that."

Bryce shrugged, "I know. But it's important and God asked me to, so."

Reese moved her spoon around in her yogurt pot.

"Reesey. Listen to me." Bryce turned so he was facing her. He knew the bell would go any minute, so he would say it quickly.

"Over the last two years, I've learnt a lot. When I was sixteen and in hospital. Last year when David came home and Ivar got married. I learnt a lot and you're gonna learn a lot too over the next few years of your life. One thing that's really important for you to learn is this Reesey."

Reese turned to look at him, for all of Bryce's goofiness and love for getting into trouble around the farm, she knew that when he needed to be, he could be serious and heartfelt.

"You're gonna need a really good harvest over your time in high school. It's tough, and in life you're gonna come up against some stuff. So you need that good ol' harvest ready. To have a harvest, you have to plant the seeds. It's just the natural way things work, Reesey."

Bryce shook his hair back away from his face and moved his spoon around his dinner tray, weirdly fascinated by the scraping sound it made against the red plastic tray.

Blinking, he smiled goofily, stopped what he was doing and kept talking, "To have the spiritual harvest you're gonna need, you have to have spiritual seeds and cultivate them by spending time in God's word, by having fellowship with Jesus, by speaking godly confessions over your life. The same way you cultivate a field."

The bell went and Bryce jumped up, grabbed his rucksack and walked with Reese to the canteen doors where Randy was waiting for him.

"Reese, just like you can't throw out seeds the day before you need a harvest and expect it to grow, you can't put the word of God before your eyes the very moment you need it and expect the harvest. You need to plant those seeds and continually water them so that when you need a harvest the crops will be ready."

Giving her a hug, Bryce grinned, shrugged his denim jacket on and jogged backwards as he called, "C'mon Reese! It's just a harvest waiting to happen!"

Note from the author

Writing this novel has really brought back a lot of memories for me as I had the illness Bryce fought when I was a little girl of eight. So the first part of this story is actually based on a true story. My story.

Bryce's miraculous healing is also true as I was called 'the miracle child' by doctors and nurses on my ward as that is what happened to me. I hope you all learn three things through this novel.

1: God's word is active and living, it's sharper than any two-edged sword and his healing power is so real, it's life itself.

2: That love, God's kind of love, is selfless. It gives of itself even to its own hurt. So many kids these days think that love is all mushy and weird. But it's not. And I've tried to give you a small look at what it's really like through Sav and Ivar and the parents in this book. Love, God's love, isn't all feelings and wishy-washy. It's selflessness. It's pure holy selflessness.

3: And three. That to have the harvest you need, you *have* to—absolutely *have* to—plant the seeds and cultivate them. If a farmer goes and throws seed in his fields the day before harvest, what's gonna happen? Absolutely nothing. Squat. Nada. Zero. Zilch. It's just the natural way things work. So go and plant those seeds, okay? Coz we all need a harvest. Today, tomorrow or next year. We all need one. Just make sure you have a crop to harvest when you need it.

I really hope you enjoyed reading about Bryce's, Aubrey's, Ivar's, David's story and in turn reading a little bit about my own. I pray that this has blessed you and shown you a little bit more about his love. He is an awesome God who touches each of his children and tenderly loves and cares for each and every one of them.

He calls us to trust him with our lives and our loved ones. He gives us peace that goes beyond all understanding of man, drawing us into a deeper and more meaningful relationship with him.

Abba Father. Daddy God.

Love,
Arialle-Lily Crick

With thanks to...

Noah Crick: for once again a breathtaking cover. Your gift really is so visible and a blessing to many! You capture the heart of 'The Rosetta Stone' in the cover so well, it's mesmerizing.

Siena W: Who, as always, blows me away with the amazing finish and edit she puts in my books. You are a gift from God! You take what I put onto paper and spin it into a picture worth reading! Xx.

To my Mama: who this book is dedicated to. Thank you. Thank you for always being strong, always being there for me and encouraging me in the Lord.

To my brothers: Y'all are a scream!!! So crazy! Three brothers, woah, how do I survive? *evil laugh* All of your character traits have ended up in so many characters. Especially you, half-pint. The littlest of us all. You are a great model of Hunter.

To all those who have read the first edition of this book and written a review on this second edition book, thank you.

To my Heavenly Father: Death cannot hold what is free! To quote 'At Dawn', death is never the end when you walk in. Thank you for being my daddy, thank you for saving my life and just being awesome like you always are. You are a loving father. You reach in and heal us from the inside-out, restoring us to yourself once more and forever. Thank you for being my anchor, my strength in the storm.

Other books by this author:
At Dawn

*Grief is something we can all get lost in.
But grief doesn't just have to be about what we have lost. We can grieve actions. Mistakes. Regrets. We can get lost in all of them.*

Mary and Martha have relied on their brother Lazarus for protection and support since the day their parents died. But when Lazarus is taken ill and passes away, the sisters are lost. For Mary, her whole world has crashed around her. She feels lost, too lost to ever be found again. Martha busies herself to lose herself in the chaos and forgets about the peace in the quiet. But when the traveling Rabbi from Galilee arrives at the tomb, everything changes. Follow the trio from Bethany as they go with Jesus and his twelve through Jerusalem. Witness the compassion they have towards orphans Michael and Amito.

Witness the death of Jesus with them as they stand at the feet of the cross. Discover that you're never too lost to be found and that with Jesus, death is never the end.

Surviving Jerusalem

Surviving Jerusalem
ירושלים שורדת

ARIALLE - LILY TEÁ CRICK

Fear can be like a cage. Keeping you locked in and unable to breathe. Regret and hate can be just as suffocating. But those you thought were your enemy, can turn and change, forgiveness and trust are powerful.

Growing up in the rise of Saul of Tarsus, Jael watches as her people and family are scattered. Terrified of losing all she has left, will she find the strength to reach out and help someone. Someone who is related to the one person who carried the most danger and threat in her life?

Printed in Great Britain
by Amazon